Prospect

Prospect

BILL LITTLEFIELD

A Richard Todd Book

HOUGHTON MIFFLIN COMPANY · BOSTON · 1989

For information about permission to reproduce selections from this book, write to Permissions, Houghton Mifflin Company, 2 Park Street, Boston, Massachusetts 02108.

Library of Congress Cataloging-in-Publication Data

Littlefield, Bill.
Prospect / Bill Littlefield.
p. cm.
"A Richard Todd book."
ISBN 0-395-49168-1
I. Title.
PS3562.17844P7   1989   88-31946
813'.54—dc19   CIP

PRINTED IN THE UNITED STATES OF AMERICA

Q 10 9 8 7 6 5 4 3 2 1

The author gratefully acknowledges the following works as sources for some of the baseball stories in this book: *The Summer Game*, by Roger Angell (Boston: Houghton Mifflin, 1972); *Dollar Sign on the Muscle*, by Kevin Kerrane (New York: Beaufort, 1984); *Ty Cobb*, by Charles C. Alexander (New York: Oxford University Press, 1984); *A False Spring*, by Pat Jordan (New York: Dodd, Mead, 1973); *Eight Men Out*, by Eliot Asinof (Evanston, Ill.: Holtzman, 1981; reprint).

For my mother and father, who took me to the Polo Grounds, and for Amy. But most of all for Mary.

Prospect

Pete

SCOUTING WAS A FUNNY THING FOR ME TO GET INTO, the way both Alice and I felt about travel. But I'm damned if the business wasn't full of guys who didn't like to fly, even though there was an awful lot of flying involved, and guys who said they hated to drive, too, though sometimes they'd drive all day and all night. There were guys who said they got stomachaches when they had to sell a boy's parents on the idea of him signing, and others who claimed they'd rather go to the dentist than fill out all the paperwork their clubs required. But we will put up with almost anything for the chance to do something that offers us joy. And when you get older you will fly, or drive, or stand on your head to be in the presence of that thing, which is a fleeting thing.

What you hear about, when you hear about scouting at all, is the big find. Signing is what the boys dream of. Signing is money. But no scout I ever knew put up with the travel and all the rest of it for money. You'd have to be crazy.

Today the younger men see it as a route to a front-office job, a step on the corporate ladder. They're not as likely as the old fellows to pull a boy aside and show him some little thing he's doing wrong. You know, show him how to push off his back leg and get his whole body behind a throw from the outfield. Watch a kid like that begin to learn to throw, just get the taste of it. The next throw's a little better, and the next one's a little better than that, and before long this kid is looking like a ballplayer. He may not be going anywhere but back to his sandlot team, but he goes back there a better thrower. He's happy as a lark. He gets that feeling from doing a thing right. When he feels that throw leave his hand and sees it take off on a line for the cut-off man, money doesn't have a thing to do with it.

I was like a lot of scouts in that I first got into the game as a player. Or I thought I was a player. I was player enough to think the scouts would come to me. A bonus was unusual in those days. Nobody'd ever heard of an agent and most boys were just crazy to sign.

I'm not one of those guys who's going to tell you those were the good old days, though. I hear a lot of old-timers, jerks on the radio or the television so dumb they'd bite the hand that feeds them, telling everybody that the man in the street can't root for a ballplayer who's making a million dollars a year. That's crap. It's only the newspaper writers and the commentators who mix up the salaries with the game. If those phony turf surfaces they play on in most of the National League parks can't kill the game, I don't see how money's going to do it.

That's not to say the old days weren't different, because they were. Almost all the boys used to have jobs in the winter, for example. The lucky ones had farms or other family connections they could count on. The sharp ones sold insurance or something else. Occasionally one would work his way through college, or even law school. But a lot of them just got on in factories or plants, one thing or another. Now most of the players who last any time at all get so that they make enough playing ball to spend the winter just working themselves into shape for the next season. They work together on equipment designed especially for them, their particular muscle strains or surgical experiments. They hire their own nutritionists and fitness coaches. They study videotapes of themselves. It's a science now, being a major-league ballplayer.

But the game's the same, and you need the same tools to play it. You have to run, throw, field, hit, and hit for power. I understood that fifty, sixty years ago, and it was no secret to me then that I couldn't run. That's the first thing they measure in the scouting camps now. They line up everybody but the pitchers and run them sixty yards in pairs. The scouts stand at the finish line with stopwatches. Boys who can't cover that sixty in seven seconds or less, they're awful lucky if anybody gives 'em a second look, no matter how well they can throw or hit. Hell, in the camps today, ninety percent of the boys don't ever get a chance to show they can hit.

Maybe it would have been different if scouts in the old days had looked at players that way. Maybe I'd have been a doctor or an accountant. If they'd only seen me run, nobody in his right mind would have given me even a Class C chance, which is what I got. But when I was playing semi-pro ball with my father, there were more scouts around. Enough so that they would drop by a high school or semi-pro game for the hell of it. When Bitsy Craig came by that one evening, I wasn't running. I was taking some batting practice. I didn't know who he was, of course, but it didn't bother me that someone was watching me hit. Lots of people used to do that. I loved to hit.

Anyway, he watched me line a couple to left center, then a couple to right center. Then I pulled a few down the line. One of the older men on the team yelled at me to get out of the cage and let someone else hit, I still remember that. I said, "One more," and dropped a bunt down the third-base line. That was a superstition I had when I took batting practice. They'd ask me to sacrifice bunt sometimes, but it only seemed to happen if I'd forgotten to practice it. I hated to bunt, so I'd always try to remember to practice one to ward off the real thing, like carrying an umbrella so it won't rain.

I bunted that last one, a good, serviceable sacrifice bunt, and when I came around the backstop, Bitsy Craig was there, squinting through the smoke of his cigarette.

"Who taught you to hit, kid?" he asked.

"My dad works with me," I said.

"Where's he at?"

"Hitting flies to the outfielders," I told him.

We both looked out along the third-base line. My father was accepting a baseball, tossed underhand by the little kid they let hang around the team as long as he chased down bad throws or bad hops. We had enough tired old or wild young arms to account for plenty of the former, and the field was full of cinders and rocks, which accounted for plenty of the latter. Dad tossed the ball up a few inches with his left hand, swung under it, and snapped his wrists. A long, lazy fly arced out into the coming twilight, seemed to hang for a second against the pale sky, and then fell into the glove of one of the cluster of ballplayers standing around in center field.

"How long's he gonna be doin' that?" asked Craig.

"Few more minutes," I said. "Till it's time to play."

"He hit as hard as you do?" Bitsy Craig was smiling when he asked, but he had a funny way of making you feel as if he really wanted to know the answer to a question, even one like that. Anyhow, all I knew how to do was be polite.

"He hits 'em hard, but not as far," I said. "Mostly he hits 'em through the holes."

"He's littler than you," said the scout, still looking down the third-base line. "Probably chokes up and punches the ball. But he still taught you that wristy swing. He ever play anywhere?"

"Just for the Ducks." I shrugged. "Just here."

By now we'd drawn a little knot of a crowd, and though they stayed at a respectful distance, I could hear one of the men behind me say, "He *is*, I tell ya. I saw him once or twice before at legion games. He was even wearing the same sportcoat. A guy who went away and played double-A up in New York State pointed him out to me."

I'd thought about the day this would happen. Everybody hears stories about a scout seeing a kid hit three mammoth home runs or pitch a no-hitter. In my mind he was going to be considerably more dapper than Bitsy Craig, though. I thought he'd be an athlete himself, gracefully grown old . . . Joe DiMaggio when he was selling Mr. Coffee. He would step up to me after the game with a contract already in his hand, the pen extended in my direction: "Sign here, son." He wouldn't smell like cigarettes or have the crumbs from a tunafish sandwich on his pants. He'd have a winning smile and all his own teeth. He'd be a shrewd judge of talent. Where his shortsighted colleagues would see a kid who couldn't run much, he'd see a man who found such pure joy in hitting a baseball that there was no choice but to sign him.

Bitsy Craig spat between a gap in his sharp yellow teeth. "Let's go talk to your dad a minute," he said.

We walked together down the third-base line. My father had finished hitting fungoes, and he was pulling on his jacket. The umpire had already shouted for the managers to get their line-up cards in.

Bitsy stuck his hand out for my father. "Mr. Estey," he said, "I represent the Lions. I heard your boy could hit. I came by tonight to watch him."

"I hope you see something you like," my father said.

"I bet I will." Bitsy smiled. "I'll buy you both a cup of coffee after the game." We went over to join the rest of the Ducks, and he took a seat in a lawn chair behind the backstop.

I had two hits that night. One was a triple that just kept rising on the left fielder, though a better athlete might have had a play on it. The other was a home run that nobody would have caught up to in any league. I could do that then when somebody got a fastball up in my eyes.

It was good enough. I learned later that a lot of the Lions scouts signed big, strong kids because people in the organization had always been fools for power hitters, same as the Twins and the Red Sox. It didn't cost them much, and they had enough farm teams to keep us all busy, shuttling us from one to another as they waited to see which of us might actually be a major leaguer. According to what I heard later, there was never any doubt in the organization that I could hit in the major leagues. Even the old boys who said Bitsy Craig was an ass to sign me granted that I could hit. But they also said I'd never run any better, and they were right about that too. I went to six spring-training camps with the Lions, and I hit the hell out of the ball in every one of them. The old folks oohed and ahhed, and the dumb writers said I'd be sure to come north with the club. The smart writers saw that I never ran any better from one year to the next. Maybe each year I ran a little worse.

I never asked to be traded, though, or popped off to anybody that I hadn't gotten a fair shot. I played wherever they asked me to play. I guess I was an organization man before I was a man. When it finally became obvious to everyone that I'd never be anything but a kid who could hit the ball a long way sometimes, they offered me a job as a scout, and showed me how to do it.

But I wasn't thinking about scouting on the night Bitsy Craig stopped by the Ducks game to see me play. Back then it didn't seem that thinking had anything to do with it. I just played ball. I was the only kid on that team, but it wasn't because my father pushed it, or because I did. It had come naturally. One day I had grown out of watching him play. Somebody long dead now had said, "Grab a glove, kid." I must have had sneakers on. I would have had my mitt. I must have trotted obediently to whatever position the man indicated, scuffing up clouds of dust as I went. My father must have been watching, even if only out of the corner of his eye. I must have been frightened — Christ, nearly to death! And I must have done all right.

My father was a shortstop, and I generally played left field, because we had a center fielder who could reach anything and all I had to do was watch the line. In a league like that you can hide a slow guy in the outfield for quite a while. You used to be able to do it in the big leagues too, until so many teams went to the plastic turf. Sometimes you can still do it for a year or so at first base.

From left field I could see my dad hunch down when our pitcher went into his stretch. I could see him begin to bounce on the balls of his feet. He rolled and shifted on stumpy legs. Nine times out of ten he knew exactly where to play a hitter, and he was rarely surprised on a baseball field. He played hard. On a short fly ball to left, he'd turn and run with his head down, arms churning, until he got to the spot where he judged the ball would come down, unless either the center fielder or I called him off. Sometimes when it was me that had to do it, my voice would crack. Didn't matter. He'd shy right out of the way like the infielder's supposed to on that play.

On that night Bitsy Craig showed up, we went back to the house when the game was over. My mother made coffee and then sat down with us at the kitchen table. Bitsy pushed the saltshaker back and forth from one hand to the other while he waited for his cup to cool. My father and I sat expectantly, still in our Ducks uniforms, his dirtier than mine. My mother watched quietly.

"Couple of ballplayers on your team," Bitsy Craig finally said to my father. "Second pitcher had a fair curveball, and a genuine change of pace. Who the hell ever saw a semi-pro pitcher with a change of pace? Center fielder was all right. Nobody hit like your boy, though."

"He's got a hammer," my father said.

"Does he want to play ball?"

"He says he does." My father nodded.

"All right," said Bitsy. "Here's how it works. I can recommend him, which means somebody else will be down here sometime to look him over. He'll hit okay no matter who's watching, so that's no particular risk. If whoever it is doesn't see anything he doesn't like, he'll send in a report and they'll offer your boy a bonus to sign. We'll do it that way if you like. Problem with it is that you don't know how seriously they'll take my report, or when they'll get around to sending the checker, or what'll happen between now and then, like a sprained ankle or the flu."

This was not the way I had pictured it. I don't know if it was the way my father had pictured it or not, but he wasn't interrupting.

"The other way it can go is that I can sign him tonight. I can't offer any bonus, but I can make him a member of the Lions Professional Baseball Organization right now. He'll be paid enough to send a hundred dollars home every month if he doesn't pick up any bad habits. He'll join our Class C club in Katalka right away, and play more games this summer than he would in three summers of semi-pro. He'll find out pretty quick how much he wants to play ball."

None of us, not even Bitsy, would have known what an agent was if one had climbed in through the kitchen window. A man with the power to sign me to a contract was making an offer. I was ready to jump at it. My father said he thought I should stay around for the last couple of weeks of school. Bitsy said no problem there, and that was that. I was in baseball.

Six summers later, in the middle of a season I was playing in Murphysburg, they told me I was going to get my unconditional release. They told me early, because at the same time they offered me a job in the organization, as I've said. I was going to be a scout.

Of course an unconditional release is still an unconditional release. The night I got the news I led off the second inning of the game with a walk. I trotted down to first, and when the pitcher was set on the mound again, I got a little walking lead. I took another step or two as he pitched, and then the guy hitting behind me — I could probably tell you who it was if I thought about it, but it doesn't matter — fouled the pitch off. I started back to first, and suddenly I was struck with the most astonishing awareness of what was going on.

As I took my little walking lead, the first baseman drifted in behind me, one eye on the pitcher in case he wanted to throw over to keep me close, the other on the batter, who might turn to bunt. The second baseman leaned toward first, anticipating the bunt, knowing me well enough to discount the steal. The third baseman edged in from his position, cheating for the extra step he might need to throw me out at second if the bunt was too hard or if I got a slow start. Behind him the third-base coach was going through the series of signs that would convey to the batter what he was supposed to do. Meanwhile the pitcher stared in at his catcher, who was flashing signs of his own. The batter guessed at what the pitcher would settle on. Under my feet, as I led off again, the dirt felt springy.

We're all in the dance, I thought to myself. I wanted to tell the first baseman. I wanted the batter to keep fouling off pitches. I didn't want to have to leave the base paths, either because I'd scored or because we were out. As long as the intricate dance was going on, I wanted in.

"Wait!" I wanted to shout. "Hold it. This is too good to lose. Don't give me that damned release now. Not now that I understand it."

I wanted to shake my teammates, some of them so talented they would later play in the big leagues for years, but so far from their own unconditional releases that they were taking all those moments for granted. The dirt just felt like dirt to them.

The pitcher turned and threw over to first. I had no intention of stealing, even in my last game, and I hadn't strayed far. I could easily have gotten back standing up, but I dove for the pleasure of diving, cupped my hand around the corner of the bag, and leaned away from the tag. I stood up, both feet on first base, and brushed the dirt from my uniform shirt. I had to work to keep myself looking the way you're supposed to look on first base. I had to work to keep myself from jumping up and down.

Pete

YEARS AGO MY MOTHER TOLD ME ABOUT A DAY ON which she'd had a shock. She'd been at a friend's house, a social occasion, and someone had decided it would be fun to have a picture. My mother was sitting on a couch between two other women, and when the picture came back — it must have been a week later — she could barely hide her dismay. She recognized her friends all right, but who was that old, heavyset, gray-haired lady between them? Her laugh was still girlish. She slept well and woke up early, full of curiosity about what the day would bring. She'd never felt dumpy or mottled a day in her life, and yet here was the evidence, smiling out at her in an awful parody of the young woman she still felt like.

They took pictures in Fair Haven too. There were Christmas pictures, in which a resident would be standing beneath the huge wreath hung over the mantel, flanked by a son and daughter-in-law, grandchildren, great-grandchildren. The oldest residents in these pictures shared the expressions of their youngest visitors. They stared in uncomprehending terror at the camera lens, while those in the middle, rational generations tried to assure them that everything was fine. "Smile, grandma. Won't it be fun to have a picture of us all together."

In the game room, where there was a Ping-Pong table that

nobody ever used and several sturdy card tables, there was a picture of me. It was a newspaper photograph. In it I am standing on the steps of the Baseball Hall of Fame in Cooperstown, New York, with half a dozen other fellows. I am wearing a straw hat.

At the end of the same hallway you took to the game room there was a screened porch with several wicker chairs. During the day it was popular, particularly with residents who had been told not to smoke and who still did. They hauled themselves out there and worked away at their contraband cigarettes. The nurses didn't bother them on the porch, either because they felt the smokers weren't doing anybody any harm or because they were tired of picking on old folks.

In the evening the porch was usually empty. Almost all the residents were watching television. That's when I'd go out there to sit. I'd close the door behind me to cut off the murmur of the six o'clock news, and bend into one of the chairs that faced out onto the back lawn. The yard was well kept, tended daily by young men in faded orange T-shirts who took their clear complexions and painless knees for granted. But by evening they were gone. I would sit and listen to the last of the evening birds. Eventually it would get dark, and the bats would start squeaking and wheeling around the building, cutting impossible corners in the heavy summer air.

Bats are the damnedest things. One night, shortly after Alice and I were married the first time, she shook me awake and said, "Dammit, Pete, there's something flying around in here."

"You're nuts," I said. But then I heard it too, flapping and squeaking somewhere in the dark. I got out of bed and flipped on the light just as the bat hooked left out of the hall and swooped into the bedroom.

Alice pulled the sheet up over her head, and that's where she stayed for the duration. "Kill it!" she screamed. "Oh God, they get in your hair!"

She was safe enough, of course. I stood in the middle of the bedroom in my drawers, wondering how to handle the bat. With the light and the screaming, it was probably a lot more frightened than Alice was. It crashed around the bedroom, knocking against the clothes tree and then the closet door with a solid *thwack*. Then it righted itself and careened hopelessly off into another dead end. There were screens on the windows, and the odds against its finding its way up the chimney in the living room, which had to be how it had gotten in, were remote.

"Don't just stand there!" Alice shrieked. "Kill it! Oh God, I hate it."

It must have been worse for her, covered with the sheet and only hearing the bat as it looped and clattered around the place, but with its wings spread, sailing close overhead, it looked pretty bad to me too. Finally I rolled up a towel and began swiping at the creature as it dipped into range. On the third or fourth pass I shortened up my swing and caught it with an uppercut. It bounced high off the wall in the hallway and dropped, chittering, to the floor. One more whack and it lay still, small and black.

"Did you get it? Is it dead?" Alice was peeking out from under the sheet.

"Deader 'n hell, kid," I said.

A week or so later I was in the dentist's office and I read an article about bats. The author was a woman vet who loved the damn things, and she was pictured with them draped around her shoulders and neck. According to her, bats were rarely rabid, and did not even intentionally swoop down into people's hair. She maintained that they were harmless and fascinating. She said that if one flew into your house you should just open a window and it would fly out. She didn't explain why it would fly in to begin with.

I suppose beauty is in the eye of the beholder, whether it's bats or whatever, and the woman who said they made great pets was entitled to her view. But that bat lying dead in the hallway, broken and black on the wood floor, could have been the devil's emissary as far as I was concerned. It was a weird construction of leather and hair, and its pinched face, dead or alive, looked up at me as if from a bad dream. I covered the body with the towel, picked the lumpy package up with a piece of cardboard at arm's length, and dumped it in the garbage can.

"My hero," said Alice when I got back in bed. "Did you wash your hands?"

"I never touched it," I said.

It was almost three o'clock in the morning, and neither of us was likely to go back to sleep right away. I tickled her shoulders, and then we made love. Before Alice drifted off, I said I'd name the kid Bat if she got pregnant that time, and we'd tell people it was after baseball bats or Bat Masterson, but we'd know different. She kicked me and went to sleep. That's over forty-five years ago.

The bats I saw from the porch at Fair Haven were harmless enough, just exercise for the eyes. I watched them until it was too dark to see them. Then I listened to them, if it wasn't too cold, or if someone hadn't come out to tell me it had gotten too cold. Generally they'd say "chilly." "Come on in now, Mr. Estey. It's gotten chilly out here."

I didn't make trouble. I would heave myself up out of my chair and come in off the porch. I would plod like a good soldier back down the hallway to my room. It was a small room on the back side of the place. It was not the kind of room they showed the families who came in to look around Fair Haven and see if that was where they wanted to drop off Mom or Pop, because it didn't get the sun. It was on the first floor, shaded by the trees out back. People feel better about leaving somebody in a home if they can say the room is bright and cheerful.

The tradeoff was privacy. That meant nobody was angling for my room, keeping a sharper eye than usual on me to see if I might be going to die, which is what happened if you lived in one of the sunny rooms up front. At meals, people would speculate.

"Who'll get 101?" an old crone would say.

"You won what, Mrs. Babcock?" her companion, Mrs. Irving, asks politely out of her deafness.

"Who'll get 101?" shouts Babcock. She wants to accommodate her friend with the hearing problem, and she herself is too blind to see that the present occupant of Room 101 — failing, certainly, but still well enough to take her meals in the dining room with everybody else — is sitting at the next table. It is Mrs. Melchiore. Though her liver has had it and cancer is crawling like black smoke around her bones, she can still see and hear as well as she could in her prime.

"Who'll get 101?" shouts Babcock again, more loudly, believing that Irving hasn't answered because she still can't hear the question. Irving *has* heard the question, and she can see Melchiore clear as day, bent over her cold tomato soup, old lips curling away from old teeth. Irving is trying to signal Babcock to shut up, but of course Babcock can't see the signals.

"Your hearing's getting worse," shouts Babcock. "I said, who'll get 101?"

Mrs. Irving finally struggles up from the table and flees the room, leaving her meal untouched.

This sort of thing went on all the time.

My small room meant that I did not have a roommate, which was unusual. I didn't have a television set, and that was even more unusual. I'm not sure whether I was the only person at Fair Haven without one, but it wouldn't surprise me. Even the folks who couldn't really see or hear enough to watch it had TV in their rooms. Some bright-eyed nurse or staff member would come in on these folks as they sat staring into space or nodding in their chairs, and the chirping would begin. "You don't want to just sit here like a bump on a log, do you? Let me find something nice for you to watch on TV." I could hear them as I walked through the halls. "Oh, here's that lovely Mr. Donahue. He's always so interesting. You'll like this." The old lady or man would stare, wide-eyed as a baby, at the flickering shadows. The nurse, well-meaning, I suppose, would tiptoe out. The television would stay on for hours, until somebody on the next shift would come in to turn it off and put the stunned viewer to bed.

I did have a radio, a damn good one. When I'd come in off the porch, I'd sometimes tune it to a ball game. I could pick up games all over the place — sometimes, if it was late at night and clear, a game from a thousand miles away. I could tell when I'd reached the right spot on the dial, even between innings. There's a kind of urgency in the sound of the commercial jingles or the station breaks, almost as if someone's saying, "Come on, let's get back to the game." Then there's the murmur of the crowd in the background, buzzing over what's just happened or what may happen next. I've heard that murmur in hundreds of different parks, and over hundreds of different radios too.

Beyond the sound of the play-by-play man's voice, the pop of the bat, and the crowd's waxing and waning attention, there were the sounds I could supply myself. Spikes on the concrete of the dugout step. I don't think there's another sound like that. It'll come back to you if you've ever been around the game. The rattle of bats in a bat rack when you run your hand over the knob ends, looking for the right club, that's another one. I could hear them.

One of those sounds, or a dream of one of those sounds, could start the memories. Then what stopped them was turning over in bed onto a shoulder that cracked like kindling. That'd bring me right back to the present: aspirin on the nightstand, next to the handmade card with the purple flowers crayoned by the little girl who comes to visit once a week after school for her Girl Scout project.

As often as not I'd fall asleep with the radio on. Then I'd wake up later to darkness and the idiot patter of an all-night talk-show host, egging on the callers to discuss their sex lives, their feelings about abortion, or the flying saucers and aliens they'd consorted with. Sometimes they'd be talking about a proposed tax plan, capital punishment, or a water shortage. The callers brought fierce, lonely energy and conviction to whatever subject they were addressing. I hated being waked up by that.

I remember newspaper writers who talked with that same manic intensity about the games they were covering. I doubt that they ever heard the spikes on the top step of the dugout or the rattle of the bats. Unselfconsciously they would hustle up to a player who'd just gone nine innings, back him up against his locker, and tell him what had been going on in the game just concluded. Some were so transparently stupid that they were easy to laugh at and ignore, but the worst of them were persistent and smart as children in knowing how to provoke the boys. They could find your soft spot. All the years around dugouts and locker rooms, from the first days of spring training until fall had blown in and the World Series was over, the reporters and broadcasters would be there to work the players over. Sometimes they were vindictive and jealous, fat, sloppy men in the territory of winners. Sometimes they were so full of self-loathing in the presence of these movie-star handsome kids that it would ooze from them like blood from a wound. Where was *their* money? And where were *their* beautiful wives? What the hell had these kids done to deserve such good fortune when they for Chrissakes couldn't even hit .300 or win eighteen games or do whatever It was they'd fallen short of doing that day? Johnny Bench used to say he could sense the worst of them hovering like swarming bugs, before he could actually see them. I have often wondered why more reporters aren't assaulted in their work.

When I was lucky, a nurse in the hallway would hear the radio and snap it off, so that it wouldn't wake me up later. If I am waked up in the night, I don't get back to sleep. It's always been that way. When I was still working, if something woke me, the travel plans and schedules would come crowding in. I'd be thinking, *If I leave the afternoon game in Columbus by the top of the sixth inning, can I get to Oxford in time to see the kid who's thrown two no-hitters already? And should I call ahead to make sure this kid will even be pitching, because wasn't there some dispute between his mother and the coach about whether he'd play on Sundays at all?* It was no good trying to go back to sleep then.

Even after there were no more schedules and no more players, it would take me a while to remember I wasn't traveling anymore. Old habits die hard, and I would lie awake. If it was a bad night, I could hear someone lost, cranky, or moaning in the hallway. If not, it was peaceful enough. If it was warm and the windows were open, maybe I'd hear a dog out there, or the wind in the trees. Then lying awake wasn't bad at all. During the day you were on the clock. If you didn't get yourself out of bed by seven-thirty, someone would come in and get you up. If you didn't get into the dining room for breakfast before eight, you didn't get breakfast. But at least there you could choose. With lunch and dinner there was no choice. Everybody was there. Refuse and they'd threaten to throw you out. Get thrown out and where would you go next? Someplace where they'd feed you through a tube.

It wasn't that they were intolerant at Fair Haven. The proprietors and the staff were just like most people, trying to get through their days without any more friction than necessary. People deciding not to eat lunch made friction. What if everybody decided not to eat lunch? Eccentricity caused friction, too. Mrs. Graham, who lived on the second floor, had cheerfully outlived her three children, all daughters. In fact, she'd outlived them by a good many years. She believed that they still came to visit her, though, from heaven or the clouds. They'd slide down the flagpole out back. Mrs. Elepolous, the day supervisor, was very strict with Mrs. Graham. She insisted that her daughters didn't visit, especially when Mrs. Graham said it would be impolite for her to interrupt a visit from one of her daughters to go to lunch.

Me, I'm inclined to give Mrs. Graham the benefit of the

doubt. If she said her daughters slid down the flagpole to visit, what the hell. She had the details to back it up. She said her daughters were often cold when they arrived and had to wrap themselves in blankets to get warm. They'd tell her it was awfully windy coming down that flagpole, and no day for her to be out, in case somebody was trying to coax her into a walk. Hell, I've known utility infielders who were a lot crazier and did more harm, and their managers didn't care if they skipped lunch, saw ghosts, and hung by their heels out the hotel room window all night, as long as they were on the bench when the game started in case they were needed. But Mrs. Graham and the rest had played out their options. Nobody has much patience with an eighty-nine-year-old free agent.

I didn't have the same problem Mrs. Graham had, at least concerning children coming down out of the clouds, because Alice and I didn't have children. We gave it a shot, but we had no luck with it. Funny as it may seem, I was the one who was broken up about it over the years when we were trying to start a family, even though I was on the road so much. Alice kept what bothered her inside, unless it was something dramatic and immediate, like bats.

Maybe that's why I took the boys I signed so seriously to heart. They were children when I found them, all right. I remember them as clear-eyed and worshipful. Some of them were cocky bastards, but those stick with me less, even though most scouts will reel off the names of the hotshots they've signed if you ask them what they do. There's a story that when Branch Rickey was running the Cardinal organization, he was once asked to write a letter of recommendation for his brother, Frank, who was his right-hand man and chief scout in St. Louis. The story says Mr. Rickey just drew up a list of what he called "Frank's boys" — Country Slaughter, Marty Marion, Preacher Roe, and sixty or so other guys Frank had found and signed, whom the Cards had either won with or sold off for plenty.

It is natural enough to dwell on your successes, but there were other stories, too. Howie Haak got famous for scouting in Latin America for the Pirates, and he sure as hell scared up some great ballplayers. He stole Roberto Clemente from the Dodgers when they were trying to hide him in Montreal, and he signed Manny Sanguillen, Omar Moreno, lots of good ones. But the story I remember best about Howie is the one about Alfredo Edmead and Alberto Lois, two kids he signed out of the Pan American Games. They were no secrets, those two, and a dozen other scouts had had a look at them. But Howie got 'em, and he was as sure they'd make it as he was of any kid he'd ever signed. Then Lois lost an eye in an automobile accident, which is the kind of thing you can understand, you know, happening to anybody. But Edmead, who was probably the better prospect of the two, and who Haak said was the best prospect he ever signed, which means better than Clemente, had it worse. In his first year of pro ball he was cruising, hitting over .330 and stealing every time he got on first base. Then one night he races in from center field for a pop-up, dives, hits his head on the second baseman's knee, and breaks his neck. It kills him. It's a wonder it didn't kill Howie Haak, too.

Maybe Alberto Lois and Alfred Edmead were like children to Howie Haak. Maybe Howie took their troubles hard. I did, sometimes, when some of the boys I found had troubles later on. Years ago a friend of mine lost a daughter in an accident. He rarely talked about it, but when he did, he mourned. It's so unnatural, he said, to outlive your children. I know it must be true, though I'll never feel it like he did. Instead I've seen some of my boys go from high school smart alecks to muscled hotshots, then on to elder statesmen of the game, reduced, finally, to tears by a standing ovation on a day arranged for them. That's the exception, of course. Most ballplayers just play out the string quietly, like most of the rest of us. Some are dragged out, kicking and screaming. And of course some of them — hell, most of them — never make the major leagues at all, and use their bonus money to go to school or open up a business somewhere. But they all had careers that came and went while I was still getting along at scouting as best I could, scrambling from ballpark to ballpark, pretty much as I had been when I'd seen them playing for the first time. And as far as that side of it went, they all died before me.

Louise rarely caught me napping. Once or twice a month, if I had left the radio on and been awake most of the night, I might fall asleep a half hour or so before she came in to check on me or straighten up.

"Huh!" she'd say. "Some old folks have nothin' to do but sleep away the day. Life of Riley."

"Huh, yourself," I'd say. "What kind of woman are you? For all you knew I might have been dead, lying in bed this late. What the hell time is it?"

"Don't use that language in front of me, Mr. Tough Guy, Mr. Baseball Locker-Room Mouth," she'd say. "We don't have to take none of your lip. We got a contract that says we don't. Residents give us any back talk, we report 'em. We report 'em enough times, they're out. You wanna be out? Now get up and go have some breakfast so I can clean up in here. It's a good day."

You hear awful stories about how old people are treated in places like Fair Haven, but most of them are bunk, the result of hallucinations or insufficient blood to the brain. Of course people are more polite to you when you can still stand, see, and talk. Once it reaches the point where they have to haul you out of bed, clean you off, and prop you in a chair without so much as a "Thanks" for their trouble, it gets less sure. Even then, though, the stories families hear are mostly nonsense.

One woman at Fair Haven complained that they were moving her bed from room to room in the night. She rigged an elaborate web of string connecting her bed to the nightstand, the bureau, the knob on the bathroom door. She slept through the racket when the nurse who came to look in on her fell into the web and nearly strangled herself. Then she swore the next morning that the whole staff had contrived to reconstruct her strings in another room. So it was not easy for Louise and the others.

I tried to be cooperative. I tried not to go crazy. I timed my rising so that I was dressed and groomed when Louise arrived, and we could talk for a while before I went for breakfast and left her to run the vacuum cleaner while she hummed and sang private tunes high in her head.

"French toast," she'd say, as if she had to convince me to eat. "I smelled it comin' past the kitchen."

"Fine," I'd tell her. "I like French toast."

"Sure you do." She'd nod. "Man'd have to be a fool not to like some good French toast. I'll have some myself on my coffee break, if you'll get along out of here so I can finish my work."

"I'm on my way out. I only stayed this long for the pleasure of your smile. It reminds me of Spider Davis's smile. He was a charmer, just like you."

"I know a lot of Davises," Louise would say, "but no Spiders. He from around here?" By now she would be fussing with the cord of the vacuum cleaner, pretending to be impatient.

"Not from around here, no," I'd tell her. "He was from up north. I found him at a tryout camp, and he was about the most eager kid I'd ever seen, ready to do anything anybody'd ask of him. Small, great quickness. He had wonderful hands. I wonder where the hell he is now?"

"This time of day, eatin' French toast, if he has any sense," Louise would say. "I'm gonna vacuum now. You got anything else to say, say it quick. How come I never heard of this Spider Davis? Where'd he play?"

"Never made it to the majors," I'd tell her. "Now, with expansion and the long season, he'd make it in a couple of years. But when I found him there were just the sixteen clubs, and most of them weren't too keen on signing black players, particularly if they already had a couple. Lot of clubs didn't want to be the first to have a whole bunch of black guys, even after Jackie Robinson. Hell, even after Willie Mays."

"Don't have to tell me about a lotta people," Louise would say.

She was an old Dodger fan, and like many old Dodger fans, she never forgave Walter O'Malley for hauling her passion off to Los Angeles. For her the Dodgers had been more than just a baseball team to follow, or even to live and die with. The Brooklyn club had inspired her love.

Willard Mullin, the *World Telegram* cartoonist, had depicted the Dodgers as bums — hapless, unshaven, big-footed clowns who always had an eye on the gutter for a serviceable cigar butt. In the imaginations of many of their fans, Dodger wins struck a blow against an establishment full of fat-cat Giants and smug Yankees. The Yankees in particular represented oppressors everywhere. Mullin's cartoons often presented a muscle-bound Yankee with a crown on his head, lording it over the lesser teams as they scrambled for the crumbs his pin-striped lordship dropped.

And of course the Dodgers had signed Robinson. Insiders knew Branch Rickey never walked a straight line in his life, but bringing Jackie Robinson to the major leagues won him more than ball games. When Louise had gone to Ebbets Field, she'd dressed as if she were going to church. Nor had she been alone. People who didn't have a clue as to what the bombing of Hiroshima meant understood well enough what Jackie Robinson signified. While tens of thousands of people watched, black men and white men played ball together under the same sun. When Robinson stole a base or knocked in the winning run, white reporters stood around his locker and yapped at him about it, same as they would anyone else.

I heard a story once about the father of Bill Russell, the great

Boston Celtics basketball player. It seems that Russell brought his dad to a game, which the Celtics almost certainly won. When it was over and Russell had showered, he found his father in the corridor outside the dressing room, and he was weeping. Russell was concerned, but it turned out his father was crying tears of astonishment and joy. He couldn't get over the fact that the same water was falling over white men and black men, and nobody took any notice of it at all.

It was like that with Jackie Robinson too, and baseball was a good deal more in the spotlight than basketball was in those days.

"No, sir," Louise would say. "You don't have to tell me about a lotta people. But no matter what, you gonna tell me about Spider Davis. So go on and get it done."

"He was an infielder," I'd tell her. "He would have made a second baseman rather than a shortstop, because he had those good quick feet for the pivot rather than a really outstanding arm."

"Monte Irvin type," she'd say.

"Smaller," I'd tell her. "And Davis would never have hit that well. He was a choke-up hitter who'd just make contact and run. His quickness was really most of the story. That, and he worked awful hard."

"Probably grew up to be a cat burglar," she'd say. She'd have her substantial back to me. And then it would start. "I ever tell you about my youngest grandnephew? Big, strong boy. Pitches, hits, does everything."

"A thousand times, Louise. I gave you the names of people to call."

"Names don't mean nothin'," she'd say, with her back still to me. "None of those names want to hear from me."

She was right, and in more ways than she knew. The names, as she called them, really didn't want to hear from her, never mind if her grandnephew could fly. The names had all bought into a centralized system called the scouting bureau, and they'd all agreed on a procedure called the draft. The former meant that all the teams got the same information on all available ballplayers. The latter meant that whatever teams played the worst got the first shot at the top prospects the next year, unless they couldn't find enough money to sign them, in which case the Yankees or the Dodgers would probably pick them up later on. Together the bureau and the draft had pretty much killed the kind of scouting that Louise was thinking still went on. Anybody she'd call — hell, anybody I'd call, for that matter — would think the tip was a crock if the boy didn't show up somewhere in the bureau's computer printout. The days of signing everybody in sight to stock a big farm system and wait for the talent to percolate to the top were over. Teams paying their major-league outfielders two million dollars a year couldn't afford much of a farm system. Nobody was going to waste a draft pick on a boy like Louise's grandnephew, and I'd tried to tell her that plenty of times. Of course I'd also told her plenty of times that I'd retired.

"You retired from what?" she'd say. "Retired from sitting in the sun, watching boys play baseball? No sense to that. That's what people retire to here in Florida. You can't retire from that."

"Shows how much you know," I'd tell her. "I'm retired from covering six states. I'm retired from driving hundreds of miles to see it rain all afternoon on a baseball field cut out of a cotton patch. Retired from hotel rooms that are all the same, with their New England scenes on the wall and their little paper strips over the toilet seats and their coffee like kerosene."

"You don't have to travel to see him, you know. He's just over at Eppis. Or I can get him to come right over here. Have him throw right outside your window. And I can go down to the kitchen and make you the best cup of coffee you ever had."

"I'm retired," I'd tell her. "Retired."

That's when she'd turn on the vacuum cleaner, and that's

when I'd go to breakfast. I got around by myself pretty well in there as long as I didn't try anything sudden. When Louise fired up the vacuum cleaner, I skedaddled and left her to her noisy labors. She'd give me hell under her breath until I reached the door, but by the time I was down the corridor a few steps, I could hear her crooning over the noise of the machine.

Louise, of course, still thought in terms of the old days and the old Dodgers. Each Branch Rickey farm system, whether he was building one for St. Louis or Brooklyn or one of his protégés was building one somewhere else, was a thing of beauty. But Rickey played pretty fast and loose with a lot of the kids he signed. Everybody knows about the special care he took with Jackie Robinson, making sure his ballplayer would be able to withstand the pressure of the insults, slurs, and threats from fans, opposing players, even teammates. Fewer know how Rickey pocketed the contracts of borderline players, neglecting to file them with the front office so he could cut a kid loose after a few weeks without obligating the club to anything. But some old players are still around who'll talk about that, and about the way Rickey would pit his boys against each other. He'd send a contract out to a guy when he was ready to come up to the majors and offer him a fifty-dollar-a-month raise over his minor-league salary, which was a joke. So the guy would complain, maybe even send back the contract unsigned, and Rickey would say, "I don't give a damn if you sign it or not. I got half a dozen guys who can probably do the job as well as you can. You want to play in the majors, sign it."

When his farm systems were going good in the Cardinal and Dodger organizations, he *did* have those half-dozen players, too. No doubt about it. And no doubt either that that's where the seeds for the players' union and free agency and the two-million-dollar-a-year ballplayer came from. There never was a union that management didn't create. You'll still hear a lot of old guys claim Rickey was a saint, but they've got bad memories, or they've been sitting hatless in sunny ballparks looking for prospects too long.

People like Louise don't know all this, of course. Newspaper writers in those days kind of worked for the ball clubs. The clubs took care of 'em, fed 'em, and took 'em on the road with the team. So writers weren't as inclined to dig up dirt as they are today. Television really wasn't in it yet, so there wasn't the pressure of competition forcing the writers to go way outside the game stories. And the players themselves weren't writing books when Branch Rickey was still operating. I think Jim Brosnan was the first of the locker-room writers, and that wasn't until, what, 1960? So there was more distance between the outsiders and the insiders, and people like Louise were the outsiders.

"I knew Jackie Robinson's average every day," she would tell me. "I watched him close on the bases, too. I could tell when he was gonna steal."

"How?" I'd ask her.

"His eyes," she'd say. "You watch his eyes shift back and forth, measuring, and you could see when he was gonna steal."

I don't know how she saw Jackie Robinson's eyes from the outfield seats, which is where she must have been when she saw him play, but memory is a wonderful thing. They say half a million people in Boston claim they saw Ted Williams in his last at-bat, even though that old park only held about thirty-two five at the time, and cold weather had kept the crowd way under capacity. Hell, the team Williams was playing for kept the crowd way under capacity. But still, there's those half a million people claiming they saw the Kid's last home run.

Louise is like those people in Boston. Even now she sees things in Jackie Robinson that the guy sitting next to him in the dugout never saw. People are like that about Ty Cobb, too . . . Walter Johnson, Willie Mays, players like that. Bob Feller was fast, but let twenty years go by and people swear they saw him throw a ball through a brick wall. They tell you how the weather was when it happened, and how much money they won by betting on it. Stay around long enough and you'll hear an awful lot of stories like that. You'll tell 'em, too.

But Louise wasn't trying to impress anybody. "Jackie Robinson just did it," she'd say. "Stole second. Stole third. Stole home, too. Stole anything wasn't nailed down. Changed the game and opened the doors for his people. Lotta folks say Mr. Branch Rickey made Jackie Robinson. They say he taught Jackie Robinson how to act like he didn't hear all the stuff people shouted from the seats. But I look at it the other way round. Mr. Jackie Robinson made Branch Rickey. He made him look like a genius and a progressive citizen. God moves in mysterious ways. You go back to work and find you someone like Jackie Robinson, the world will never forget Mr. Pete Estey."

"That's a theory with a lot of holes," I told her many times. "One is that only one guy can be first. Second is that there aren't a whole lot of young fellows with the kind of tools Robinson had. Then there's the small matter of my being retired. I think I've mentioned to you once or twice before that I'm retired."

As I said, that's when she'd turn on the vacuum cleaner. It was my signal to go to breakfast, which is still my favorite meal. I am not picky about who I eat with, though I've never liked grumblers, particularly early in the morning, so I try to find cheerful company. Mrs. Graham was frequently alone at the breakfast table, and I would join her sometimes. Her talk about daughters coming out of the clouds put some people off, and the management didn't like it, but as I've said, I've known utility infielders and certainly left-handed pitchers who were crazier. Mrs. Graham was always cheerful, and she ate quietly. On the morning when Louise recommended the French toast, though, I began to think I'd have to start picking my companions more carefully. Mrs. Graham was more outgoing than usual that day.

"Mr. Estey," she chirped when she saw me coming, "I knew you'd be here for breakfast this morning."

"I try not to miss breakfast," I said. "It's paid for."

"Of course," she said. "Of course. But I meant today, especially. I have a message for you."

"Oh?"

"And it's a good thing you *are* here, because I might forget it anytime. And it's good news."

"What's the news?" I asked.

"Do you know someone named Jackie Robinson?" she inquired sweetly.

"Well, I used to know him a little," I admitted. "Back in the days when he was still playing ball and that was my business. But Jackie Robinson's been dead for years."

"Well of course he's dead," Mrs. Graham agreed. "Otherwise what would he have been doing in the clouds? But he certainly surprised me when he came down the flagpole yesterday afternoon. I was expecting my youngest daughter."

"Mrs. Graham," I said quietly, "you've been talking to Louise, haven't you?"

"Sarah," she said.

"Sarah?"

"My youngest daughter's name is Sarah, same as mine."

"Yes, but about Jackie Robinson. Louise put you up to that."

"Louise . . . ," said Mrs. Graham meditatively. "I don't think I know a Louise. My daughters are Sarah, Alice, and Faye."

"And my wife's name was Alice, and we've discussed that before," I said. "But we've never had Jackie Robinson come up in the conversation. What brings him up?"

"Down," said Mrs. Graham. "He was looking for you. You weren't in the garden, so he spoke with me. He told me to find you and tell you to keep the faith."

"That doesn't sound much like the Jackie Robinson I knew," I told her. "Are you sure that's who it was?"

"That's who he *said* he was," she said. "Why would he want to come down and fool an old woman?"

I sipped my coffee. I ate a bite of French toast, which was as good as ever. Around me the chatter rose and fell. Silverware tinkled and cups clacked in their saucers. The sun streamed magnificently over white heads, white tablecloths.

"Mrs. Graham," I said, "if Jackie Robinson shows up again, you explain to him that I've retired." She looked puzzled. "You know," I went on, indicating the rest of the people in the room with one arm, "retired. Like everybody else. No meat left in the grinder, as some of the fellows used to say. No mileage left on the tires. That's all you have to tell Jackie Robinson if he shows up here again. He retired, too. He'll understand."

"Who?" asked Mrs. Graham.

They can insult you in a million different ways, if you let it happen. They can kill you with it. Sometimes the way it happens will surprise you. George Peck, who was a fine sportswriter, was in a place like Fair Haven before he died, and his wife gave him a harder time than anybody else. She'd gotten to the point where she couldn't take care of him, and toward the end George needed a good deal of care, but she'd visit him all the time and give him hell when he didn't remember something. He'd confuse who was married to whom, or who had what children, and it would drive her to fits. I saw this myself, because I visited George a number of times and she was usually there with him.

He'd been an elegant man. He always wore a tie in the press box. Now his clothes were frequently soiled and his hair was unruly. That drove her nuts too.

"George," she'd say, "won't you at least sit up straight? Can't you keep your shoes tied up?"

Then he'd get a date wrong, or a place, recount something that hadn't happened or wonder how a house looked that had burned down thirty years earlier, and she'd be all over him.

"Think!" she'd shout. "Concentrate! Don't be so lazy!"

More than once she created so much uproar that the other patients would begin to moan and cry out in sympathy. Someone would have to come and ask her to leave.

Who can tell why she did it? God, it was something to see, but who can tell? Maybe she was afraid that one day her own brain would close up shop, and all she could do about it was try to bully her husband's slipping mind back into action. George went on in that way for a number of years, and his wife gave him no peace as far as I know.

Back in Fair Haven, when you lost it to the extent that George Peck had, you generally had to move out. They didn't let you stay in the residence hotel part of the place once you couldn't limp to dinner and feed yourself. On bad days you could feel them watching you sideways for signs of weakness. Did you slur that word a little? Or look a tad disoriented when you reached that crossroads in the corridor? If you were lucky — and never was *lucky* such a relative term — there'd be an opening on the other side of the building, where the machines stood ready should you throw up blood or stop breathing in the night. On the other side the halls were covered with linoleum rather than carpet, and they were empty except for the people who'd been wheeled out of their rooms and left for a change of scenery. They sat and jiggled their bony hands at whatever went by. Their mouths gaped, toothless and nasty. Orderlies pretended to tap their cigarettes out on the quivering gums. One trip down those corridors and George Peck would have pulled himself together quick.

The other side of the building hung over the residents of Fair Haven like a threat. There was little voluntary traffic from our side to theirs, and none the other way. Everybody knew what was over there, and even those who were most afraid to die hoped that something crucial would quit fast and hard before the slow tide of diminishment landed them in the empty hallways, blind, deaf, drooling, and lost. The staff was on the side of the living, and most of them would go out of their way to help you hang on. Mrs. Graham had her visitors from the clouds, but as long as she could get herself to the table and her appetite was okay, they'd let her stay. On occasion Louise, who was not even a nurse, would briskly rub the legs of a resident who complained that she couldn't get out of bed. With her own meaty hands she'd coax blood back into the pale limbs and bully her charge off to breakfast. She worked on both sides of the building and she hated to see anyone slip, though she'd sigh and say it was God's will when it happened. But I'd hear her sometimes in a nearby room, even lifting somebody out of bed because she figured, *Damn, if I can just get the feet on the ground, they'll know what to do.*

I was careful to give the staff no reason to look at me too closely. If I was dizzy when I came into a room, I looked for things to lean against casually. In the morning I usually got up in increments, before there was anyone around to wonder what was taking me so long. I was careful to eat well, even to exercise a little bit. Each morning after I'd gotten out of bed I stood as straight as I could, then I bent slowly toward my toes. Sometimes I nearly got them, and if the rush of blood to my head wasn't too dramatic, I'd do that several times.

There was a pool, not much of a thing, but clean. Heated, of course. Most mornings I'd try to get down there. Nobody used it for rehabilitation until the afternoon, so many times I'd have it to myself. I once knew a poet who said he could compose verse in a pool. The rhythm of his strokes started the words coming. I'm no poet, but sometimes I kept my mind occupied by thinking through the line-ups of old ball clubs: pitcher, catcher, first to third, then left to right in the outfield. Tigers in 'thirty-four had Schoolboy Rowe, Mickey Cochrane, Hank Greenberg, Charlie Gehringer, Billy Rogell, Marv Owen, Goose Goslin, Jo-Jo White, and Pete Fox. That's a pretty easy one, because it was a championship year for Detroit. The hardest are the war years, when there were a lot of guys in the majors who'd never have been there if the better ballplayers hadn't been called into the service. Even as late as 'forty-six, Mel Ott fielded a team with only one guy who hit over .300. Can you imagine how that must have galled a hitter like Ott? They had Dave Koslo as their best pitcher, and I'm sure he lost more than he won. Walker Cooper caught. Then it was Johnny Mize at first (he was the .300 hitter), Buddy Blattner at second, Buddy Kerr at short, and at third Bill Rigney, who nobody would ever have remembered except that he stayed on in the game as a coach and manager forever. Then it was Sid Gordon, Willard Marshall, and Goody Rosen in the outfield — a far cry from a few years later, when the Giants had Willie Mays, Monte Irvin, and Don Mueller out there. Clearest memory I have of Don Mueller was one day when he got furious at a pitcher trying to feed him an intentional walk, and he reached out across the plate and hit a pitch that was two feet outside into left field for a single.

That's how I would occupy myself when I was swimming short laps in that warm pool. Every once in a while I would try it with a more recent team, but that was pushing it. There's the problem of short-term memory, of course, though I doubt mine has really begun to go yet. There's the natural fact that I remember the players I knew best, and they were the older players. But the real problem is that players don't stay with the teams they come up with anymore. It used to be that a trade was a big deal, you know. Now you kind of expect one every time a guy gets toward the end of his contract. Some teams will trade away a guy as punishment after he beats them at arbitration. Some players demand trades, give the club a list with three or four teams they're *willing* to go to. A few years ago, when Carl Yastrzemski retired, everybody celebrated the fact that he'd played his whole career with one ball club. Before free agency, of course, that was the normal thing. Whatever else you might say about the game before free agency, it was an awful lot easier to remember who played where from year to year.

I'm not suggesting that the game's no good anymore. I'm not one of those fools who spends his time snarling about the money the players can make now. I'm just saying that forty or fifty years from now, old guys trying to recreate line-ups while they swim laps are going to have a tough time of it.

My swimming helped keep the staff happy. More than once while I was paddling around in the pool I saw one of them open the door and point me out to a prospective customer. I wasn't pretty — an old man, drawn and slack, gray hair pasted across my ears — but I was good copy. "We like to keep them active. We like to encourage all kinds of activities," they'd say. The prospective customers were always the sons or daughters of the old folks who'd be moving in. I was one of the few to have checked into Fair Haven myself.

"That's why you're crazy," Louise would tell me. She had strong views on retirement. But the truth was more complicated. I'd come to a kind of compromise with my employers, the Lions, about the matter of retirement. They'd offered not to fire me as part of their program to save money if I'd retire at the end of that year. Hell of a compromise. They'd had to join the scouting bureau, as everybody else had. There was no Branch Rickey heading the ball club, of course, only Rusty Phelan, who couldn't stand the idea that some of his scouts might be duplicating the bureau's efforts. Rusty shivered at the possibility that the club might pay twice for the same information. It didn't work that way, but Rusty was no baseball man, and cross-checking for him was a waste of money. So he decided all he needed was a few suits who could read the bureau's printouts well enough to tell him who the best kids were when it came his turn in the draft, and he cut the full-time scouts loose. Some of them caught on with the Phillies, the Cubs, or other teams that had brains enough to maintain decent-sized operations of their own. Some of them got jobs with the bureau itself, and learned how to talk to the computers. Some of them retired.

Of course it was more complicated than that. There was the wear and tear of the road, too, but there were worse things. One afternoon, hot as the devil, I was down in the southern part of the state, looking over a boy named Lane. He was a kid who eventually came up and played parts of two seasons with the Royals, though nothing much came of it. He was pigheaded about his fastball, and when he got where he couldn't just throw it by everybody, he came unglued. He never developed any confidence in another pitch, but even after he got released he still looked like a ballplayer.

Anyway, this one particular day Lane was drawing a lot of attention, and I was with a couple of other boys, in behind the backstop. That's the best place to watch the movement on a kid's fastball, no matter what some of those guys who go leap-frogging around the place looking for all the angles will tell you. I was sitting next to Whit Cullinane, who'd been scouting for the Phils for about a hundred years, and alongside him were several of the newer boys who were getting their feet wet, some of them attached to teams and some just tagging along. This kid we were watching knew who we were, of course, at least in a general way, and he was reaching back for all he had with every pitch. He had a good enough fastball that some of the boys began to compare it with fastballs they'd seen more of.

"He's got a little of the young Tom Seaver," said one. "Watch how he gets his power out of his legs, like Seaver."

"Oh, for Chrissakes," said another, "Seaver was a student of pitching. Seaver was a damn machine out there. He wrote damn books about pitching. This kid can't find the same release point two pitches in a row. You better look at him real closely today, because if he keeps coming across his body that way, he isn't going to throw a fastball again for a month."

"Ah, I just meant the legs," said the first guy.

"Seaver . . . Jesus," said the second.

This went on for a good long time, with a couple of other boys chipping in to say who they thought Lane looked like. I made a note to check on whether there'd be a tournament later on in the league he was pitching in, so I could see him throw against a few more hitters who'd stand in against him and not give him so much of the plate to aim at. I looked over at Whit because I thought maybe he'd have a schedule with him, and he had the damnedest look on his face you ever saw. First thing I did was look off down the right-field line where he was staring, figuring he must have seen something that had scared the hell out of him. There was nothing there, though. Just the white baseline straight as a string in the brown dirt, and beyond that the clipped green outfield, and two hundred and sixty feet away the right fielder, with his hands on his knees, and then the wall, and then you couldn't see any further.

"Whit, what the hell," I said. "You look like you've seen a ghost."

"Jeez, Pete," he said, "I shit my pants. Help me outta here, will ya?"

I got up and gave Whit a hand, but there was really nowhere to go. It was just a park field we were on, and there was no clubhouse to take him to. Not even a public john. The other boys must have known what had happened, because once Whit got up from his chair, nobody could have missed it. They let me do the work, though, looking at each other and then out to the mound, as if they'd all suddenly found some new problem to study in Lane's motion.

Whit and I started for the parking lot, him leaning on me, heavy and unsteady. "What the hell happened?" he kept saying. "What the hell happened?"

His car was closer, so I got him there, but it was plain he couldn't drive. "Look," I told him, "I'll run you back to your motel where you can change. Then I'll get a taxi back out here and pick up my car."

Whit nodded weakly. He wasn't going anywhere by himself.

By the time I got him back to the motel, he was shivering. I'll bet it was ninety degrees, but his teeth were chattering. He still had that same bewildered expression on his face.

"You have a doctor?" I asked him.

"Pete," he said, "I'm a long way from home. Jeez, what the hell happened?"

His room was stifling, airless. The windows didn't open. I made a move toward the air conditioner, but he said he was still cold. Yards away there were children in bright bathing suits, splashing in the motel pool. Their shrill voices cut through the heat outside, but in the room they were muted and indistinct. I remember a funny thought I had then — how I'd spent thousands of days or nights in rooms just like that one, with the same children screaming in the same hysterical games, though many of them must have been grown by then, married, divorced, cursed, blessed, and dead.

"Pete," said Whit from the bed, "I feel a little better now."

He didn't look any better. His color was gone under his tan, and gray stubble showed on his quivering cheek. Even under the blanket you could see his hard little old man's paunch bobbing with the effort of breathing. There was nothing to make the room his but a plaid suitcase at the foot of the bed and a cracked leather shaving kit on the shelf behind the toilet.

"Listen," I said, "I think maybe I'd better go for a doctor. Either that, or if you really are feeling better, we'll get you to a hospital and let them take a look at you there."

"Nah, nah," he said. "I'll just rest here a while, be okay."

"Whit," I said, "I really think I ought to get you to a doctor."

"I'm awful tired," he said. He rolled onto his side, and the bed was covered with blood. He closed his eyes and died.

Even so, I had no romantic notions about being carried off on my shield. Some people might think an old scout would just as soon die in harness at the ballpark, but I don't know as it's so. Die in a crowd and you're a sideshow, flopping around on the dirty concrete. The ballpark's a good place to make a living, all right, but no place to die, or even to start dying. A motel's almost as bad, with the two glasses wrapped in paper on the bureau, the heavy orange bedspread, the one empty, uncomfortable chair in the corner. A hospital's not so good either, though at least you're not liable to surprise anyone, and you won't die alone unless you want to. But I'm old-fashioned or superstitious enough to want familiar things around me when I go. I made a nest at Fair Haven, though a small one, I'll grant. I put a picture of Alice on the bedside table and hung another one on the wall across the room. I brought a rug with me that we got in Mexico when the Lions sent me down there to scout one winter. That was before the scouting bureau, of course, but after everybody else seemed to be coming up with an infielder named Hernandez or Davillio or Salazar who could go nine miles into the hole and throw you out balancing on one leg. Rusty began to see that happening over and over to our big, slow kids, and finally he told me to get the hell down to Mexico and see if I could find some of those boys for him. I saw a couple of pretty good players, but the Lions lost them because they didn't take care of them, didn't bring in any Spanish-speaking coaches to the minor-league clubs, let a couple of the best of them survive on ham and eggs and cheeseburgers because that's all they learned to say. Finally they got homesick enough to jump ship and go back to Mexico.

So Rusty didn't get anything much out of my trip, but Alice and I had a wonderful time. You never saw such colors in your life as they have down there. Markets full of ripe fruit, yellow, orange, and green. Whole blocks of blankets, red and black and white, and sometimes a guy standing around in costume, Indian headdress and all, colored feathers sticking up every which way.

Alice was trying to take me up on my offer to share baseball with her on that trip. Most mornings she'd pack up a lunch for us. She spoke Spanish beautifully and could find whatever we needed. The two of us would sit in that Mexican sun and eat enchiladas or whatever, and all around us the men would look over at me and wonder what I'd done to deserve this strong and beautiful woman and this job of sitting on my tail watching kid ballplayers try to impress me. I felt like a damn king.

At Fair Haven I had that rug, which I'd grown used to over the years, of course, the way you do until you don't see it anymore. But if I thought about it, I could bring back that stretch of days in Mexico, and I used to think that wouldn't be such a bad thing to remember if you were dying.

Whit Cullinane's funeral was well attended. I told Louise about it once when we were discussing the issue of retirement, and she was impressed.

"People from all the ball clubs." She nodded. "That's good. Like a military funeral. March him under an arch of baseball bats."

"No," I told her. "I only said well attended. It was no circus. Mostly a lot of old men standing around, wondering who'd be next."

"I read about Babe Ruth's funeral once," Louise said. "It was a hot day, and all his old teammates were outside the church in the sun. One of 'em said, 'I'd give a lot for a beer right now,' and another one said, 'So would the Babe.' "

"Waite Hoyte," I said. "And he said, 'Christ, I'd give a lot for a beer right now.' "

Louise frowned, but she said, "I cried when I read that. Funny the things you cry about."

"I might have cried about Whit Cullinane dying in a motel room. I should have cried at that."

"Nothing to cry about in that," Louise said. "Lord don't care where he finds you when it's your time. You trade in your rags for a heavenly crown, wherever you are."

"Maybe so," I said.

"No maybes. Your Mr. Cullinane didn't care where it was he died. He was lucky enough to have someone beside him."

"I don't want to die on the road," I told her.

"We all on the road," she said.

Louise

I HAVE A LOT OF PRAYERS. I USE DIFFERENT ONES FOR different people, depending. I started a special one for Mr. Pete Estey, though, almost the day I met him, and it never changed until the Lord saw fit to move him out of Fair Haven, where he never did belong. Imagine a big strong fellow like that, nothing wrong with him but age slowing him down a little, sitting around with a lot of sick people and feeling sorry for himself.

My prayer for him was about community. "Lord," I said, "show Mr. Pete Estey about community. Show him we can't just quit on life — retire, he calls it — and sit back and watch it go by. Community means we help each other out by doing what we can do. Mr. Pete Estey helped boys multiply their talents, just as it says to in the Bible. Don't hide your light under a bushel. He found them wherever they were, and he helped them along. He did that for years. He got discouraged, Lord, by changes. People didn't seem to need him after a while. Friends died. I think maybe he got fired, too. But show him about a bigger community, Lord. Show him how people still need him if he'd pay attention, and it's not enough to just keep himself afloat at Fair Haven, hanging up his shirt and jacket so carefully every night, cleaning his teeth like he was a jeweler working on precious stones, preparing himself to die like he was getting ready for a dance. Show him how we got to prepare ourselves to die by living, Lord."

People say the Lord works in strange and mysterious ways, but I think maybe it's the other way around. People make strange and mysterious what the Lord would just as soon leave simple and clear. Mr. Pete Estey had his love in life, his game of baseball, and he had no excuse to quit on that. You get him talking about it and you can still see the love in his eyes. I could do that with other folks at Fair Haven, too, but mostly by leading them on to talk about their children, even though some of them were bitter about being at Fair Haven and blamed their children for that. Love survives, though, if you give it a chance. Most of the folks I listen to are still proud and loving, whatever else they are. Get most people talking about their children enough and they light up, even if they don't get visited as often as they'd like or find anything when they shuffle down to their mailboxes at one o'clock every afternoon.

Mr. Pete Estey was that way with baseball. It hadn't rewarded him as it had some. I don't believe he was ever the type who'd go out drinking with the boys all night, then talk years later about all the friends he'd made in the game. Baseball maybe even wrecked his marriage, twice. He says he never did like traveling around different cities and towns all the time, and his wife liked it a whole lot less, but that's where the game was. And then the drug stories, the owners who didn't know enough to keep him on the job, the players who forgot him and cut him dead or the ones who were bitter because they thought he hadn't given them a chance. All these things tested his love, just like a child that disappoints you or neglects you or makes you weep. But he was still listening to the games late at night at Fair Haven. He was still at least half in love with his game. And though I saw him fall asleep over the paper a hundred times, it was never until he'd been through the sports section, at least in the baseball season.

"Speak to his love, Lord," that's what I'd pray. "Show him community."

I didn't talk a lot about God's love to Mr. Pete Estey. I didn't talk about God to him. But I talked about Mr. Pete Estey to God all the time. I suggested to him that maybe Mr. Pete Estey should be a special project, because even God doesn't often have the opportunity to take somebody out of Fair Haven except feet first.

Of course I talked to God about some of the others at Fair Haven, too. I even begged him to take some of them to their reward. I don't know if that was right or not, and maybe it was weakness that made me do it. God's ways are not for us to understand, and he knows even about the sparrows, but I'd tell him sometimes about the ones in such terrible agony that they cried all day, or the ones who rocked and fidgeted in their chairs and snapped at you in an awful despair because they didn't know where they were; the ones who lay on their backs like abandoned ships, empty of everything but the wave of the stubborn heart-beat. They all needed help and they all got the best care God could provide with his humble servant, but I had to speak to him about it sometimes.

"Lord," I'd say, "all right, it's your mystery. Maybe it's just like earthquakes, floods, and doors slamming in the night. There's more than we are meant to understand. Maybe you're reminding us of something, in case we forget what we are in the circus and noise of all that snazzy TV. We're flesh and blood that's bound to fall into decay, so we better see about the spirit. We're here to lend our poor strength to those who need it, each in our turn. But I'm weak too, Lord, and sometimes I come to doubt. When I see some of those people shrieking with pain the doctors can't touch, I come to doubt. Maybe it's a test of my faith when an old woman falls away to bone and silence, and her children have long ago died, and the breath rattles in her throat like straw. I lift her, change her, tell her about the weather outside. She is dead to my touch, but her breath still comes. Maybe it's your test of my faith and my strength. But," I'd say, "then there's Mr. Pete Estey. He could be one of the strong. Speak to his love, and teach him community."

I'm not on the earth to tell the Lord his business, I know. My faith tells me he knows what he's doing. But I'm only flesh like everybody else, and I get impatient. I can't sit and watch waste. I can't keep my mouth shut. And even so, I never said half of what I had it in mind to say to Mr. Pete Estey or to the Lord. I felt it in me to ask them both what they were sitting around wasting time for. But I held my tongue, at least as far as the Lord was concerned. Time's not precious to the Lord, because he's got plenty of it, and if it starts running out he can make more and put new people in it. With Mr. Pete Estey I had less patience. "You could at least take a look at the boy playing ball," I told him. "Maybe you can help him with something."

"You told me he never lost. You said he threw ninety miles an hour, nothing but strikes," he said.

"That's right." I nodded, because I'd seen it.

"What's anybody going to tell a boy who can do that?" he asked. "What kind of help do you think he needs? You want me to tell him not to get old?"

"I want you to tell him how to get to the big leagues," I said. He was making fun of me, as usual, but I tried to hold my temper. Mr. Pete Estey could be the devil for making you lose your temper.

"Louise," he said, "I've told you I'm retired. I'm not retired just because I want to be. I'm retired because nobody who could do your boy any good would listen to me anymore. The business outgrew me. Or I outlived it. Nobody who could help him would know me from any other old man sticking his nose into somebody else's business. The old days are gone. I'm not going to make a fool of myself bothering people who'll think I'm a crank and laugh at me later over drinks. I've told you about the tryout camps. Tell your grandnephew to go to them. If he's any good, he'll get a look, maybe. If he doesn't, tell him to go to another one."

For a long time our conversations ended like that, because I couldn't let on that getting somebody to pay attention to Jack was only part of my plan. The truth is, I didn't know whether the boy could do like I said or not. Like Mr. Pete Estey, I'd put my baseball days behind me. Brooklyn was a long time ago. But the other part of my plan was to get Mr. Pete Estey out of Fair Haven, where he shouldn't ever have been in the first place. Of course I couldn't come right out with that, or he'd have dug his heels in even harder, just for spite. But I thought, *Now, if I can just get him back to work, back to feeling useful and productive, that'll be all he needs to get going again.*

The praying was part of it. I'd never be fool enough to take on a project like that without God's help. But you've got to help yourself, too. So I pulled tricks. I don't deny it. I'm not above tricks. I nagged him, too. I couldn't have told him more often that he didn't have no more slowing him down than I had weighing on me, and he didn't see me quitting. But he'd say, "Louise, you can't rile me," and sometimes I'd despair.

What I calculated was that if I could just get him to take a look at Jack, he'd feel the itch to do something about him. You know, he'd just see how easy that boy threw, and he'd say to himself, "Yes, there's a young fellow who *should* be in the big leagues. Why isn't anybody paying attention to him? I'll have to get to work on it." There wouldn't be anything else he could do.

But things don't always work according to your plans, so that's not the way it happened. How it happened was the fire.

Now, first of all, it was not as bad as it could have been. When a building full of old people catches fire, it could be awfully bad. It started in the back of the building, in a trash barrel, they think. That's the side of Fair Haven that Mr. Pete

Estey's room was on, the old side. Down below it is the trash in cans that are supposed to be covered. They say probably one wasn't on the day of the fire, and someone walking through the yard flipped a cigarette into the barrel, where it probably started things smoldering. Then sometime in the night it caught fire.

I was there when the first smoke alarm went off, like a bugle from hell. Everybody at Fair Haven was afraid of fire, of course. We'd all been told over and over what to do if it happened, and I walked as fast as I could to the back of the building, same place where I cleaned, even though it meant passing the doors of people who were crying for help.

"What is it?" they were shouting. "Is it a drill?"

Somebody turned all the lights on, which was good. Behind me I could hear the nurses and orderlies helping out people who said they had to look for their teeth, or who wouldn't go into the corridor without their clothes on. There was no panic, even though the alarm was screaming. It was something.

Some of the back rooms, the only ones that did get burned, were on fire when I got there. Mr. Pete Estey's room was the first one I came to, and though I thought he'd be out, I stopped just to be sure. There he was, flailing away with a towel at an old rug that had caught on fire from the cinders coming in through the window. It was a picture, Mr. Pete Estey hammering and stamping at the flames. He was giving that rug some powerful licks, old as he said he was, and he was busy enough at it so that he didn't hear me at the door. It didn't look dangerous, even back there, but I wasn't going to take any chances. "You old fool!" I shouted at him. "Get out of this place! It's on fire!"

He looked over his shoulder at me as if I'd just called him for supper. "Why, hello, Louise," he said. "What are you doing on the night shift? I assumed you'd miss the excitement."

I charged across the room at him and grabbed the towel out of his hands. "Get out of here!" I said. "You see those fire engines out there? What do you think they're here for?" By then the engines had pulled up behind the building, and the firemen were running here and there, hooking up their hoses and shouting directions to each other.

"I'll be damned," said Mr. Pete Estey, looking out the window. He was rubbing his chin. I said he could be the devil for making you lose your temper.

I was about to throw him over my shoulder when he said, "Maybe you're right, at that." We walked out together, and even though there was more smoke now and flames in the windows, still nobody was panicking. In the yard we could see just the fluttery confusion of the old people, who kept wandering into the way of the firemen and stumbling over the hoses.

I was mad at Mr. Pete Estey for still being in his room when I got there. The blood was pounding in my ears like ocean waves. Later I found out that at the first sound of the alarm, he'd walked the length of the back hall, making sure everybody else was being attended to. Then he'd gone back to his room, where I'd found him. To this day I never got him to admit that he didn't go back there because he knew I was coming and it would drive me wild.

As fires go, it wasn't much. More smoke and noise than anything else. But once the firemen finished breaking the windows out back and filling the rooms on that side with water, it was a pretty mess. The ground was littered with bed linen and sticks of broken furniture. When the firemen had gone, it looked like a hopeless yard sale after a bad wind.

But the kitchen was all right, so the staff made up coffee and sandwiches for everybody who didn't go right back to bed. Mr. Pete Estey, living at the back of the building as he did, had no bed to go to. I found him with a coffee cup in one hand and a cheese sandwich in the other, listening to Mrs. Sarah Graham, who said she was too excited to eat.

"I won't die by fire," she said. "I know that, anyway. This makes three fires I've lived through, so that's that."

"It must be a comfort," I said. "Of course, some don't think

they'll ever die at all, so they stand around in burning buildings
to test their luck."

Mr. Pete Estey smiled up at me, serene as a cat.

"But one of those was just a kitchen fire," Mrs. Graham was
saying. "Just a grease fire that caught on some of the wallpaper
before the girls could put it out with water from the sink. We
didn't even have to call the fire department. I wonder if that
counts? Do you suppose it counts if the fire department doesn't
come?"

"Absolutely," said Mr. Pete Estey. "Fire is fire. You're safe on
that score."

Mrs. Graham relaxed then. She closed her eyes and nibbled
on a sandwich.

"What about you?" I said to him.

"This is my first fire, Louise," he said. "So I guess it's something I still have to worry about."

"That's not what I mean," I said. "You know that's not what
I'm talking about. What are you going to do now? You can't
move back into your room. What do you think you're going to
do?"

He couldn't hide his worry then, slick as he could sometimes
be. Maybe he'd been assuming they'd have somewhere else to
put him while they cleaned up the rooms on the back of Fair
Haven, but Fair Haven was full up and there was a waiting list,
too. Most places like it are the same way. People sign up for
them years before they need them, or someone in the family
signs up for them. More and more old people all the time.

"I hadn't thought about it," Mr. Pete Estey said.

"Well, I thought about it," I told him. "It's going to be a
while before they get the stink of smoke out of those rooms and
get the walls painted up and the new windows in. The insurance
people have to come in and look everything over, and after that
the work takes time. I've got a spare room. You come on and
live with me while you're waiting on it."

You see how he couldn't turn me down flat, like he had every time I'd suggested that he shouldn't be retired. He liked his nest, but his nest was a shambles right then, and he couldn't just stay there. He was going to move or be moved somewhere, like it or not. And he was a kind man, you know, who'd realize pretty fast that if the people at Fair Haven didn't have to worry about him, they could think more about someone else who'd been burned out and was worse off than he was. He had all his sense and the words to hold off the fear. And I offered it as a choice. Besides, it was temporary.

"That's very kind of you," he said. He wasn't being funny now.

"It's just good sense," I said.

"I'll have to think about it," he said.

I got up out of my chair and told him, "All right. You think about it. While you're doing that, I'll go on home and get your room ready. When you're done thinking, I'll come back and get you."

That part of it was a gamble. I was just hoping that he'd take one look at the room he'd been in and want to get away from it. Everything would be sooty and damp. Lord, that smell after a fire is a terrible smell. Everything would have to be carted out for special cleaning. Maybe it was already gone. Maybe he'd just see the bed frame tilted up against one wall, the mattress gone, the closets empty and the doors hanging open, just the wire hangers left. They wouldn't have had time to even begin cleaning, and the black streaks, like the shadows of flame, would still be under the window.

But what happened was, they never even let him go back to his room. They said the back hall was just closed off, and he shouldn't worry about it. The insurance would take care of cleaning all his clothes. Whatever else was in the room, they'd rescue what they could. He could claim it later. Meanwhile, they'd assigned him to another room where they were sure he'd be happy, with a roommate they were sure he'd like. The part about the roommate was what made up his mind.

When I came back to Fair Haven, he was sitting by himself in the lobby, what they called the reception room. He wasn't reading the newspaper or anything, just sitting, kind of folded in on himself. He looked like a little boy about to go off to summer camp, and he wasn't sure he was going to have such a good time.

"Come on," I said. "Let's get this show on the road."

"Louise," he said, "you don't have to do this."

"You don't have to thank me," I told him. "You'll be good company. We can talk baseball."

We walked out to my car and the sun was shining. You couldn't believe there'd been something as nasty as that fire just a few hours before. He was shading his eyes against the glare, half looking like he thought maybe he should go back inside.

"The door's open," I said. "We'll go on home and I'll make you some coffee and French toast."

"Well," he said, "I like French toast."

"Sure," I told him. "Man'd have to be a fool not to like some good French toast. And you'll get my coffee, too."

"All right," he said. "I'm sure it will be excellent."

"The best there is," I said.

Then he said, "Oh, Jesus," and he began to cry. He put his head in his hands, right there in the front seat of my car, and wept. We hadn't gone anywhere. We were still sitting at the curb. The sun was hot, and the car was stuffy. I waited, and after a while he finished and dried his eyes. "Damn," he said. "I'm sorry."

"Cry all you like," I told him. "Man's been burned out of his home, he's got a right to cry."

"I've lived too long," he said. He was refolding his white handkerchief now, so it would stick out of his pocket. "I'm like a child again. I'm not even sure what there is to cry about. Fair Haven wasn't my home, really. I was a boarder, like everybody else. It was just a place to wait. No more a home than all the hotels I've checked in and out of. I haven't had a home since the second divorce. But, goddammit, I thought Fair Haven would be a place to finish. It was comfortable enough."

"Huh," I said. "You keep talking like that and I'll be insulted. I'll let you go right back in there."

"They'd put me in with someone else, Louise," he said. "Some other old fool without brains or luck enough to have anywhere better to go. Some other idiot who's lived too long. He'd have a television on all the time, and he'd turn it up loud because he'd be deaf. He'd have a collection of pictures of children and grandchildren who are too busy to take care of him. He and I, we'd fart away our days, each wondering if the other'd heard it, until we were too lost even to notice that. Let's get out of here."

I started the car and off we went. He didn't say another word until we were home. I took him in through the front hall and directly to the spare room, which is off the kitchen. It was neat and clean and small, with one window that looked out on the gray house next door.

"The bathroom's the door we passed in the hall," I said. "You have this floor all to yourself, and the kitchen handy if you get hungry in the middle of the night. My bedroom's upstairs. The landlord lives in the other half of the house sometimes, but he has some other houses too. He's not around much. The bus into town stops right at the end of the street, in case you need anything when I'm out. If the bus pulls up and you haven't gotten as far as the corner, just wave at the driver and he'll wait for you. They're used to old people around here."

"Louise," he said, "thank you. You didn't have to do this."

"I'm going to make coffee," I told him. "See if you don't like it as much as I said you would."

He hadn't brought anything with him, of course, because of the smoke and water. There was nothing to unpack. I left him sitting on the edge of the bed and went into the kitchen. I heard the springs complain, as if he was testing the mattress with his hand. Then I heard his footsteps, just three or four across the wood floor, and figured he was looking out the window. What he would see wasn't much, just another two-family house like the one we were in, but needing a coat of paint even worse. Then I heard the closet door open, and I wondered what Mr. Pete Estey would think of what he found there.

"You might try something on from in that closet," I said from the stove. "Never can tell but that something might fit. When you're ready for it, come get some coffee."

"Whose clothes are they?" he asked.

"My husband's," I said, "but he don't need 'em. I kept 'em after he died. I don't know why. I took 'em down and hung 'em all in that closet. I hadn't thought about them for a long time until I heard you open the door. He was a sharp dresser. See what you can find. There's shoes in there too, but they probably wouldn't fit any feet but his."

He came in and sat down at the kitchen table then, and I handed him his coffee and pulled up a chair myself.

"How long ago did your husband die?" Mr. Pete Estey asked.

"Twelve years," I said. "Some of those suits may be cut a little funny for today. But maybe they'll do for just walking around."

"Tell me about him," he said.

So I did. I told him about Edward Baker Brown, who I always called Brown. I told him about being married for forty years and never spending a night apart except when Brown was in the war. I told him about two children, both long ago moved away, married, bringing up families of their own, and about moving to Florida with Brown after all those years in Brooklyn, both of us feeling like we'd earned the warm weather and easier life. Then Brown had died, and I'd found there were plenty of people who needed taking care of in Florida, just like everywhere else, so I'd gone back to work.

When I was all finished he said, "My God, Louise, you must be almost as old as I am."

"I suppose so," I said. "I don't give it a whole lot of thought."
"I'll be damned," he said.

I didn't say anything then, because I didn't want to start an argument or get him kidding me about being sensitive. He'd just gotten there, you know. Hadn't even finished his coffee. But I made a little note to the Lord that I'd get around to working on Mr. Pete Estey's language when the time was right.

"How old *are* you, though?" he asked.

"I told you," I said. "I don't give it much thought."

"That's nice," he said. "Probably that's the way it should be."

"Why does it matter?" I asked him. "Where's the point in counting all the years?"

"Just habit, I guess. When I was a boy it mattered because I was waiting until I was big enough and strong enough to be taken seriously as a ballplayer. Then after I signed, I had to hope they'd pay enough attention to me while I was still a prospect. Once you get a few years on you, you're just a career minor leaguer. Then after I quit playing it didn't matter for a lot of years, except when Alice and I were trying to have children. We ran out of time on that. And when the Lions and most of the other teams started cutting down the payroll for scouting, it mattered again. It was the old boys they let go. The ones who weren't so comfortable with the computer printouts. It sure as hell mattered in Fair Haven, too, once I checked in there. You watch the people fail — stop seeing, start falling down in the bathroom, whatever — and you sure pay attention to the years. Particularly when some of the ones babbling at the walls are younger than you are."

"You know," I said, "it's a miracle nobody was hurt in that fire. Everybody got out okay, old as they are. God's still watching over them."

"God would have been doing some of them a favor if he'd let their hearts burst," he said.

"What are you going to do with yourself today?" I asked him.

"I hadn't thought much beyond this cup of coffee," he said.

"Well, I'm going shopping," I told him. "When I come back, I don't want to find you just sitting here at the kitchen table, staring into space. Go out and get yourself a walk. Or if you want to stay in, look over those books in the living room. Brown was proud of his library. You'll find something."

"Don't worry about me, Louise," he said. "I've gotten used to being alone."

"Whatever you say." I nodded, even though I didn't intend for him to be alone for long.

Pete

THE FIRE CERTAINLY BOLLIXED UP MY PLAN TO DIE quietly, beholden to nobody. You'd think that would be a simple enough ambition, particularly for a man who'd lived as long as I had. But that's not the way it was.

Years and years ago, my father told me a story about a relative of ours, a woman whose name I can't even remember. In fact I can't remember much about her except that she lived in Maine in an old house with a barn chamber, the splendor of which my father never tired of describing in a hokey Maine accent. So I remember her barn chamber, and I remember the simple elegance of this old woman's plan. On her sixty-fifth birthday, she decided that she would live another five years. She and her husband, who'd died some years before, had owned the old house in Maine outright since their marriage, and she'd lived alone in it long enough to have gotten comfortable all over again. When she turned sixty-five she sold or liquidated everything — stocks, bonds, insurance policies, a few animals, other odds and ends — everything but the house and its contents. Then she divided the cash into five parts and deposited each part in a separate savings bank. Her plan was to empty one account each year and to die when the fifth account petered out, probably on the same day. I don't know why she used five different banks. She was an old woman. I remember it, though, so maybe my father stuck it in just for that reason.

The great thing about this old relative of mine was that she made her plan work. She didn't make seventy. She died in her sleep in that big house in Maine, leaving just enough in that fifth bank account to bury her.

Now, of course, dying like that would be a neat trick. Quick as your heart stops these days, they drop in a new one. Catch your breath in your sleep and they hook you up to machines that breathe for you. It's simple enough to say you can avoid the extreme measures by staying out of hospitals and nursing homes, but it's not so easy to do it. Once you get old, a lot of things can land you in the hospital. A cold can turn into pneumonia. Your circulation can crap out. Arthritis can bend your fingers into terrible claws, and the drugs they give you for the pain can drop you right on your back. That'll put you in the hospital, too. When you get old you stop sleeping through the night, and if your teeth go bad you don't eat well, because it hurts. That's two things that'll make you dizzy during the middle of the day, and if you tell a doctor about it he'll slap you into the hospital for tests.

I know a guy who ignored a blister he got trying to rake leaves, and it got infected and ran a red streak right up his arm. He ended up in the hospital, because the only way they could knock out the infection was to give him penicillin through a tube. Once he was in the hospital, he had a stroke.

Then there's always falling down stairs, which will put you in bed with a broken hip. That'll lead to pneumonia more often than you think, too. That's at least two ways to get pneumonia.

It's no picnic being old. There are a lot of jokes about it: "If you're over seventy and you wake up in the morning and nothing hurts, you know you're dead." Stuff like that. People in their eighties have written that sort of thing, but when they haven't been writing they've probably been struggling to get out of chairs on legs gone numb, or squinting through cataracts that have grown like scales across their eyes, or wondering forlornly what someone on the other side of the table is saying under the buzzing that fills their ears all day long.

Get old enough, and unless you're luckier than all but a few, you'll lose control. One way or another, somebody will end up taking over for you. That's why I like the story my father told me about the old woman up there in Maine. She made a decision while her mind was still sound, and somehow, over a few years, she got the message down into her blood and her bones, where it would do some good. And she got it there in time. It was a neat trick. There was nothing morbid about it, at least as it was told to me. She had it under control. How did she do it? I'll never know. All I could do when my friends began dying and my own collapse started to whisper through the wires was look for a warm, dry spot and hope the end would come quickly. Fair Haven was as good a place as any in that respect, better than most. I could have made my stand there, such as it was, even without the magic knowledge that told that old woman in Maine how long she was going to last. I had a measure of control there, because I'd recognized my limitations. I didn't run sixty-yard dashes. I didn't hurry anywhere. Louise once said I moved like a turtle. I never tried to see anyone who didn't want to see me.

But the fire changed everything. There I was in Louise's kitchen, holding somebody else's fifteen-year-old suit in my hands. My choice was to stay dirty in the only clothes of my own that I'd have for at least a week, or put on this dead man's pants. Not much control there.

In Louise's neighborhood, just taking a walk would be risky. Fair Haven was laid out so it was impossible to get lost, and the paths around the place were cunningly designed so that no matter which way you turned, you'd bump into something familiar and end up back where you'd started. There wasn't much adventure in it, but who needed adventure at my age? Here, anything could happen. If I went for a walk and started dreaming about Alice's kitchen or the day I almost got called up to triple-A with the Lions, I could wake up lost. Who'd help an old white fool with fear in his eyes? I didn't even know the name of the street Louise lived on.

Even if I stayed put, there were dangers. The room was full of mysteries. The stove was gas, but who knew whether you had to light something under the burner if you wanted hot water? I didn't want to fiddle with it. I could have read, except that my glasses were back in my room at Fair Haven, on the bedside table, unless the firemen had knocked them off and stepped on them. I sat in the kitchen and listened to the busy hum of the refrigerator until it quit and left me in silence. Wasn't even my silence.

I must have fallen asleep at the table, because the next thing I heard was someone rattling the outside door, and I thought Louise had come back awfully quickly. But the steps in the hallway weren't hers. Then I heard a key in the lock, and there was a young black man, maybe in his late teens, maybe early twenties. He looked like a ballplayer.

"I'm Jack Brown," he said. "My Aunt Louise called me to come and see if you needed anything. Said she had to go back to work for a while to help get people settled."

Well, I thought, she hadn't wasted any time. Maybe she was worried I'd get skittish and go back to Fair Haven, roommate be damned. Or maybe she hadn't liked the way I'd looked when she'd got me out here, and was afraid I'd fall dead before I could do her grandnephew any good. What a piece of work she was.

"So," said Jack Brown. "You okay?"

"Louise has told me about you," I said. A man's got to know when he's licked. "She says you're a ballplayer."

"She told me about you, too," said Jack Brown. "Said you

were with the Lions. But I looked you up in the *Baseball En-cyclopedia,* and I couldn't find your name."

"I was in the Lions organization," I said. "I never played for the big club. Good hit, no speed."

"So now you're a scout," he said.

"You and your great-aunt." I snorted. "Now I'm a retired scout."

"Well, that makes more sense," he said. "When she told me, I couldn't see how you could scout from Fair Haven. I thought probably you were crazy, or just bullshitting her."

"You know her well enough to see that I couldn't do that for long," I told him. "I'll bet nobody ever has. I don't know whether she really thinks I can do you some good, or whether she just thinks that trying to would be good for me. It's her show, though. That's pretty obvious. And now I'll bet this fire will have her convinced that God's on her side with it."

There I was, you see, at her mercy. When I was still in Fair Haven, I could hold my ground. But now, for the time being at least, I had no ground to hold. I was sitting at her kitchen table, and soon enough I'd be in her dead husband's suit. She knew I wouldn't say no to her when she'd taken me into her home. She'd unretired me, whether I liked it or not.

"So who'd you sign?" asked Jack Brown.

"Mostly boys you never heard of," I told him. "Did you know that ninety-two percent of the ballplayers who sign contracts never make it to the major leagues?"

"Is that what you told the guys you were trying to sign?" He laughed. "Shoot, it's a wonder you got anybody."

"No, I didn't necessarily tell them that," I said. "But I didn't sweet-talk anybody much either. With the real good ones, I'd say they had a chance to make their living in a great game."

We sat across the table from each other then, neither of us saying anything. At Fair Haven they would be taking naps. Jack Brown was too restless to sit for long, and eventually he got up, opened the refrigerator, and drank some milk from the carton. Then he leaned against the counter. What a young man he was. How comfortable in his skin.

"So do you need anything? Anything I can get for you?" he asked.

"Nothing I can think of," I told him.

"You want to see me pitch?"

"All right." I nodded.

"You be here in the morning? I'll bring somebody by to catch for me if you will."

"I'm not going anywhere," I said.

"Okay," he said.

That's how easy it was to be back in it. But even then I wasn't quite admitting it to myself. After the boy left I thought, *Well, maybe he won't be any good. Maybe he'll just be a kid who thinks he can throw.* God knows, of the thousands and thousands of kids I saw play over all those years, most of them weren't nearly good enough. The game you see major leaguers playing may look like the same one you played in high school. It's the same distance between the bases, same number of men on a side. But most kids don't even have the eyes to pick up a major-league fastball as it comes in on them.

There's more to it than that, though. The Twins brought an outfielder up a few years ago, an early draft pick who could hit and throw and run. He'd played in their system for a couple of years, until they felt he was ready for the big leagues. The first game he started was in Fenway Park in Boston. He was in right field. Bottom of the first inning he's out there pounding his glove, picking at the grass, checking the wind like any outfielder, when all of a sudden he starts shaking. His teeth are chattering as if it's December and he's out there in his undershorts. The shaking moves right down his arms and legs, and pretty soon it's evident to the pitchers in the bullpen, which is in right field in

Fenway, that this guy is really in trouble. His breathing is all out of control. He's gasping for breath as if he's drowning, right out there in the outfield.

Finally somebody in the bullpen calls the dugout and they stop the game and bring this kid into the clubhouse. They get him lying down and the trainer has him breathe into a paper sack to control the hyperventilating. Eventually he stops shaking and his teeth stop chattering, but by then of course the game is on again and the Twins have got somebody else in right field.

Nobody wants to make a big deal out of what happened. Maybe it's the flu or something. The kid sits on the bench for a couple of days and he seems to be okay. He comes up as a pinch hitter once in the third game in Boston and gets a sacrifice fly, so everybody figures what happened his first time out was some kind of fluke. An allergy or jitters in front of a big crowd.

Next stop for the Twins is New York, and they put this kid out in right field again. Right field in Yankee Stadium has seen some real butchers. Reggie Jackson played there. Maybe the kid will be okay. But while the pitcher is still warming up, the shaking and the gasping start up all over again. The fans in New York can smell blood, and they start howling at this guy who's heaving for breath in the outfield. This time somebody must be watching from the dugout, because they get time called and get him off the field quicker than they did in Boston.

The doctors back in Minnesota tried rest, tranquilizers, and psychotherapy. They examined the kid's diet and tested his blood and urine to make sure he wasn't taking something. Some fan wrote in and suggested that they send him to a hypnotist, so they tried that. They might have taken a chance on voodoo and exorcism too if they could have found someone to give it a shot.

Nothing worked. The kid was okay at bat, but every time they put him out there in right field he fell apart. He could hit major-league pitching. He ran well. He looked like a ballplayer, too — slender, but with the good wrists and arms. It was a terrible thing. *So, I thought to myself as I sat at Louise's kitchen table, maybe this boy Jack Brown won't have something it takes besides arm speed, an idea of the strike zone, and enough sense to recognize good advice when it comes along.*

I was still hoping, you see, that I could find some reason pretty quickly to head off really getting involved. Otherwise, now that I owed Louise, how was I going to avoid having to drag my old self out into the sun to watch Jack Brown pitch? And if he was half as good as he and his great-aunt thought he was, how was I going to avoid having to call a lot of people who didn't want to hear from me, who didn't know I was still alive, or who didn't even know who the hell I was, and didn't care? It was a wrong thing to do to an old man who only wanted to retire. Who knows what might have happened to that old woman in Maine if somebody had insisted that she start coming to exercise classes at the Senior Citizens Center or take a lunch-hour job as a volunteer crossing guard? She might have lost her balance in the street and been run down by a school bus. She might have been taken all broken and bleeding to a hospital, to live out her remaining days in crippled misery, always waiting for somebody to bring her this or wheel her there. Worse, she might have become vigorous in the flush of her pushups or the sunshine of her outdoor work. She might have lost the concentration essential to her five-year plan. Then she'd have outlived her money, and unless she was willing to take charity and lucky enough to find it, she'd eat cat food through her last days. She'd have lost her control.

I could see how it would happen to me. When I went out there to watch Jack Brown pitch, maybe it would be evident right from the start that he was no better and no worse than lots of other healthy youngsters, his chief characteristic being that he had a great-aunt who was more ambitious and energetic than most other pitchers' great-aunts. Then I would have to say to him that he'd better forget it, find something else to dream about.

I'd done that plenty of times, and seen boys react to it all kinds of ways. One socked me in the jaw — fortunately, when I was a much younger man.

It would be bad enough to tell another boy that he wasn't the player he thought he was. Nobody likes to hear it. But it would be worse to find that Jack Brown did have enough talent to justify the next step, because that would land me on a ballfield full of boys so young it would make me weep. I'd be hobbling up to a scout who was doing what I once did, pulling at his sleeve for the attention I thought Jack Brown should have. And he'd be thinking, *Christ save me from old farts.* All around us boys would be stretched on the grass, rocking on their perfect hamstrings. They'd be carelessly making circus catches under the sun, while I examined the ground before me for holes or ruts that would pitch me forward on my face. If I was lucky, when I fell two boys would be there to pick me up like a bundle of twigs and send me tottering on my uncertain way.

Over in St. Petersburg there is a league of old men. They have some cute name for themselves, and they play softball games for crowds of people even older than they are. Some of them muster surprising ferocity. Those over ninety get especially big hands when their names are announced as they come to the plate. I only know this because once, by awful coincidence, I walked by the field they were playing on. It was a terrible parody of the game, all rigid struggle and groping for the ball. At the worst moments, men who had once been real athletes tried to leap for balls over their heads or turn other tricks they could no longer do. I watched with horror from behind the backstop.

Once I heard a story about Casey Stengel's participation in an old-timer's game at which they were honoring Connie Mack. Through some grotesque mix-up, Mr. Mack was left alone and unattended at the pitcher's mound when the ceremonies had concluded. There he stood, swaying in the heat, lost and blinking. "Jesus," Stengel said from the dugout. "Somebody help me get that old man out of the sun."

That's what I wanted to say that day I saw this league of old men. But I was an old man too. Anyone who heard me would have thought I was nuts.

The last place I wanted to be was out on a ballfield. It had never felt right to walk across a diamond in street shoes, but that would be the least of my problems now. Any outfield would be full of ghosts — bad territory for old men. Besides that, a stray ground ball could knock me in a heap. Even just standing out there in the presence of all that healthy muscle and blood would seem a kind of insult to what God had created in those strong boys. The sun would shine down on them in the glory of their sweat and their ease, and I would gape and gawk like a flightless bird, and probably forget what I'd come for.

I must have fallen asleep worrying about it, because the next thing I knew there was another key rattling in the door. Louise was back, with two bags of groceries. "If you were sleepy, why didn't you go in the bedroom and lie down?" she scolded.

Still lost in dreams of humiliation, I hadn't the wit to answer. Boys in knickers walked around me wide-eyed and wondered what God had wrought. Where was I? Ballplayers hadn't worn knickers in sixty years.

"Things are kind of turned upside down at Fair Haven," said Louise. "Fire marshal's been out interviewing people. Newspaper people sniffing around. Even the TV station had someone out there with a camera and lights and everything. Mrs. Sarah Graham was all upset because they wouldn't wash her hair so she'd look her best on the evening news. The TV reporter heard her complaining and figured maybe he had a story about Fair Haven's abusing the residents, so he rushed over with his crew and started asking her questions. When I left she'd just begun telling him about her daughters coming down the flagpole. You can probably see it at six o'clock."

"Your nephew was here this afternoon," I told her.

"Jack Brown," she said. "I asked him to come by and see if you needed anything. I thought you old baseball men might find something to talk about."

"I never liked matchmakers," I said.

Louise began emptying grocery bags on the counter. I hadn't touched her with my comment. Maybe she hadn't even heard it, or if she had she wasn't going to allow it to interrupt her. At Fair Haven I'd picked fights with her whenever I'd wanted to, but here she could see she had it all her own way. Her plan was rolling. Cranky remarks weren't going to get in the way.

I sat and watched her as she sorted and stored boxes and cans and put on the hot water for tea. For some reason I thought again about Alice in her kitchen, going through the same motions. When I was on the road, which was most of the time, Alice ate omelets or had a hamburger somewhere with a friend. She said there was no fun in just cooking for herself. But the first thing she'd do when I'd come home was go out grocery shopping. She'd stock the cabinets with cans and the icebox with steak and ice cream, and when she was finished she'd sit back and put her feet up on a kitchen chair, full of that good feeling that comes from being prepared. As the week or two weeks I'd be home passed, the food she'd stocked would dwindle to leftovers and snacks, and she'd get gloomier. It was the traveling that broke us up both times we got divorced.

For a long time Alice was after me to get a job outside of baseball. My halfhearted efforts at it only made her bitter, and they made me ashamed. I'd interview for a job and then hope like hell they wouldn't offer it to me. We both hated the dishonesty of it, though I'd never admit straight out to her that I wasn't really trying. Sometimes baseball would make me so mad I really would go out looking for something else, but never for long. Never for long enough. It is a sustaining game.

You see how hard it was to be in Louise's kitchen? I didn't

want those memories of my wife's home. I thought I'd left them in the past. At Fair Haven the food was monotonous and bland, but the kitchen was behind closed doors that I never had to go through. They probably wouldn't have let me in if I'd asked, and I never asked. Now here I was, surrounded by full cupboards and coffee cups. Only Louise was trying to argue me back *into* the game. Or not really having to try anymore, because she knew she'd already won. Maybe she'd known that since before I'd known there was a struggle.

"I thought we could all have lunch together, after you watch Jack Brown pitch," she said.

"You know about that," I said.

"You see if he isn't something special," she said.

We had tea then, and later dinner. Louise made roast chicken with gravy, roast potatoes, green beans, apple pie for dessert. Coffee with plenty of milk. Nothing was too good for the old man who was going to see that her grandnephew Jack Brown became a famous pitcher.

When we were through she invited me to sit with her and watch television, but I said no. She shrugged, and cleaned up the kitchen with the same competence and care that characterized whatever she did. Then she headed for the front of the apartment, leaving a light on in the bathroom in case I needed it during the night.

On my back in the strange bed, I was aware of strange sounds. A couple of doors down the street somebody was hammering erratically in the moonlight, trying to patch his steps. Somewhere else a woman was calling a dog named Fitzie or Fritzie, whistling between the shouts. For the first time since I'd checked into Fair Haven, I was smack dab in the center of somebody's neighborhood. The sounds of Fair Haven were those of any hotel — water running somewhere else in the building, a muffled cough, in the hallway the monotonous hum of nighttime television.

But here in Louise's spare room I heard the voices and chatter of men and women she probably called by their first names.

During the times when Alice and I were trying to be a happy couple in the middle of the block, I heard the same sounds. We giggled in bed about the man a few doors down who came home from work at six, set up ladders, scaffolding, and spotlights, and painted his house for an hour before dinner. He did a little, perfect patch each night as long as the weather stayed warm enough. When he was finished with the house, it was time to start again.

We heard the runaway dogs and cats, too, and the children clattering up and down their driveways in wagons. More children all the time. In the morning I often woke up before the alarm. While Alice slept I listened to the soft *plop* of the newspapers falling on doorsteps up and down the block. When I heard my own paper fall, it triggered some tiny, harmless sense of pride. I too was established enough to have a paper delivered. It would be there when I walked out to get it. The illusion of substance.

Why hadn't our life turned out like those of the other couples, the other families on the street? We loved each other more than most, if I was any judge at all. We had no children, and they did seem to be the glue that held much of it together for many of the others. So much to keep track of while children are growing into and out of clothes and shoes, learning to use the toilet, needing braces or glasses or discipline or love.

Alice could have filled that gap by being herself in the world and a wife to me. She faced up to disappointments, took them on squarely, maybe raged against her life without whatever it lacked, but stayed planted where she was. I was the one who was always leaving to watch baseball games, just as I'd once left to play in them, wherever they told me to go.

In the afternoon Louise had spoken with such frank love about her husband. Almost the first thing she'd mentioned after his name was that they had been apart only when he'd been in the service. Lying now in her spare room, I found myself thinking what a lucky man Edward Brown must have been, to be able to find such sustenance in another human being who loved him so well and so long with her warm arms and her heart so steady in the world. What constancy they'd made for each other, and how nuts they must have thought anyone who couldn't find nurture and satisfaction as they had in each other. How they must have laughed at the folly of men who chased women, women who took many lovers, sharpies, pros, and hustlers always looking for an edge. What a simple completeness they'd found in one another, and what a comic mystery that so many others were rushing and rioting around without it.

I couldn't be a smart aleck about a marriage like that, you see. I couldn't dismiss it as timid. Ballplayers I'd known had joked a lot about their marriages, claiming it was only long months in spring training and on the road that allowed them to survive. My marriage had ended twice because I couldn't leave the game alone. Lying there in that spare room, I admitted to myself that Alice, twice my wife, might have spoken of a better husband the way Louise spoke of hers. I never doubted my wife's strength and devotion, but I couldn't provide them with an object. Put simply, I couldn't sit still when baseball was going on all around me and somebody was willing to pay me to play it or watch it. And I thought, *Jesus, what a sweet and precious thing you've blown*, but I knew as quickly as the thought came that it wasn't that simple. Only a child would think it was.

Now it was late enough so that the hammering had long ago stopped and the dogs and cats were in or out, where they belonged. Occasionally a car hissed on the road out front, and the reflection of the headlights glanced off the window and found the corner of the small room. Otherwise it was still in Louise's home.

When Alice and I lived together before the traveling ruined it, or during the times we both believed I was looking for a job that would keep me home — or when I half believed it, anyway — we slept curled up together. It became a habit, and even now I couldn't sleep any way but on my right side, bent into a kind of half-circle that she would fit into. I pulled myself into that position, and the moon coming through the window was full in my face. I remembered a superstition, an old wives' tale, about how a woman who wanted to get pregnant should show her belly to the full moon. Now here I was, old beyond the promise of children, old almost to where the distinction between old man and old woman disappears, and here was the moon, more barren than any desert we know and linked with fecundity, romance, and spooning in June.

Under that moon I let an old man's mind sink. I wondered whether that business about the belly and the full moon was an innocent superstition. Maybe not. Maybe it was the bitter old joke of a bitter old woman, an old wife who had no pleasure left but to make fools of those who were young and strong and beautiful to their husbands and lovers, while she was a dry stick who'd outlived her passion and pleasures. Maybe it was a tale born of viciousness, an old woman's impossible attempt at revenge. Maybe she hoped the full moon would fill a wife's womb with crazy tides, and any child born out of that salt and empty ritual would make its mother yearn for lonely peace.

I could understand such an old woman, even though I'd have laughed at her for thinking she could ever get even with the young. There is much on earth to make us bitter. Hadn't I been forced to choose between two loves? And hadn't the one I'd chosen — the one that chose me and hung on with a steel grip — jilted me when I was old and useless? Hadn't the gods for their perverse amusement sent me a woman who could tolerate anything but baseball, the only mistress I had? Weren't there men, middle-aged and older, lying in their beds under the same night sky, still convinced in their hearts that they'd have been in the big leagues if I'd given them another chance to run sixty yards, or dropped a kind word to someone about them, or even for Chrissakes been willing to come back to an old park somewhere to see them hitting on another day, against another pitcher, under better lights, or when they'd gotten rid of the hangover? And who knows but that some of them were right. There were so many of them.

Weren't there men out there who'd married younger women and then been absent-minded enough to grow fat or bald or slow, and who'd seen their women run on them? Weren't there women who'd strained to bring children into the world and to stretch money that was never enough into food for everybody under the roof, only to find that somewhere else their men were betting on slow horses or buying beer for women with shrill laughs?

In my game, wasn't there plenty to make you mournful and bitter on your bad days? Wasn't there Lou Gehrig, an iron man in his day, dead young of a disease that mocked and wasted his wonderful ballplayer's body? And Roberto Clemente, killed in a plane that he'd chartered to help feed earthquake victims in Nicaragua? And what if you did beat the diseases and the plane crashes? Then you were Willie Mays, hobbled and sore in the outfield at forty-two, such a sad shadow of the boy who had laughed and sprinted in the sun of the Polo Grounds that in the last years New York fans would look away with tears in their eyes when the ball was hit to center.

For an old man like me, weren't there tribulations and pests? Wasn't it a mean life when you couldn't even retire?

I lay there under the moon, curled up and waiting for sleep. That same moon had shone down on Fred Snodgrass, I thought, after he'd dropped a routine fly ball to put the tying run on base in the seventh game of the World Series in 1912. That same moon had shone down on Carl Yastrzemski after he'd popped up to end another one-run game at the end of another World Series sixty-three years later.

I let other players come to mind: Bill Lee, who was about as unlike the grim Yastrzemski as any man could be, but who'd pitched so well on those same Boston teams that could never quite get over the top. And that reminded me of Thurman Munson, whom the free-spirited Lee had called a Nazi, and who had died in a plane crash on a trip home to see his family. And that reminded me of the Hall of Fame in Cooperstown, where there was a corner containing Munson's locker and uniform, a kind of shrine to bad luck.

Munson was a tough character, which is maybe why the next guy to come into my head was Gaylord Perry. He hung on and hung on until he'd won over three hundred games, and then he retired to North Carolina and did a little public relations campaigning to try to spiff up his image, but it didn't take. I remember him warming up in some bullpen when he was pitching for Texas, giving an old usher hell for not keeping the kids with their scorecards and pencils away from him. Perry'll be in the Hall of Fame someday, but not for being a nice guy. He won 314 games before he was through.

Perry was a spitballer, of course, and I found myself thinking about how they'd outlawed the spitball but couldn't really stop a smart guy from throwing one. You could always load a pitch with something — hair grease or spit or Vaseline from inside the heel of your glove. Or you could cut it on your belt buckle or with a little piece of emery board you had tucked away somewhere. Or you could get a catcher to scuff up a ball if you needed it once in a while, and that might help you hang on for a year. But eventually, if you hung on long enough, you'd get traded to six teams in three years, the way Perry did. And then you'd be gone.

Since it didn't look like sleep was going to come, I finally fell back on the same trick I'd used in the pool at Fair Haven when I wanted to just quietly occupy my mind without giving it anything really worrisome to chew on. I set it to running down the line-up of the Brooklyn Dodgers the year they finally won a World Series, in 1955. Their catcher was Campanella, who was later crippled and confined to a wheelchair. Johnny Podres was their ace in that series, a boy who could have been the mayor of New York when it was over. Years later he became a mean bastard of a pitching coach. Pee Wee Reese anchored the infield at shortstop, and after he retired people bought bumper stickers that said "Pee Wee Should Be in the Hall," meaning the Hall of Fame, of course. Eventually he made it, and on his plaque it says he helped ease the way for Jackie Robinson. Robinson played third base and stole home in that series, which is sure something you don't see much of anymore. Jackie had a son who was a dope addict. He himself died of a stroke.

Duke Snider, Carl Furillo, and Sandy Amoros played in the outfield. Amoros made the catch off Yogi Berra that saved the series. My God, that was something. Afterward all the writers gathered around him, and somebody asked Sandy whether he'd thought he had a chance for the ball as it started hooking away from him toward the left-field foul pole.

"I donno," said Amoros, shaking his head. "I just run like hell."

Junior Gilliam played second base, and Gil Hodges was at first. Gil Hodges could have been mayor of New York too. Both of them are dead now.

I'd gotten to the rest of the pitching staff — Carl Erskine, Clem Labine, Don Newcombe — and was just trying to remember the name of the right-handed kid they traded to Baltimore the next year when I realized that all the names I could call up were attached to Jack Brown's face, and I guess that's when I finally slept.

Louise

JACK BROWN'S FATHER — MY EDWARD BAKER BROWN'S brother's son, Malcolm — was not all that he might have been. He was a fine tall man, like his uncle, and he had the same deep voice that he could make you feel right along your spine if he wanted to do it. But where my Brown was content to work hard and tend his own garden, Malcolm had a snazzy streak. Both of them liked good clothes, but Malcolm was a flashy dresser. He was lighter than the rest of the family, too, and dated white women sometimes, just to show he could. Jack is even lighter than his father was.

Brown and I got to know Malcolm again when we moved to Florida, though we'd known him as a little boy. He'd come down south ahead of us, him and a white partner, and they'd got into land speculation and real estate. Malcolm Brown could sell anybody anything, and for a time Florida was his easy pickings. It came and went, though, and Malcolm Brown was broke as often as he was flush. But he was always confident and never lost his smile. He was always just on the verge of something big, at least to hear him tell it.

Brown got letters from him, or from his daddy when he was still alive, and while he was reading them he'd frown and mutter. When he was finished, he'd put down the letter and begin very solemnly to tell me about his nephew's latest disgraceful adventure. But before long he'd be laughing despite himself at how Malcolm had bought some worthless piece of property from someone who thought he could see a sucker coming a mile away, then had sold the same land back to the same man six months later as a goldmine or an oilfield or the secret site of some lost Indian treasure. Pretend as he might to be unhappy with his nephew's business, Brown would laugh in his eyes, and the laughter would wash over his disapproval like water bursting down a dam, and he'd roar at the idea of that dumb speculator up to his elbows in alligators, digging around in the swamp for the money that wasn't there.

Malcolm Brown was as casual about his women as he was with his money. He'd joke that he had bastards running all over Florida. But his only legitimate child was Jack Brown, who was still just a little boy when his daddy was shot. His mother moved back north then, back to New York, and took Jack with her, of course. But Jack had had enough of warm weather and baseball games the year round to know he liked it, and as soon as he could leave home, he did it and came back down. That was several years ago. His mother called me then — I hadn't heard from her since Malcolm's funeral — and asked me could I kind of keep an eye on Jack, since she couldn't do anything with him and he was heading in my direction.

I didn't know what to expect. Brown was dead by then, and I wasn't even sure I'd know Jack by sight, since the last time I'd seen him he was still hanging on his mother's skirt. When he showed up, I did recognize him, though. He'd got the deep voice by then, and the height and shoulders of his daddy and his great-uncle, though he was heavier than either, kind of *strong* heavy. When his mother finally quit trying to convince him to stay in New York and keep at school, she told him to look me up, figuring maybe he couldn't be quite as wild if he knew he had some family in town.

But Jack Brown never showed even a sign of wildness to me. He stayed with me, in the same room I gave Mr. Pete Estey. Jack was there for about a month before he came in one afternoon and said he'd gotten himself a job that paid enough so that he could afford to share an apartment with a friend, and off he went. It turned out the job was in one of those service stations open day and night, and he worked the day shift sometimes and the night shift other times. He'd joined two baseball teams, which was where he'd found the friend. One team played its games during the day, the other at night. He'd pitch for whichever he could according to when he was working, and to hear him tell it, each was happy to have him whenever he could make it. That's when you could hear his daddy's voice in him.

I asked him sometimes how he got along without sleeping, and he said it was just a matter of making the most of the time you had. It was all planning, he said. Like making sure he had the right uniform with him to change into after work, so he could cut out the trip home if he was playing ball nights. He must have been a fair mechanic and a quick learner for them to put up with him at the station, but when he talked about how he managed to work and play on two ball teams and still drop by and see me occasionally, you could close your eyes and hear Malcolm Brown. He could do all he wanted and come through trailing the clouds of glory, to hear him tell it. Other than that, though, and the size and the deep voice, of course, I never saw any of his father in him.

I don't think it was just that the work and the baseball left him no time for meanness. Jack Brown was always a good boy. But he never did go back to finish school. He seemed happy enough just playing baseball and fixing cars, and in that he was about as different from his daddy as he could have been. Malcolm Brown wanted people to know his name and shout it out whenever he came into a barroom. He had a smile wide as a brick and never lacked a spit shine. There were rumors that he was connected with the Mafia on land deals and other networks of crime and mischief, and he relished the stories. He told them on himself out of the side of his mouth and laughed like a madman. He thought they gave him romance. You might worry about him, but you couldn't help but laugh when he was telling stories. Jack Brown had some of his father's confidence, but he wasn't the kind of talker Malcolm was. Nobody was.

Of course, for me Jack Brown was special. Brown was gone, and none of the family was too much inclined to visit Florida. My own children thought I was crazy for staying there alone and were always asking me to come live with them, but they had their own lives and I had mine. If I was alone, I wasn't lonely. Working over in Fair Haven would cure anyone of that fast. But Jack Brown coming along when he did was a nice surprise. While he lived here we talked about family. He found out early that I wouldn't push him any way he didn't want to go. It wasn't that I didn't care whether he went back to school or whatever else he did, but I could see he would be fine whichever way he went. A boy's parents can't see his best side sometimes, they're so worried about his future. I could look at Jack Brown from arm's length, even though he was family. And he could stop by for a cup of coffee without the strain that'll come into the talk between mothers and sons.

His mother, naturally enough, was worried that he'd turn out like his father, which she thought she could avoid if she could get him through school and college. She was wrong. There's lots of college-educated crooks. But she was doing the best she could by her lights. She couldn't see all that Jack Brown had going for him, because it wasn't just what she wanted for him. Jack was a natural who moved like a big cat. He was handsome and friendly. His mother'd had a husband who'd traveled in fast circles and got himself shot. She wanted a safe life for her son and no more funerals. When Jack Brown came south, she despaired. Florida was bad news, probably worse now than when she'd left it. Jack Brown's father's genes might mix him up with Cuban criminals and cocaine now instead of Hollywood swamp speculators, but for her it would all come out the same. She was afraid, and she couldn't see the *good* news, which was that she had herself a good boy. Jack Brown didn't seem to need money like his daddy had, and when he was playing ball he sure was happier than his daddy ever had been.

So you can see why I wanted to mix Mr. Pete Estey up with Jack Brown. It seemed to me it couldn't help but do them both good, but even if it didn't they'd have plenty to talk about. Baseball hadn't changed so much.

It was funny, though, how thinking about Jack Brown coming by in the morning to show Mr. Pete Estey how he could pitch had me awake before it got light out. I don't know what there was to worry about. It wasn't like I was trying to arrange somebody's marriage. But I just lay there and thought about it in the dark, and the thought that came to me was did I really have any business messing around in people's lives that way?

The thought didn't stay with me long, though. The Lord smiled down on me and he said, " 'Course you do."

Jack Brown, I thought in gratitude and wonder. *Jack Brown, carrying the genes of a swindler and worse, a red-headed, smiling Negro who couldn't keep it in his pants. How much of the father is in the blood, Lord? Jack Brown, tall on the pitcher's mound, looks big as John Henry when he leans toward the hitter, swings into that spare delivery, stings the inside part of the plate with his fastball. Big as Marcus Garvey.*

Carrying the genes of a daddy shot by a man he fooled as bad as Jack Brown can fool a hitter. How much invisible conked red is in this boy's woolly black hair? How much of his daddy's wandering eye and his agitated walk and his nervous glancing at

the shiny gold wristwatch because there was always someone
waiting to be taken on a corner across town, someone sucker to
a line of patter fast as any fastball, crooked as any curve?

Jack Brown, Jack Brown, smooth as brown butter. Carrying
the crazy genes of a man you may not even remember, legendary
con man, desperado, and moving target. What has your mama,
timid and shivering up north, told you about him? What do you
know of the history of the face you carry into the sunshine every
day?

Jack Brown in your service station overalls, happy enough to
be working for wages and eating pepper-steak sandwiches or fried
fishcakes, as long as there's a ball game to pitch tonight. Happy
enough to drink Coca-Cola when it's over.

Jack Brown, did your mama ever take you to the El Dorado
Motel, where your daddy lay on a worn green carpet with a bullet
hole in his head and another one in his ass, nothing but silk
shorts on his wasted frame? He picked the wrong man to sell
swamp to, finally. An Alabama farm boy with a gun, and
patience enough to come back and reopen the deal, and eyes
sharp enough to recognize the Lincoln parked out front. Still, he
might not have shot your daddy without a word, he might have
gloated over finding him again or screamed for his money back
or rolled up his sleeves and taken a poke at him, if it hadn't been
a white woman in bed with Malcolm Brown when that Alabama
boy kicked the door down.

How much do you know, Jack? How much mean is in you?
What will you show Mr. Pete Estey when he stands out there
under that hot Florida sun, shading his eyes with that brown-
spotted hand, measuring you against a thousand forgotten boys
who thought they could pitch?

Jack, do you remember the sirens? Can you see the police
standing around, leaning against their cars, smoking in the hot
night? Can you hear the creak of their boots and the crunch of
the wheels of the cart on the gravel driveway as they pull the body

out of the back of the El Dorado Motel, no hurry now and no reason to be gentle? Can you see the big eyes of the people in the crowd? And the big eyes of the manager out front, trying to explain to the detective with a notebook how he'd never have rented your daddy that room if he'd known?

You see why the Lord gives me the go-ahead to do my work? See why I know I'm all right bringing Mr. Pete Estey into my home and telling him all about Jack Brown? See why I know the Lord smiles on me when I work on getting these two together so that they'll both be doing what they're supposed to be doing?

Too many things dragging us down to that green carpet in the El Dorado Motel. Too much bad gravity in the midnight parking lots. Police blotter's full up with people with plans all their own. All of us be better off with a little help when there's somebody willing to give it.

Amen.

Pete

I WOKE UP COVERED WITH SWEAT, THE SUN IN MY eyes. I couldn't see in the glare. I didn't feel like I could move. *My God,* I thought, *I've had a stroke. I've finally had a stroke.*

Then I heard Louise humming in the kitchen and found I could wiggle my toes.

Louise had apparently put a blanket on me after I'd gone to sleep. I struggled out from under it and dropped my legs over the side of the bed. Out of habit I sat there for a while, taking it slow in case I felt dizzy. But I was all right. I pulled the sheet around me and took a deep breath.

Louise, who must have heard the bedsprings complain, appeared in the doorway. "You'll want to take a shower," she told me. "I'll hold your breakfast till after that."

"I guess you're in charge," I said.

"You don't want a shower?"

"I'll take a shower," I said. "I don't know about any breakfast yet. What time is it?"

"You got time," she said. "I already talked to Jack Brown this morning. He traded shifts with another boy. I'll take you over to the park so you can meet him by nine-thirty, before it gets too hot."

"It's too hot now," I told her. "Where'd this blanket come from?"

"I looked in on you last night and you had the sheets all kicked out to the sides. Look like you been fightin' something in that bed. I didn't want to wake you straightening those sheets out, so I put the blanket over top of you. Can't sleep naked to the world. Not in my house."

She turned and went back into the kitchen, and in a minute she was humming again. She'd left towels and a safety razor on a straight-backed chair in the corner.

When we got to the park, her boys were already there. Jack Brown and his friend were lounging under a tree.

"What the hell is this?" I said. I was surprised by the irritation in my voice, and beside me Louise jumped a little. But there it was, like a little hot spring gurgling up out of nowhere.

"What?" said Jack Brown from under his tree.

"Most scouts would leave right now," I said. "Turn on their heels and walk right away from you as quick as they could. Who wants to scout a boy sitting on his ass under a tree?"

Jack Brown got up and dusted himself off. The other boy stayed at his ease and squinted at me speculatively.

"You look too old to be a scout," he finally said.

"I am too old," I told him. "I've been trying to tell that to this boy's great-aunt for months now. Maybe years. But here I am, and I'm the best he's got. What do you do?"

"I'm a catcher," said the boy.

"Well, you don't look fat enough to be a catcher," I said. "But we'll go over to home plate there, and then you can show me if you're a catcher. I'll try and show you that I'm really a scout. Or was one."

I couldn't blame him, though. I must have looked even older and sillier than usual. Louise's husband's short-sleeved white shirt hung off my shoulders like a tent, though the suit's pants fit. There was room in those shirtsleeves for several pounds of muscle I'd never had, even in my prime.

Jack Brown's first pitch hit home plate, skipped by his catcher, and caught my left leg, just below the knee. I stayed up, though I don't know how. "Warm up slow," I said.

"I warmed up before you came," he said.

"Then you went and sat under a tree. Warm up again. Slow."

When he relaxed, he had a fine, natural motion. He used his legs well for leverage and his stride was modest. He came from a little more than three quarters of the way over the top, and his motion was consistent. His timing was good, and he released the ball from the same point on most of his pitches. Either somebody had showed him how to save his arm, or he'd learned it out of self-defense, pitching for two teams, sometimes at night, sometimes during the day.

When he'd thrown easily for a few minutes, I held up my hand and walked out to the mound. "All right," I told him. "Keep your motion easy like you have been. Over the next ten pitches, build up to your fastball. Bring it in as close to knee high and straight as you can. I want to see if it naturally does anything on its own."

"Knee high's all right," he said.

In a few minutes Jack Brown was popping fastballs into his friend's glove. His motion stayed tight and contained. His rhythm was workmanlike, consistent. From what I was able to see in a few pitches, his natural fastball would ride up just a little and bear in on a right-handed batter. It was not the sort of movement that would dazzle anybody, though. For most boys the fastball is what you use to gauge talent and potential. Jack Brown's was respectable, but nothing more. It wasn't devious, or scary, or humbling. It didn't hiss as it went by, or echo out over the park like a rifle shot when it hit the catcher's glove.

If I'd had to guess right then about Jack Brown's future as a pitcher, I'd have said he was a lucky man because his natural, easy motion would keep the arm injuries down and his sense of the plate would have semi-pro teams competing for his services as long as he could still walk out to a mound. He had the means and the discipline to pitch for a good long time and have a life in the game, but not in the major leagues.

"All right," I said. "What else do you throw?"

"Curveball," he said. "Screwball. Knuckleball."

"Change-up?"

"Never tried it much," he said.

"Okay," I said. "Show me the curve."

He threw three curveballs. That's all it took for me to see that his curveball *was* his change of pace, whether he knew it or not. It didn't have the bite or dip to be a real curveball unless the guy he was throwing it to was still looking for a fastball, in which case he'd help out by lunging and make that pitch look a lot better than it was.

I walked out to the mound again. "Show me how you hold your curve," I said, and Jack Brown obliged by sticking out his right hand with the ball in it, then rotating his wrist in a slow-motion demonstration of the way he thought you should break off a curveball.

"Like this," he said.

"I'm not worrying about how you throw it yet," I said. "Just how you hold it."

He held the ball out and I used my thumb and forefinger to pull it looser in his hand. Or I tried to. I had no real strength in my fingers.

"You see what I'm trying to do?" I asked him. "Loosen up your grip. You grab it too tightly back there in the heel of your hand and you flatten it out. The way you crack your wrist when you throw it, a good hitter will pick it up right out of your hand when you let it go. If you can't make it *do* something, you better forget that pitch."

"It curves," he said.

"Yeah." I nodded. "It moves a little on the one plane, the horizontal plane. But that's the easy movement to pick up. A good right-handed hitter will pick that little wrinkle up, wait a beat, and slap it into right field, even if it is moving away from him a little bit. A good left-handed hitter will drool if you throw him one of those things, especially if you get it up in the strike zone like that last one." I put his fingers around the ball again, but this time I stuck my thumb between his palm and the ball. "Hold it from there," I said. "Hold it like if you squeeze it too hard it'll break and cut you."

I walked back behind the plate and watched Jack Brown throw a curveball that dipped at the end, like a bird somebody'd shot. His catcher missed it completely, and the ball kicked up off the plate and hit the inside of his thigh. "Shit!" he said, and he jumped back from the ball as if it were a snake that had bitten him and might not be through yet.

"All right," I said. "Now all we have to do is find somebody who can catch it."

On the mound, Jack Brown looked like a magician who'd just made a quarter disappear and didn't know where it had gone. He couldn't wait to get the ball back to throw the curve again.

The next one sailed outside, two feet beyond the catcher's reach. A major-league wild pitch.

"Don't foul up your motion," I said. "Throw it out of your natural motion, same as your fastball. Don't throw it harder. Let it take the movement from your wrist. Don't overpower it. It ought to be a couple of feet shorter than your fastball getting up here. That's the whole point. You want to keep the hitter off stride. Keep him swinging early at your curveball, late at your fastball. Move 'em in and out on the plate. Simple as that."

The catcher was back with the ball. Jack Brown was ready to go again. "You want to see the knuckleball?" he said.

I held up my hand to stop everything. I walked out to the mound, favoring the leg Jack Brown had hit with his first fastball. "Leave the knuckleball alone," I said. "Leave the screwball alone, too. Throw your fastball and that curve I showed you.

Practice a change-up until you can keep it low. Ten years from now, when you can't throw the fastball past anyone, start worrying about a knuckleball."

"Okay," he said. "Now what?"

"Now I sit down before I fall down," I said. "Jesus, it's hot."

As it turned out, Jack Brown had promised to help the catcher with his car, so he didn't come back with us for lunch. It was just Louise and me at the kitchen table with cold cuts, potato salad, and iced tea. She kept herself busy with setting the table and laying out the food and wrestling with the ice tray for as long as she could, which was longer than I'd thought it would be.

"How come you haven't said anything?" she finally demanded. "Ever since we left the park, I been waiting for you to tell me Jack Brown has a Rex Barney fastball."

"Oh, Christ," I said. "Rex Barney." He was a Brooklyn pitcher who had Bob Feller's speed but mysteriously lost his control before he could develop into the kind of pitcher everybody who ever saw him was sure he would be. His fastball was just a natural gift. After he lost his sense of where the plate was he went to psychiatrists and tried hypnosis and all kinds of damn things, but he never got it back. He was out of baseball at twenty-six, which was a damn shame.

"Jack's got better control than Rex Barney had," I said. "He pays more attention when you suggest something to him, too. He's a good listener. Rex Barney was a lousy listener."

"That's not what I'm talkin' about, and you know it." Louise snorted. "Jack Brown's got a good fastball he can throw for strikes, right? And you wouldn't have taught him that curveball if you didn't think it could do him some good, so you must think he's a pitcher, right? Now how are we gonna get him noticed and signed and headed for the major leagues?"

"How many camps has he gone to?" I asked her.

"How'd you know he'd been to any?" she said.

"He wants to play ball. He can read the newspaper. If he couldn't, you'd read it for him and make sure he was there on time. How many has he gone to?"

"Four," she said.

"What did they tell him?"

"Said to keep working on it," she said. "That's not so bad."

"What else?"

"One said he probably threw right now as well as he was ever gonna throw, and it wasn't good enough."

"How'd Jack take that?" I asked.

"He's still pitchin'," Louise said.

"You know," I said, "if it was twenty-five years ago, when everybody had a slew of farm teams all the way down to Class D ball, Jack Brown would have a job in baseball. He's eager, he throws strikes, and he can take instructions. But he's as big as he's going to get, and he won't throw any harder. Scouts looking at him today won't get stars in their eyes."

"How can you be sure of all that, lookin' at him for fifteen or twenty minutes? You can't *know* he's as good now as he'll ever be."

"I'm just telling you what I'd put in a scouting report if I was working," I said.

She left the kitchen and went out to the front room, where the phone was. I could hear her dialing, and I guessed she was calling her grandnephew to talk about what I'd had to say. It was pretty much the same thing I'd told him at the park when I'd seen enough, though I hadn't asked him how many tryout camps he'd been to. I hadn't enjoyed telling him what I thought, but it hadn't been as bad as I'd anticipated, either. Young as he was, Jack Brown took it better than a lot of fellows. Or maybe he was just looking me up and down through it all and laughing to himself, saying, *What could this old fart know about how good I can be?*

Anyway, I was relieved that that part of it was over. Now I'd told his great-aunt too. And another feeling had come into it, which I hadn't anticipated at all. I was feeling kind of excited that I could still do my job. I really hadn't had to watch Jack Brown for long to know what he could do and what he couldn't.

And then I found that I was hungrier than I'd been in a long time. When Louise came back into the kitchen, I'd started building myself a sandwich that would have lasted three people three days at Fair Haven.

Louise took one look at my efforts and said, "This don't appear to have hurt your appetite any."

"No," I said. "Isn't it the damnedest thing? Look at that sandwich."

"Well," she said, "baseball men must be made tough. Jack Brown has no hard feelings either. He has to work tonight, but tomorrow he'll be on the day shift and then he'll be playing ball at eight o'clock. He wants you to come out and see the game."

"Fine," I said. "I'd like that."

All this was very curious. I hadn't gone to a ball game since leaving the Lions. Hadn't had any desire to do it. At Fair Haven I'd listened to games on the radio, but maybe it had been more for the company than anything else. Now here I was feeling real anticipation. Hot damn. I was going to a ball game. Buy me some peanuts and Cracker Jack. And I was chewing on the biggest sandwich I'd seen in years.

Then I had an idea. "Louise," I said, "let's see if some of the other folks at Fair Haven might like to go and see this game."

Louise

MRS. GRAHAM WAS THE FIRST PERSON WE SAW, BE-
cause she was sitting out on the front porch like she always was.
In profile she looked like a bird. A bird with brittle bones,
perched on the edge of the old green bench on the porch as if
she were waiting for a sign. She was staring out over the grass
like somebody having a vision, and when Mr. Pete Estey stepped
onto the porch and called her by name, she gave a little hop in
her seat.

"Mr. Estey!" she said. "Isn't that a marvel! I was just saying
to Sarah this morning that I certainly hoped I'd see you again
before too long, or I'd forget the message."

"You mean about Jackie Robinson looking for me?" Mr. Pete
Estey asked gently. "You've already given me that message. 'Keep
the faith.' "

" 'Keep the faith'?" Mrs. Graham asked absently. "Oh, no,
I'm sure that wasn't it. It was longer than three words. What
was it, now?"

"Well, listen," Mr. Pete Estey said, "you come to the ball
game with us tonight and maybe you'll remember it. We're
going to see Louise's grandnephew pitch, and you ought to come
on along with us."

"I don't have anything to wear." Mrs. Graham smiled.

But she was ready when we came back later to pick her up. She and an old man named Mr. Moses Labine, whom Mr. Pete Estey had also convinced to go. He'd wanted to invite more, but Mrs. Graham had complained that if he did there wouldn't be any room in the car for her daughters, in case one or two or all three of them showed up at the last minute.

I'd been to a number of Jack Brown's ball games before, of course. His team that played at night used the high school field sometimes if the school boys weren't using it. It was an awful pretty place, the grass as green as any park you'd ever see. The field stretched out flat forever, like the rest of Florida, but for baseball they had a wooden fence that they ran around the park, a temporary fence propped up on the outside. There were wooden bleachers along the first and third baselines, but we'd brought lawn chairs from Fair Haven. Mr. Pete Estey and Mr. Moses Labine set them up just beyond the first-base bleachers, and there we sat.

Along the first-base line some of the boys on Jack's team were warming up, frisky as colts. Some leaned this way and that, stretching their legs. Others played catch to loosen up their arms. Then they leaned back to throw; they pointed their toes, like dancers in their tight pants, and exaggerated each movement, like slow motion. Then they snuck looks at their girlfriends in the wooden bleachers.

They made Mr. Moses Labine uncomfortable, and he said so. "They're awfully close to be throwing so hard," he complained. "One of them could throw a wild one and crush your head like a walnut."

"Didn't you bring your mitt?" asked Mr. Pete Estey. "Jeez, I assumed you knew enough to bring a mitt when you went to see these wild boys. I figured you knew how to protect yourself."

"What the hell are you talking about?" asked Mr. Labine. That was real concern replacing his usual cranky self. He probably hadn't owned a baseball glove in fifty years.

"Ah, well, maybe we'll be lucky," Mr. Pete Estey said. "Maybe they'll hit all the foul balls the other way."

Jack Brown's team took the field, with Jack on the mound. If Mr. Pete Estey's opinion of his future as a pitcher had discouraged him any, he didn't let it show on his face or in the way he carried himself. He looked sure and smooth as he warmed up, and the first batter couldn't manage anything more off him than a little foul pop-up, which the catcher handled without any trouble at all.

"Don't he look slick," I said.

"He looks like a ballplayer," Mr. Pete Estey agreed.

"But not like a pitcher," I said.

"He's a good pitcher right here," said Mr. Pete Estey.

"But not like a major-league pitcher," I said.

"I remember now," shrieked Mrs. Sarah Graham, and several people nearest her in the bleachers looked at her and wondered what was up. "It was Babe Ruth. Isn't that right? Haven't I got the name right?"

"Babe Ruth?" said Mr. Pete Estey.

"Wasn't that his name?" asked Mrs. Graham, who had doubt in her eyes now. People paid no attention to so much of what she said.

"That's a ballplayer's name, all right," Mr. Pete Estey said. "Maybe the best there ever was."

"Skinny legs and a big barrel chest?" The excitement was back in Mrs. Sarah Graham's voice. "Sort of a baby face? Walked kind of pigeon-toed?"

"Oh, for God's sake," snorted Mr. Moses Labine.

"That's Babe Ruth," said Mr. Pete Estey. "What about him?"

"Why, that's who came down the flagpole with the second message for you. That's what I was trying to remember. He said his name was Babe Ruth."

Like I said, Jack Brown was sharp that evening, and by the time Mrs. Sarah Graham had remembered that it was Babe Ruth who'd come down the flagpole and given her a message for Mr. Pete Estey, he'd retired the side in the top of the first inning. That meant that by the time she remembered the message, Jack Brown was kneeling before us in the on-deck circle, like a statue of a strong boy. It wasn't unusual for him to be batting second. Jack could hit with power, like a lot of boys on his team could. It was a hitter's league. But he also controlled the bat pretty well. He could bunt, and he ran well enough so that he didn't clog up the base paths. So he often hit right after the little shortstop, who led off half the games he started with a walk. And so there was Jack Brown, big as life, with two bats on his shoulder.

"I don't know why I couldn't remember it right away," Mrs. Sarah Graham said. "It's not a very long message. He just said to tell you that he once thought he was a pitcher, too."

Mr. Pete Estey heard that the first time, and he looked at me as if he couldn't decide whether to laugh or kick my chair over. "Louise," he said finally, "what the hell's going on here?"

"I don't know what you mean," I told him.

"What are you up to with Mrs. Graham, here?"

"What's she got to do with it?" Mrs. Graham said, apparently mystified.

"Yeah," I said. "What've I got to do with it? Now watch this game. That littlest boy got himself another walk. Jack Brown's up to bat."

"Boy, it's a load off my mind to remember that." Mrs. Sarah Graham sighed. "When I can't remember things, sometimes I worry that my mind's going."

"Your mind's as good as anybody's," I told her.

Jack Brown could hit from either side, though he didn't much like hitting left-handed unless they asked him to bunt. In this game he was up right-handed anyway, because the other team had started a left-hander, and Jack's team always scored runs, so nobody was gonna ask him to bunt in the first inning. What I liked about watching him hit was his stillness. A lot of boys kick at the dirt, dig in their toes, stretch their necks like they slept wrong. They've got all those wristbands and batting gloves to straighten out before they'll step up to the plate. Jack Brown stood still, square to the plate, feet not too far apart. Sometimes if a pitcher took too long he'd step out and spit and step back in again, but mostly he just stood there, like he knew the other boy was gonna have to throw it and he didn't mind waiting.

He didn't have to wait this time up, though. That other boy who was pitching was maybe still thinking about the boy he'd walked to lead off the inning, because he looked like he was in a hurry to do something right. Jack Brown was a big strike zone for him, too, so maybe he was encouraged. Anyway, he reared back out of his stretch and threw a fastball over the plate, and Jack Brown let it go by. He just watched it right into the catcher's glove, like it was a bug or a bird he was pretty sure he was already familiar with but he'd give it a long look to make certain. He didn't step out after the pitch, either. Just stayed loose and still at the plate and let that pitcher hurry up into his stretch and throw that same fastball again, only maybe up a little higher, letter high, and at the last second Jack Brown swung and hit that fastball about nine miles. It got out over the fence so fast that nobody knew quite what to make of it for a few seconds, and then they all jumped up in those wooden bleachers and started to shout, clapping and shouting Jack Brown's name. He didn't waste any time getting around the bases, and he was back in the dugout before the shouting was over.

"What do you think about that?" I asked Mr. Pete Estey. "Ever see a pitcher hit like that before?"

"Sure," he said. "Babe Ruth. But you already knew about that, didn't you?"

"Who's Babe Ruth?" said Mrs. Sarah Graham.

I could always watch a ball game. It didn't have to be Ebbets Field, though there's never been anything like that since. But you put me alongside any park, big or little, where there's a ball game about to start and I'll be happy. Some people say baseball's a boring game. I have to give them the benefit of the doubt and some human charity and assume they say that because they don't know the game. If I weren't inclined in that way, I'd say they were fools. Once you know the game a little, you see that even when nobody's throwing the ball or hitting it, there's plenty going on. You've got your pitcher trying to set up the hitter by throwing inside and then outside, up and then down. Hitters are trying to guess what's coming next, or at least some of 'em do that. Fielders are shifting here and there according to who's up and how many are out and who's on base and what's the score at the time.

And each of those boys out there, at least the ones that know the game, is doing what he can to help. That littlest boy that hit in front of Jack Brown would have to bat four times to hit one as far as the home run Jack hit, but he was smart enough not to try. He was smart enough to know his run counted just as much as the one Jack Brown scored behind him. He hit out of a funny little old man's crouch and got on base with walks. And if the pitcher threw him strikes, he looked over the infield to see if he could find somebody slow or lazy somewhere and bunt his way on. If the third baseman and the first baseman both looked like they were on their toes and watchin' him, he'd climb right up almost on top of the plate where an inside pitch might nick his shirt, or where he could lean a little and just poke at an outside pitch with his choked-up bat and cozy it over the second baseman's head like Wee Willie Keeler used to do.

And all that was just when this littlest boy was up at bat, because there were a hundred other things he'd always be trying to do in the field to help out. Before a pitch he'd jump back toward second base to take a step away from a runner who was leading toward third. He'd shout who'd be playing where when there were men on base, and on a ball hit to the outfield he'd be in line to cut off the throw. You couldn't watch that boy for thirty seconds and say there was nothing going on out there, even if they were only changing pitchers while you were watching. Not if you were really watching him. And even I could tell that as far as his gifts went, he was no kind of prospect at all. He was playing just as high up as he was ever going to play. I didn't need a scout like Mr. Pete Estey to tell me that. But, my, that littlest boy playing shortstop was playing it with all there was of him. He loved the game, and that love shone on him through the dirt of each slide and the sweat of his hard running.

Once you learn to see, you know, you can't be bored. Not at a baseball game. Mrs. Sarah Graham hadn't seen a lot of baseball games before, but she caught on to that right away. It appeared she could have been content right through a double-header, surrounded by all that color and noise, and getting up to shout when the folks behind her did. She'd have something to tell her daughters about all right, she said.

Mr. Moses Labine wasn't so content, though. He complained that one leg of his lawn chair was sinking into the ground and he might fall over. After I got up and helped him straighten that out, he said if he'd known the sun would be so strong, he'd have worn a hat. Mrs. Sarah Graham pointed out to him that the sun had gone down some time ago, that it was the lights overhead that were so bright, and that besides, he *was* wearing a hat. That kept Mr. Labine quiet for another half an inning, but by the time Jack Brown had shut down the other team in the top of the third inning on nothing but an infield single, he was complaining again. There were some young boys hooting and carrying on in the bleachers behind us, and Mr. Labine said it wouldn't be long before one of them would slip up and stick a knife in his back and take his wallet, because it happened all the time.

"I'm not finished here," said Mr. Pete Estey.

"Well, you're a hell of a host," said Mr. Labine. "Here we

are, sitting ducks for thugs and muggers. The blood's left my feet. We never should have come, if you ask me."

"Relax and enjoy yourself," said Mr. Pete Estey.

"Sure, relax," Mr. Labine grumbled. "Relax in this goddamn chair that's cutting off my circulation so I'll probably get gangrene. Relax until somebody chasing a foul ball trips over me and tumbles me over and breaks every bone in my body."

"Oh, for God's sake," Mr. Pete Estey finally said. "Louise, why don't you take Moses and Sarah back to Fair Haven? You can pick me up on the way back, if it's not too much trouble."

"No trouble at all," I told him. I didn't want to walk away from the game, but I'd seen Jack Brown play lots of times. I'd see him play lots more.

Mr. Moses Labine and Mrs. Sarah Graham and I got ourselves straightened around, our chairs and sweaters and caps accounted for, and headed for the parking lot. I let them get a step or two ahead, Mr. Moses Labine carrying on about how dark and dangerous it was, and I stopped and looked back at Mr. Pete Estey on the first-base line. He was hunched forward in his chair now, with his chin in his hands. He was concentrating on the batter, I guess, though from where I was the bleachers blocked me from seeing just what he was looking at. He was as still in his seat as Jack Brown at the plate, like he wanted to make sure he wasn't missing a thing. He didn't look like he minded that he had no company now. Maybe it had just been him and the ball game anyhow, and now he didn't even need to be polite.

I watched him like that, leaning toward the field like a doctor, or a professor. Then I caught up to Mr. Moses Labine and Mrs. Sarah Graham in the parking lot. I got them back to Fair Haven in nothing flat, and turned right around in case I could get back in time to see the end of the game. On that return trip I probably even drove too fast, Lord forgive me, but I hated to miss the game.

Luck wasn't with me, though. Jack Brown and that other boy

pitching must have been too good for either team to fool around with relievers. It was a quick one. As I pulled into the parking lot, the other cars were pulling out. But the lights over the field were still on, and I didn't suppose that Mr. Pete Estey was going anywhere without me.

I walked toward the diamond in the warm night, ready to hear all the stories of the game I'd missed. Several little boys were running around the bases now, shouting and sliding to beat imaginary throws, while their parents sat quietly in the bleachers, enjoying the time under the stars before they went home.

I didn't see either Jack Brown or Mr. Pete Estey until I'd come all the way around the bleachers on the first-base side, where the lawn chair I'd left him in sat empty. Then I saw them both, behind the backstop, talking to each other, I guess, but looking out at the field as if there were still something to see out there, still a game going on. Neither of them noticed me at all until I was right beside them. Mr. Pete Estey had a bat in his hands.

"You telling him something about hitting now?" I asked him.

Mr. Pete Estey didn't answer me right away. He was fiddling with that baseball bat, flexing his old, bony fingers on it, smiling like he could remember his own hitting days. Or maybe he was just enjoying the feel of the wood. Maybe he just liked touching that bat. Anyway, he was in no hurry to answer me, but when he finally did turn toward me, it was with the kind of smile you give to somebody who's made a joke but doesn't know it.

"I don't have anything to tell this fellow about hitting," he said quietly. "And I'll tell you something else. I'd step right into the way of any other guy who thought he could tell him anything about hitting, too. Punch him right in the nose if I had to."

Jack Brown went on home then, saying he had to be at the station in the morning.

We watched him walk away under the park lights. When he had disappeared beyond the far end of the parking lot, Mr. Pete

Estey suddenly snapped awake and said, "Damn! I forgot to ask him when the next game is. When does he play again, Louise?"

"You're gonna see him before he plays again," I told him. "You can bet on that."

"What do you mean?" he asked.

"Look at you," I said. "You still got his bat."

Pete

YOU KNOW THE WISH YOU HAVE SOMETIMES THAT YOU could cut all the crap away from your life? Simplify everything? You look around at the clutter you've accumulated in the normal days of living, the drawers and cabinets full of things, the shelves and closets and attics crammed with all the baggage of a life. And maybe you say, *I could do all right with one plate, one mug, a knife, a fork, and a spoon. I don't need all these appliances waiting to break, all these scraps of projects abandoned in the basement and boxes half full of one thing and another from the hardware store. I could shed this junk. I could go live in a cabin on a mountain.*

People say it. *I don't need this.* But the world is relentless. It piles things on.

And it isn't just what builds up in the corners. It's the scuffling with the phone company or the gas company over whether you've paid the bill. It's the dripping faucet and the car that clanks mysteriously when you drive it back from the service station and the pipes that back up on Sunday. The shoes that pinch and the paint that flakes off and the raccoon in the garbage can again. It's insurance forms, madmen on the bus, or an odor you can't quite put your finger on that might kill you in your sleep.

But we don't, most of us, go off to live on a mountain. We subscribe to all the aggravation. I've known men who sat in traffic jams for two hours twice a day. Each morning they got up, they knew they were going to do this.

Jack Brown swung his bat that night and there, clear as ice water, was the antidote. No clutter. He hit like he was born to it. He hit like some women dance.

Twenty-five years after he retired, Ted Williams was still going to Winter Haven, where the Red Sox trained, and working with the young kids in the system, trying to show them something about hitting. Paunchy and belligerent, he looked ridiculous in that double-knit uniform they'd given him. Or at least he would have if you didn't remember that he was Ted Williams. And he'd badger and cajole those kids, and grab the bat out of their hands to show them how he had done it. Any kid who actually tried to listen to everything Ted Williams had to say about hitting would go away with his head spinning, convinced that hitting a baseball on the button was as complicated as getting to the moon. And Ted was an aggressive teacher, too. He really would grab the bat right out of their hands. So he cowed a lot of kids who'd tighten up about it, even while he was shouting at them to relax. And of course the funny thing was that while Williams played, you never heard any of those complicated theories he came up with later. He just used to say he saw the ball and hit it.

What the Red Sox should have done was set up an endless videotape of Ted Williams, aged twenty-three, swinging the bat in games. The picture of Williams doing what he did better than anyone has since might have helped. No noise. Just the picture, clear and simple.

But Jack Brown hadn't studied hitting, hadn't paid any particular attention to anyone else who was trying to do it except for the boys he was trying to get out, one at a time. As far as he was concerned, he was a pitcher. But something in him smarter than whatever thought he was a pitcher worked the message out to his eyes and his wrists and his hips that he was a hitter. And though Williams was always represented as the man who'd gotten hitting down to a science, that was the way it had been with him, too. He could talk to you forever about how he shifted his weight or held his hands or swung up to make sure he maximized his chance of getting the fat part of the bat on the ball — whatever — but what he did when he swung . . . you could no more take that apart and explain it with physics than you could reduce to a formula the act of love.

I don't mean Jack Brown hit like Ted Williams. He *was* like a lot of great hitters you might have seen, but then he wasn't. In the smooth, unhurried swing there was some Ernie Banks, but he was bigger than Banks. In one at-bat that night I saw him do something Hank Aaron could do when he was in his prime. His wrists were so quick that he could wait on a pitch, wait, wait until the catcher thought he had it in his mitt, then he'd roll those wrists and drive the ball right out of the park. I'm not exaggerating. I've seen catchers watch Aaron's drives sail out, and then look into their gloves, the way a man who discovers his wallet's been lifted will keep patting his hip pocket after he knows damn well there's nothing there.

But what Jack Brown did wasn't sleight of hand or magic. It was just right. You look back at all the junk, as I said, or the traffic jams, or all the clumsiness and false starts in a life — that's what's unnatural. Jack's swing was the pure act, unencumbered. Up on a mountain, alone, it would have been lovely. But in that ballpark, a place designed for his swing just in case it might come along someday, it was a kind of fulfillment.

Of course, even on the night I first saw all this, I worried that it might be just an old man wanting what he saw to be special, because it might be the last special thing he'd see.

The bedroom off Louise's kitchen was just barely large enough for me to swing a bat in if I choked up a little. For some time

before I went to bed that night, the night we'd seen Jack play, I
stood, feet planted, and tried to duplicate Jack's swing, first in
slow motion, teaching myself again, and then to the beat of
imaginary pitches, fastballs, one after another.

In the morning I walked into the kitchen as if the hanger was
still in my shirt.

"What's the matter with you?" Louise said when I sat down
at her breakfast table. "Sleep on the wrong side of the bed?"

"That must be it," I said.

"Should we get you a board for that bed? Maybe it's too soft."

"It's fine," I said. "The bed's fine. The fellow sleeping in it's
too old to be swinging a baseball bat before he gets in it, that's
all."

"That's right." She nodded. "Just stick to being a scout. No
need to come all the way out of that retirement to your playing
days."

She put three pieces of French toast in front of me, already
buttered and covered with syrup. I looked at her and didn't have
to say a thing.

"I know, I know," she said. "It's a lot of breakfast for a morning
in the middle of the week. But you gotta keep your strength up.
There's a lotta work to do, now that you discovered Jack Brown's
a hitter."

"When'd you discover it?" I asked.

"Discover what?" she muttered. Her back was to me now. She
was fussing with something at the sink.

"Oh, I see," I told her. "You never knew what he was either.
As far as you were concerned, he was going to be a major-league
pitcher. Even though you saw Jackie Robinson hit. Probably saw
Joe DiMaggio and Willie Mays, too. Probably saw Sweet Billy
Williams. Hell, probably saw Josh Gibson."

"I saw Satchel Paige," she said.

"Yes, but we're not talking about pitchers now, are we?" I
said. "We're talking about hitters. My question was, when'd you
see that Jack was a hitter?"

"Oh," she said.

"Yes, oh," I said.

She sat down with a cup of coffee. She never ate much breakfast herself.

"I could have fooled you, Louise," I said. "I could have gone out on that damn high school field the other morning under all that Florida sun and pitched a fit in the dirt. I could have fallen down with sunstroke and come up babbling, useless to you. You'd have deserved it. It was a cruel thing to put an old man through that charade."

She sipped her coffee. She looked as if she was considering what to say next, considering from a distance. Sizing me up, maybe. What a gulf there was between us.

"You wouldn't have believed it," she said.

"I went to see him pitch," I said. "I went out in the sun of the morning and damn near fainted and watched him pitch, on your say-so."

"I wasn't so sure myself," she said. "I wanted to see what you'd make of him as a hitter, just seeing him cold like that."

So you see? There is no escaping what life lays on us, is there? The best of us is treacherous in a pinch, and I was feeling sorry as hell for myself. That stream in the mountains would run soapsuds eventually. From that cabin you'd hear, distant at first, the murmur, then the rumble, then the crash and roar of the bulldozer, come to clear the way for hamburger joints. Or else you'd betray yourself. You'd get out there among the daisies and the grazing deer, and you'd miss something too much to stay. Something trivial. A TV series, or a newspaper comic strip. Beauty and truth wouldn't be enough after all.

But meanwhile here was Jack Brown, banging away on cars all day and hitting baseballs on the nose at night, or vice versa. Even pitching well enough to keep him in somebody's uniform for twenty or thirty more years, well after he'd stopped dreaming his major-league dreams. And here was his great-aunt, devious as a sneak thief, backed by God and good intentions. How did she keep a straight face at the breakfast table? She knew I'd made a fool of myself, knew I'd had that bat in my grip long after the lights in the neighborhood had all gone out, knew I'd been reaching back for a groove that hadn't been there for half a century. The results were before her. *Ecce homo ignoramus*, back bent, hip throbbing, wrists like two peeled sticks.

But how long until Jack turned an odometer back, started selling the inventory out the back door, chopped a stolen car one night and found out how easy it was? How long until Louise went the Lord's way entirely and turned to choirs and scripture instead of baseball dreams? How long until my heart opened one heavy-lidded eye, took a long, dreary look at what it was pumping life through, and found the mercy to quit?

"It didn't matter that it wasn't my idea," I said. "It doesn't even matter now."

"What does that mean?" Louise said cautiously.

"It's like they say in the movies," I told her. "It's bigger than both of us."

So that morning, after breakfast, I made a phone call. I'll tell you how lost I was with the whole business, how long since I'd paid it any attention. I didn't even know for certain who to call. But when I'd reached the Lions, who'd moved to Washington since I'd had anything to do with them, I found out it was still Emmett Flanagan who ran their scouting, and he was polite enough to act as though he was happy to hear from me.

"We really lost touch with you, Pete," he said. "We don't like to do that, you know. You're part of the family."

"All right," I said. "How's the family doing?"

"Oh, hell," he said, "this is the sweetest setup you ever saw. The commissioner wanted a franchise in D.C. so bad he just about paid us to move. Got a hell of a fine ballpark, never rains in here. No complaints at all, 'cept we could use a left-handed reliever, but so could everybody else. What have you been up to?"

"Well," I said, "I saw a kid play ball the other night, and you might be interested in him."

He must have known when I called that I thought I had a prospect for him. Why else would a retired scout call the team he'd worked for? But even so, I hadn't given him time enough to figure out exactly what to say. Still, Flanagan was a pro, so the uncomfortable silence only went on for a few seconds, and then he said, "Well, Pete, what's his name? Where is he in school? I'll call up his file."

"His name's Jack Brown and he's playing semi-pro down here in Florida. But he won't be in your computer."

"Oh, you'd be surprised," he said. "Where in Florida?"

"Vernon," I told him. "And I sure would be surprised. He dropped out of school up in New York and came down here. He hasn't played any organized ball except this semi-pro for a couple of teams."

"What's Vernon near?" he asked.

"Tampa," I told him. "St. Pete."

"And you say Brown's his name? How old is he?"

"His aunt says twenty," I said.

"He have a middle name? Social security number?"

"I don't know," I said.

I must have sounded half apologetic, because he said, "Aw, don't worry about it. Just might have been able to punch up his file faster if we knew. Don't matter." Then there was another pause, and he said. "Yup, there he is. Says he's a pitcher."

"I'll be damned," I said. "Yes, that's what he says too."

"Not much that's promising, though, Pete. He's gone to a couple camps down there, and he didn't show much. Nobody thought he was any good."

"You keep files on guys who aren't any good?" I asked.

"From this I'd say he throws easy, like he knows what he's doing. But he doesn't have a big-league fastball."

"That's right enough," I said.

"So, what the hell, Pete?"

What the hell, indeed. What was I going to tell him, the man and his machine? That I'd seen Jack swing a bat and it had made me dream? Emmett Flanagan wouldn't be impressed. And if I told him I'd grabbed hold of a bat myself, he'd be sure I was nuts.

"What I liked when I saw him was his bat," I said. "I like him as a hitter."

"Well," Flanagan said, "I'll tell you what you do. You write up a standard report on this guy. I'll send you the new form. You gotta put him in a position somewhere, because we already know he isn't a pitcher. And then send the report up here, and put to my attention on it, okay?"

"All right," I said.

"Guess who I heard from?" he'd be saying later on that day, if he remembered it. "Old Pete Estey. He's somewhere down in Florida. Must still be watching ball games. Calls here today with a kid he saw. Say, who'd he ever sign, anyway?"

And somebody else would say, "Jeez, Pete Estey. I thought he was dead."

Then they'd go back into their offices, where they'd shuffle papers and make some phone calls and peek at their watches every now and then, like people who work at desks anywhere else.

It would surprise people to know how dull the business of baseball is. In the papers you read about the salary wars and the holdouts, and it sounds pretty dramatic. Or every once in a while a general manager will do something stupid, like miss a deadline for sending out a contract and lose a player, the way the Red Sox lost Carlton Fisk in the middle of his career. Then poor Haywood Sullivan looked like a fool. But most of the people who work for the ball teams are no more or less stupid or interesting than people who work anywhere else. They may value loyalty more, in a peculiar way. They will talk pretty solemnly about the traditions of whatever club they're working for, what it means to be a Dodger or a Yankee or an Oriole. But when they switch jobs, they slip right into the new club's traditions, or help make some up if that's what they're hired for.

Beneath Dodger Blue or Yankee Pinstripes or the Oriole Way, most people who work in baseball do feel loyal to the game itself, and it's this loyalty that sustains baseball men, who make up a fraternity based on about equal parts love of the game and gratitude for a job in it. That means baseball men — and I don't mean players now, but old men who can't play anymore, some who never could — are pretty clannish, more so than members of the Elks or the Rotary or any country club. They're suspicious of change, outsiders, and even insiders who don't behave themselves. Pitchers, especially left-handed pitchers, can get away with being goofy for a while, but eventually any ballplayer who even reads is liable to be labeled a flake.

Anyway, the idea, of course, is for the team to win on the ballfield, but only four of the twenty-six teams win division championships each year, and the idea in the offices upstairs is to keep the customer more or less satisfied and to make some money, just like it is in any other business. That means looking like you're trying to make trades to improve a bad team, even if you aren't, which has some of the excitement of show business about it. It also means lining up advertisers and talking to writers all the time. It means making sure the concession stands are stocked and the city's going to okay the new parking and the hot-water works in the locker room. It means double-checking the hotel reservations and the flights between cities, and talking to doctors and trying to guess which pitchers are whining and which ones are really hurt. It's everything from that to worrying about whether the kids you hire to clean up are smoking dope in the stalls or selling pills to your players.

And a baseball office goes along like any other office, too. Lots of owners of ball teams have reputations as crazy, irresponsible, self-indulgent children, and some of them deserve it. Some of them are as hard to work for as the papers say. But even so, there aren't many people who really get fired in baseball. Oh, managers and coaches get fired, of course, but they generally get hired again pretty quickly somewhere else in the game, even the bad ones. Check Don Zimmer's line in the *Baseball Encyclopedia* and see how many teams he's worked for. General managers, public relations men, broadcasters, and traveling secretaries, just the same. Most of them get along by going along, and when they're finished getting along in one organization, they move over to another one and get along there. Wherever they're working, they're liable to move into their new offices and find people they've worked alongside somewhere else. Then they all give each other a fifth of bourbon for Christmas.

There's a phrase you hear a lot in baseball, "catch lightning in a bottle." It means a team suddenly starts shining in ways nobody can quite explain. Several players start hitting a little better than anyone ever thought they would, and the balls that have to stay fair to win ball games do. Nobody who's pitching well gets hurt for months at a time, or if they do, somebody comes up from triple-A and pitches even better. When a team catches lightning in a bottle, it can win the pennant, even if everybody figured it for fifth place before the season started.

But front offices don't catch lightning in a bottle. Front offices don't even like surprises, and a scout who used to work for them calling up about a kid he's seen play is a surprise. Who needs to hear from an old guy who might as well have been dead for all anybody knew? Especially an old guy who got canned?

Old people are another group that doesn't need surprises. When you wake up with a peach-sized bruise on your arm and you don't remember banging it on anything, that's a surprise. Or when you're having a dream that you can run, and you wake up with your legs aching in the rainy dawn. So I admit it. I was relieved when the phone call to Emmett Flanagan went the way it did. No real surprises. He hadn't told his secretary to say he wasn't in, which wouldn't have surprised me, but he'd brushed me off. I knew that while I was talking to him, and knew it again when no form had arrived two weeks after I'd talked to him.

All right, I thought. *That's that.* And I said to Louise, "Look, they've got Jack in the computer. The only way to get anywhere is for him to go to another tryout camp, only this time as a position player. Then he has to run and throw well enough to get a chance to play in a simulated game. Then in the one or two at-bats he'll get, he's got to hit the ball hard enough to impress the scouts as much as he's impressed me. Then he'll be in the computer as a prospect. Not just the Lions' computer, everybody's computer. And maybe somebody will look at their screen when he's on it and like what they see. That's the way we'll do it."

"I think maybe it's time for a trip," she said.

"We'll play by their rules," I said. "Jack will do fine at a tryout. It's just a matter of waiting for another one to come along, and meanwhile we'll get him to work on a position with one of those teams he's already playing for."

"A trip north would be nice this time of year," she said.

"What are you talking about?" I asked her.

"Talking about going up north to see the Lions play," she said.

"Oh, look," I told her, "hell, I'll call them back again. Maybe they really meant to send that form down and it just got lost under something on Flanagan's desk. I'll call them and stir them up."

"We'll bring Jack Brown," she said. "He should see a big-league game."

Louise

THEY HAD FAIR HAVEN FIXED UP FASTER THAN YOU'D think. Or at least they thought they did.

First the insurance people came in and sniffed around a little. Mr. Moses Labine pulled one of them into his room and said how he thought it was hoodlums and gangsters who had set the fire. "Almost certainly Negroes," he said. I heard him. But the insurance man was black and didn't pay any attention to Mr. Moses Labine.

Then a bunch of boys came in and ripped out the charred wood, which made a racket for a couple of days. Had everybody wandering into everybody else's rooms, saying "What's goin' on?" or banging on the ceiling with canes and broom handles because they thought it was the folks upstairs.

That noise and confusion looked like it was the worst part of it, but it didn't last too long. Then the carpenters and painters took over, and before you knew it, looked like the whole place was ready for business as usual, back end and all.

Only thing was, first night after all the workmen had gone on to somewhere else, Mrs. Sarah Graham went and pulled the fire alarm in the hall. That emptied the place again, and once everybody was outside the nurses and aides went through it, but nobody could find a fire. So we went back on the porch to see who had pulled the alarm, and by and by Mrs. Sarah Graham remembered that she was the one who had done it. We gave her a little time, and she even remembered why she did it, which was that she smelled smoke.

"And then," she said, "I wasn't sure whether I only smelled it or saw it too. Or whether it was just smoke or fire. Or burglars. So I thought I'd better pull the alarm."

That opened the door, and half the rest of the people on the porch started saying how they smelled smoke, too. Smelled it even right there, standing in the air out on the porch.

Now they were right, of course. You get a fire in a house, it'll smell like smoke for a while, no matter how you clean it out. Some days it won't seem to, but then let it rain and be humid, and the smoke smell comes back on you, like a bad memory. Anybody's ever stayed in a house where there's been fire can tell you that.

But at Fair Haven it was worse, because nobody had anything much else to keep their minds off it. Smoke smell was the big story. So the next day another crew of workers came in, and they were from something called Fire Restoration Services, with a shiny truck and uniforms to boot. They came in with masks, tanks on their backs, little black hoses, and those black rubber boots on their feet, like men from outer space. Then the dumbest thing they did was tell anybody who'd listen — which was everybody, because folks in Fair Haven who could still listen didn't have a whole lot else to listen to — that they were gonna break up the molecules that were smelling so bad. That's what they said. Break up the smoke molecules.

Once they talked like that, 'course whether they could do what they said they were gonna do or not didn't make any difference at all. While they went to work in their boots and their masks, the residents were already turning over the news in their heads. I could see it. Only thing left to find out was who'd complain first. Turned out it was Mrs. Eunice Babcock, who couldn't see much anymore and had to walk right up against you to make sure she was talking to who she wanted to be talking to.

"Louise," she said to me, with her nose up under my chest, "my molecules are breaking down. I'm a goner. Too old to move anywhere else, too blind to see my way out. But if you're smart, you'll skedaddle away from here before yours start coming apart too. Before your teeth fall out and you leave your toes in your shoes one night when you take 'em off."

A few hours later and that's all you could hear about. People who complained before about arthritis or bleeding gums or sore feet, they said now their molecules were broken. Headaches, spots in front of their eyes, couldn't keep their breakfast down — it was all the broken molecules.

I told 'em hot tea and bed rest was good for that. Tea would soothe those molecules and get 'em back together. I walked 'em around in the halls to try to get their minds off the molecules, too. But whatever those boys in their uniforms did spray all around the place, and whatever else it was doing, it smelled pretty bad itself. Smelled like living near a chemical plant on a wet, hot day. Thick as syrup, so you almost tasted it. Worse than the smoke, which was sneaky. Sometimes it was there, and then again maybe you only thought you smelled it. This spray smell while the molecules were breaking was *there*, and no doubt about it, like somebody drove a truck full of fruit right up to the door and let it stand there in the sun too long. I heard one of the men say that was the lemon scent.

Finally they had to clean the place out, top to bottom. People who had family near enough went to them for a while. People who didn't went to another home or a hospital until they could get the smell of the spray out. It was like the man who gets cats to get rid of the mice, then dogs to get rid of the cats. Anyway, we all got a little paid vacation.

So I said to Mr. Pete Estey that we'd go on up to Washington and see that man he knew and show him he couldn't just tell

us he was gonna mail us a form and we'd wait for it until we
forgot that he was supposed to send it or what we were waiting
for in the first place. We'd walk right into his office and say,
"Here's Jack Brown, take a look at him. Give him a chance to
show how he's gonna knock the cover off the ball for you."

I'm always watching and listening for signs and indications.
Be a fool not to. It took the fire to get Mr. Pete Estey out of
Fair Haven and off the idea that all there was left for him was
just to wait and die. I knew once he saw Jack play, he couldn't
let it alone, and that was just how it was. Now here came some
time with nobody to care for but me and him, at least for a little
while, and get paid for it too. I could take care of him on the
way to Washington and back as well as anywhere else, and Jack
would be along, just in case.

'Course I didn't expect him to agree to go right away. But he
didn't put up the fight you might think, either. He moaned and
groaned for a while about traveling, what a trial it was. Said
how you didn't just walk into the office of a baseball team and
sell them a player like you were a salesman with a vacuum
cleaner. But right in the middle of it he got this funny look in
his eye that was something like "I'll show this foolish old woman.
I'll go along with her crazy plan, and it'll come to nothing, and
then we'll go home and do it my way."

I didn't care about that. Didn't matter one way or the other
how we got there. Didn't matter when he showed me in the
paper that the Lions wouldn't even be in Washington when we
could go. They'd be in California and Texas that week, on a
road trip. "We'll see 'em play another time," I said. "Maybe
when Jack Brown's already helpin' 'em. This time we'll just go
up there and take a look around and say hello."

It used to be when you traveled, you saw the land change as
you went along. Take the train south from New York, see the
land spread out as you go. Take the train north and watch it as

it gets so full of people, the land itself seems to tighten up instead of spread out. Seems to clench its fists and hunch its shoulders, so by the time you get in toward New York you aren't even surprised there's little boys standing up on the trestle throwing rocks at the cars going by. Bus or car, it's the same way. You see the land begin to stretch and breathe, start to grow things, as you go south of the big cities. Coming north you see it clench up tight with all the steel and concrete that's laid over it.

Florida's different, of course. I remember when Edward Baker Brown and I first came down and it was a wonder. One thing I remember was grapefruit, broken and rotted, lying right by the side of the road. Walk down the sidewalk, you could kick it. "Look at that," I told Brown. "What do you think? So much food growing wild down here, falls off the trees and nobody even to pick it up. Just grows and falls. Like the Garden of Eden. Like the promised land."

"Can't live on just grapefruit," he said. "Better find a hamburger tree, I guess." He said it just to devil me.

Next thing I remember when we first came to Florida was the trailer parks hard up against the highway. There was nothing but a fence with green strips of plastic in it to keep the highway out. Buses and cars bringin' more folks in every day, all that road noise all day long behind whatever you were doing in your trailer. Row after row of trailers, hundreds of 'em, sometimes, people sittin' outside, under the plastic awnings, drinking until they fell asleep. It made me think the old people's homes down here weren't as sad as the ones back in New York, where folks could only lie in bed all day or hope somebody would visit and you felt they were missing out on something. Down here so many of the folks who were still outside the homes were doing just the same as the folks in 'em.

But Florida's a crazy place in lots of ways. Seems like somehow the state skipped the middle of everything. In Tampa, St. Petersburg, the other cities I know down here, everything looks like it just went up yesterday and it might blow down tomorrow. Not just the hamburger places, the used-car lots, and the blocks of condos. Even the banks look like plastic banks, like some giant child with a railroad train is gonna come along to play with them anytime. Then you get outside the cities, there's swamp that's been the same for a million years, bugs as big as your fist, alligators that got frozen out or stomped out or skinned out everywhere else a long time back. They're still slippin' around in the swamp, lookin' like dinosaurs, every once in a while eatin' somebody's dog just to show we can't pave it all over and cover it up with red and green and yellow plastic. Alligators crawl up and snap their teeth, just to remind us. Alligators and the big bugs are the old ones. New buildings, new trailers that rust with the salt overnight, new cars, new machines for everything you need to do . . . take your money out of the bank anytime you want, plastic heart if yours quits, new church every time you turn around, too, and it's made out of plastic, same as the others.

It's the middle that's missing. You have as hard a time finding a farm that's been in a family for generations down here as you have finding a brownstone building on a street made of bricks. Same with the people, mostly. Springtime the colleges let out, boys and girls come down here, drink in the streets, make fools of themselves, fall out the hotel windows on their heads sometimes. And then the baseball players are down here in March. And there're all the folks who did all the work somewhere else until they got to quit or had to quit or couldn't feel their feet in the cold winters up north, and they come down here. The ones who bring a lot of money find a house on the water, or they build one in some space where nobody managed to build anything yet, and then sit and look out at the sea. The ones who don't bring a lot of money get a trailer and sit on the plastic deck and look out at the highway full of cars full of people just like them. They stare at each other and think their thoughts, and the cars go by too fast for any advice or wisdom or even good wishes, if there were anything to say. After a while the people on the decks or under the awnings don't even wave anymore. And along the road all the McDonald's and Kentucky Frieds and the others just gleam in the sun and multiply, and in the swamp the bugs crawl and the alligators go *snap, snap.*

So a trip was a fine idea. Mr. Pete Estey, for his own reasons, went along. Like I said, he was sure it would just mean we'd come home and do it his way, because he doesn't have any use for signs and indications. Ignores 'em, like he does prayers. Just like Edward Baker Brown used to be. So he called his friend, Mr. Emmett Flanagan, and said we were coming, and then what could *he* say but "You come on in and we'll talk about it."

Then I surprised him. I said, "Look, we're gonna do this trip the right way. No old bus for us, and not a train, either. We'll fly up to Washington. Only takes a couple of hours, I found out. With my time off, we'll get the middle-of-the-week fare. It's lots cheaper than a bus and a hotel. Fly right up there, do our business, fly back."

"Now that's funny," Mr. Pete Estey said. "I kind of had you pegged for somebody who'd want to make the most of a trip like this. I thought you'd want to visit the Lincoln Memorial and climb the Washington Monument. Take in a wax museum, maybe. I thought you'd want to stay in town for a while."

"Jack's got baseball games to play," I told him. "Besides, he's got the garage. He's still gotta work, even if you and I don't."

So it was all set and established. And I guess I just put it out of my mind that I never had been up in an airplane before. I didn't even think about it until we were in our seats, Mr. Pete Estey and me side by side. Jack was off somewhere else, because something in the computers was wrong, they told us, so the seats they said we had weren't on the screen there, not three together, and Jack said, "I don't care where I sit, ma'am," so they put him somewhere else.

And then all of a sudden I did think about it. Couldn't help it. I heard those big motors start to cough out on the wings and then roar, and it flashed before me that we'd just start down that runway and get going faster and faster, noisier and noisier, and we'd never fly at all, just roll along that ground faster and faster until we hit whatever it was we'd hit — you can't see out except to the sides on an airplane, so no use to try to tell what might be right there in front of you — and we'd just hit it and blow up. Flames coming down that plane from the front, everybody'd be trying to get up and squeeze out in that little narrow aisle, hardly room to put your hat up over your seat and somebody to get by at the same time.

I could see it. So we started to roll, and I began to shriek. I don't know what all I said, might have been awful. But the next thing I know, here's a lady running down the aisle at me, looks like I'm the last thing she wants to see, and then Mr. Pete Estey takes hold of my arm and pulls me back into my seat — I guess I was standing — and he says, "She'll be all right, miss. I'll take care of her. She's with me." I remember just how he said that.

The stewardess looks like she's not sure, looks at Mr. Pete Estey and at me. I guess I'd shut up by then, or I was only just sobbing. She looks back at Mr. Pete Estey again, like she can't understand what he's saying.

"She's with me," he says again. "We're traveling together. She'll be fine."

Next thing I know, I'm back in my seat at least, and Mr. Pete Estey has both my hands in his, and he's bending his face in close to mine and saying, "Tell me about your children."

"My children!" I say. "My children gonna be orphans! Listen to that thunder. Feel it push you back in your seat. We're goin' fast, but we're not gettin' up. Gonna hit somethin' and die!"

"Tell me about their births," he said. "Tell me about the first one first."

"She was the hardest," I told him. "Lord, when is this plane gonna rise? Just listen to all that noise."

I guess he had to pull my hands off my ears to keep talkin' to me. "First one is always the hardest, I've heard." That's what he said next.

"Yessir," I said. "That's right. First is worst. Poor Brown had to wait overnight and most of the next day for her to come. Told me later it was harder than being at war."

"A long labor," Mr. Pete Estey said.

"Didn't I just say that, fool?"

"But everything was all right."

"Eleven *pounds* of all right," I told him. "Eleven pounds that baby weighed. Nothing all right about that, believe me."

"But ten fingers and ten toes," he said. "You know."

"Plenty of fingers and toes." I nodded. "And a funny thing about Caroline, too. She got to be long and tall right away. Never was a fat child. Narrow waist when she grew up, too."

"And the next one was easier, I'll bet," Mr. Pete Estey said.

"Just quicker," I told him. "None of 'em are easy. Second was Anne. She started out fine, but then she kept us up with colic all night until she was six months old. Kept me up, anyway. Brown slept right through it unless I kicked him to get some company, though he said he never did. Caroline slept through it too."

I don't know how long it had been since I'd talked to anybody about when my children were born. A long time. And maybe never to any man who wasn't a doctor. Brown had no stomach for it, that's for sure. He loved his children. He held 'em, sang to 'em, carried 'em around on his shoulders until he was about to fall down. But he wouldn't stay still for talk about how it was when they were born. I'll say for him that that was before men came right along into the delivery room and did breathing exercises or whatever it is they do now. Men just waited outside then, and that suited Brown fine. Just like the Indian men who'd wait around the campfire smoking their pipes while the women went off in the bushes somewhere to have children. Braves, they called 'em.

But here I was on that airplane for the first time, tellin' Mr. Pete Estey all about those children and those days. Tellin' him things I didn't even know I remembered. And then when I'd got through with it, he said, "Look at that, now," and pointed out the window where I was sitting. We were sailing through the clouds by then, and in the breaks between 'em you could see the land pulling away from us, cars like toys on the ground, so we were up after all.

When Washington got a team the third or fourth time, whatever it was, they put it in a new building with a roof, air conditioning, plastic grass, and all. Mr. Pete Estey said it was because the owners figured the teams that had left for places like Minnesota and Texas had already proved Washington was no baseball town, so they had to have football, soccer, car races, everything you can think of going on in there when there wasn't baseball to watch. Only way to make any money, they said, and nobody didn't know that's why they were in it in the first place, even with all the talk about the tradition and Washington deserving a team and all that. So they got the new stadium out west of the city — not in the city at all, like the old ballparks were — and they put a lot of parking around it, because that was another thing you had to have if you were going to make money.

When you came up on Ebbets Field, of course, you didn't even see it until you were right in front, except for the lights standin' up on top, if you were lookin' for 'em. Mr. Pete Estey says that's the way it is with the old ballparks that are still left, too. Boston, Detroit, Chicago, places like that. But the folks in Washington plunked that big dome down where there was nothing around it but the parking, because that's how they do it now. So it looks like some kind of flying saucer or something, landed in a big empty field. Made Mr. Pete Estey just shake his head.

"I hate these things," he said. The taxi was driving around it, looking for a gate that was open into the parking lot.

"But, Jeez," said Jack Brown, "look at the size of it, will you?"

"Seats sixty-eight thousand for baseball," the taxi driver said. "Up to eighty thousand for concerts, revivals, things like that . . . when Billy Graham comes in or something. They almost filled it for the Grateful Dead a couple weeks ago. Closest they ever came. Next night it was about ten thousand to see the Lions play."

We were still driving past the closed gates, one after another, round and round. "I never been here when the place was so locked up," the driver said. "You sure they know you're comin'?"

Then we finally did find an open gate. And the next thing you know, the taxi's gone and there we are, Jack and Mr. Pete Estey and me, standing in front of this stadium like Dorothy and her friends waiting for the Wizard of Oz. I don't know how long we all just stood there, probably with our mouths hanging open. Then finally Mr. Pete Estey said, "All right, let's go," and in we went. Inside we followed the arrow that pointed to "Club Offices," which you had to take the elevator to get to, and go past a security booth before that. But we had an appointment, Mr. Pete Estey told 'em, so that was all right.

Then upstairs I wished I'd bought a new dress for the trip. That was the funny feeling that came over me. The carpet up there was new, and the girl at the desk was pretty as a model. And behind her, through a glass wall, that baseball field was green and beautiful, even if Mr. Pete Estey said he didn't like it indoors. It sure was something, four stories down below, and all those empty seats wrapped around it in rows, red, blue, and gold.

"We're here to see Emmett Flanagan," Mr. Pete Estey told the girl, and he said who he was.

"Please have a seat, sir," she told him, pointing out one of the red leather couches, same red as the Lions' hats. From there you could look down on the empty field. We all sat, and Jack Brown was still gaping. I was too. Meanwhile the phone calls were comin' in, and that girl answered 'em, "Lions, can I help you?" She was a looker, and a voice to match.

After we sat for a little while, another woman came from down the hall and stopped at the desk. She looked at us, and then she looked at the girl who was answering the phones, and then back at us again. "Mr. Estey?" she said. She was all business, you could tell, and older than her friend out front. She was dressed in a dark suit, and one eyebrow kept jumping, like somebody was pulling it up on her forehead with a string.

"Mr. Estey," she said, "Mr. Flanagan isn't here. You said you had an appointment. Are you sure you've got the right day?"

"Yes," Mr. Pete Estey said. "I called him from Florida."

"Well, I'm terribly sorry," she said, and she didn't sound any kind of sorry. "Mr. Flanagan isn't in the office. He left no word on when he'd be back, nor any indication that he was expecting you."

That was how she said it. Like she was reading it from a book.

Jack Brown sat looking at his feet. Maybe he hadn't really thought anything would come of the trip anyway.

And Lord help me, for a long minute I didn't do a thing either. I found myself just staring at the picture of Walter Johnson behind the big desk where the woman was still answering the phone with the voice like silk on satin. There he was, with his big square head staring into the camera, proud and quiet, like after all the years of being the best pitcher there was for such a bad team, he didn't have to say anything. He'd done all there was for him to do. His old flannel uniform had the Washington "W" on the chest, but it didn't have anything to do with *this* Washington team, with its indoor stadium, glass offices, and the lady in the dark suit with the eyebrow like an old teacher in a room full of schoolboys. I was thinking maybe he was looking so sad in the picture because he could see out the window and it wasn't grass anymore on the field. Wonder how he felt when the office was empty and the ballpark been turned over to the bands all night long. Wonder how much use did Walter Johnson have for rock and roll and the Grateful Deads? I was thinking old Walter Johnson would have been a pal of Mr. Pete Estey's, I bet, if he had known him. And maybe he had, at that.

So there I was, no help to him, just like old Walter Johnson's infielders and hitters let him down, or maybe he'd have won a hundred more games. I sat and watched his gray eyes, gray in the black-and-white picture, anyway, and Lord help me, I was blank as any fool.

"So, Mr. Estey," the woman with the eyebrow was saying, "perhaps you'd care to leave a message for Mr. Flanagan. As I mentioned, I really have no idea when he'll be back in the office. But when he does return, I'll see that he gets it."

"Louise," Mr. Pete Estey said, "let's go."

And finally I woke up. The woman with the eyebrow had already turned back down the corridor, but I chased right after her, moving along pretty good, since I had no high heels to worry about. Another few minutes and we'd have been calling for a taxi, or the one with the voice would have called one for us, kind as she could be, once we were going to be gone. But I caught up to the one in the suit and grabbed her arm right there in the corridor. "Miss," I said, when I had a good tight grip, "you think about this again, now. You know who you're talkin' to here?"

Mr. Pete Estey was up beside me right away. "Louise," he said, "there's no point."

"Huh!" I said. "There's a point, all right. Point's common courtesy."

"Would you take your hand off my sleeve, please?" Miss Eyebrow said.

"Lady," I told her, "I'm tryin' to do you a favor. Your Mr. Flanagan forgot he had an appointment today. That's his mistake. But when he comes back, if he finds out Mr. Pete Estey was here and you sent him back home to Florida, that's gonna

be your mistake. You'll be answering the fan mail from somewhere in the rookie league, then."

"Louise," Mr. Pete Estey said, "give it up. I shouldn't have
let it go this far. I don't know why I thought I had to prove to
you that this trip was a bad idea."

I still had hold of Miss Eyebrow's arm. She was too polite to
struggle. "Bad idea or good," I said to Mr. Pete Estey, "we're
here. Rode up on a plane, too. And Jack Brown here might like
a look around, even if you're too old to care." I turned back to
Miss Eyebrow and said, "You don't see any harm in it, do you,
miss? It was your boss who stood us up. Maybe had an accident
or something, we don't know. But here we are, and here's what
we'll do. You got a man here gave some of the best years of his
life to baseball —"

"Louise —" Mr. Pete Estey said, but I put one hand on his
arm too, to stop him.

"I say *some* of the best years," I told Miss Eyebrow, "because
he still got some good ones left to give. Still workin' for you,
even if you don't know it. Still watchin' ballplayers you wouldn't
know a thing about, and won't ever know a thing about if you
push him out the door now because your boss forgot he had an
appointment this morning."

"Miss," Miss Eyebrow said.

"Mrs.," I told her. "Mrs. Edward Baker Brown. You can call
me Mrs. Brown."

"Mrs. Brown," she said, and her voice was a slow second to
her friend on the phone. "I don't want to have to call the security
guard."

"Call him," I told her. "Call him right up. He can show Mr.
Pete Estey and Jack Brown here around downstairs. Take 'em
out on the field. I bet this boy wonders what it feels like to walk
on that green carpet down there, and even Mr. Pete Estey's
probably curious. I know he never played on that phony grass.
And you and me will sit right here in case your Mr. Flanagan

remembers where he's supposed to be and shows up. We can call down for these boys if he does."

"You leave me no choice," Miss Eyebrow said. She got on the phone and barked at somebody on the other end.

"Ah, Louise," Mr. Pete Estey said. "Now we'll be lucky to avoid arrest. How much bail money are you carrying?"

"Can't arrest you for speakin' your mind," I told him. "This is America, even if it is Washington, D.C."

Then the security guard came down the corridor, and I don't know who was the more surprised, Miss Eyebrow or Mr. Pete Estey. I wouldn't want to be the judge.

Mr. Pete Estey took one look at the guard and said, "Well, I'll be damned."

Meanwhile, Miss Eyebrow was pointing the guard toward the three of us. "Show these people out," she told him.

Then he looked Mr. Pete Estey up and down, but there was no showin' out goin' on, so Miss Eyebrow tried again. "Show these people out *now*," she said.

Finally that ol' security guard turned around to her and looked out from under the brim of his security guard's cap, and he said, "Aw, shit, ma'am, I can't do that. This is Pete Estey. He signed me to my first contract."

"I want them out of here, now!" Miss Eyebrow said. She had on those pointy-toed high-heeled shoes, or I bet she would have stamped her foot down, too.

"What the hell are you doin' up here, Pete?" asked the security guard. "I heard you were in a rest home or some damn thing."

"I'm living in Florida," Mr. Pete Estey said. "This is my roommate, Louise Brown, and her grandnephew, Jack." I know he said that about the roommate just to get me wild, but I didn't give him the satisfaction. I looked him right in the eye until he quit his foolin' and introduced his friend. "Louise," he finally said, "a baseball fan like you ought to remember this fellow. Lou Rucker was a pretty good pitcher up here for a couple of years."

"A pretty good pitcher and a hell of a drinker," Mr. Lou Rucker said. "Now I'm a damn fine security guard. Pleased to meet you, Mrs. Brown. Jack."

Miss Eyebrow looked like she'd been biting on her cheek as she watched the reunion. Now she tried one more time. "Mr. Rucker, are you going to escort these people off the premises or not?" she asked him.

"Come on downstairs, Pete," Mr. Lou Rucker said. "I'll buy you a cup of coffee and show you and your friends around the place. There's people call it the eighth wonder of the world, or the ninth, after the Astrodome, some damn thing."

Miss Eyebrow turned on her heel and made off down the hall where she'd come from. Mr. Lou Rucker led the way out of the office toward the elevator, with his arm like a log over Mr. Pete Estey's shoulder. Jack and I followed behind, and as I went through the door I looked back once at the lady who had been answering the phone all the time we were there. I caught her eye, maybe because she was surprised I was looking. She hadn't made a sound except answering the phone, and didn't so much as say goodbye now, but maybe it was because she couldn't. I think maybe they got a special training course for telephone answering. Because even though I still couldn't hear anything from her, she was laughing so hard the tears were coming down her face, mascara and all.

Down on the field it was a wonder of the world, I guess, just like Mr. Lou Rucker had said. When they first built the Astrodome, the first place they played baseball indoors, they tried to grow grass in it, he told us. The grass turned brown and died. Anybody who'd troubled to think about it could have figured out that would happen. And anybody who'd troubled to think about it would have said right then, "Well, that's that. It was a foolish notion to begin with, wasn't it? Playing baseball indoors!" But the dead grass didn't stop 'em. They just changed it for plastic and went right ahead.

Mr. Lou Rucker said the stadium in Washington showed they'd learned all kinds of things since the grass died in Houston. They had a roof that you weren't supposed to lose a fly ball in, though Mr. Pete Estey said he didn't believe it. They had the speakers tucked away in foul territory where hittin' em wouldn't matter so much, and some kind of mats or pads or something under the turf so it didn't beat up the players' knees. Mr. Lou Rucker called it turf, anyway. It looked more like little short bits of that green paper you used to find in Easter baskets. And when you got up real close, it smelled sort of like a dentist's office. (I confess it. When no one was paying much attention to me, I did get right down to smell it.) But the fact is, the whole place smelled kind of funny. Sort of too clean. First I thought maybe it was just because it was empty right then, but Mr. Lou Rucker said no, it always smelled clean, because it had an air-conditioning and heating system that was always making new air somehow, taking out all the smells and any humidity you might not want. They knew from tests they did that there was a perfect humidity, perfect temperature, perfect atmosphere for watching baseball, he called it, but I don't remember what it was, exactly. Also he said you had to filter the air all the time or the kids who came to see the bands would fill it up with marijuana smoke. "And then where would we be?" he said.

Mr. Lou Rucker showed us how the outfield walls were on tracks, so you could move them out of the way when you didn't need them for baseball. There was a control board somewhere upstairs where you could lock and unlock them. He said those walls were covered with a special plastic, so if you ran into them you wouldn't be so likely to knock yourself out. He said they also thought about putting in something he called a wall sensor, which was kind of like a radar that went *beep*, *beep*, *beep* when an outfielder got close to the wall, so he'd know to slow down or he'd bang into it.

"Thing like that might have extended Pete Reiser's career indefinitely," Mr. Pete Estey said.

"Oh, hell, no," Mr. Lou Rucker told him. "Wouldna helped a guy like that. Reiser'd heard that beeping, he'd a figured he was runnin' outta time to catch the ball and run harder. He was crazy for walls, that guy. Anyway, they never did put it in, so now we'll never know. They were going to, though. Had these guys from Japan runnin' around here measuring and stringing wire for a week before they decided against it."

"Looks like they didn't miss much else," I said.

"Oh, no, ma'am," Mr. Lou Rucker said. "Everything's up-to-date in Kansas City, like they say. Or in Washington, anyway. Besides the walls that move and the dome and all, you got your digital scoreboard, instant replay screens all over the park . . . got your luxury boxes up there" — he was pointing at a half-circle of glass walls up another level from where the stands behind home plate ended — "you can sink down into a sofa and watch the game on TV up there if you want. Don't even have to be out here with the common folks."

"Or *in* here," Mr. Pete Estey said.

By then we'd walked halfway around the place, and we had our backs to the center-field wall, if it was still there. So we noticed, or I did, that there were two men back in the dugout on the first-base side. It wasn't really a dugout, like they are on a normal baseball field, because it was on the same level as the field. But two men were in there, anyway. Mr. Pete Estey must've seen 'em too, because he was studying them, but I knew he couldn't tell much about them from that distance.

"You a ballplayer, Jack?" Mr. Lou Rucker was asking.

"Yes, sir, I am," Jack Brown said. "But I sure never played in any place like this. Pretty hard to imagine it, even though I see it."

"What's your position?" Mr. Lou Rucker asked him.

"Pitcher," Jack said. "Twice a week or so it's pitcher, anyway. Then the other days wherever they need somebody. Infield sometimes, outfield other times."

"He's a shortstop," Mr. Pete Estey said, "even though he

doesn't acknowledge it yet. An untutored shortstop. Be a great addition to some lucky organization, because he has no bad habits to break. They teach him the way they want him to come across the bag on a double play, he'll learn it that day, because nobody ever taught him another way." He was still talking to Mr. Lou Rucker, but he never looked at him. He was watching the two men on the other side of the field. Now they'd come out of the dugout, and one of them had a bat.

"Shortstop on this club's a pip," Mr. Lou Rucker said. "Elio Mañanas. He comes from that little town in the Dominican Republic where they grow all the infielders, San Marco something."

"San Pedro de Macoris," Mr. Pete Estey said.

"That's it." Mr. Lou Rucker nodded. "Those boys come up from there with the quick hands and feet. That's what you need to play ball in here."

"Might as well play in the parking lot," Mr. Pete Estey said.

Mr. Lou Rucker shrugged. "World changes, Pete," he said.

"I bet you get a clean hop on it, though," said Jack Brown. It was the first time he'd said anything except to answer a question since we'd got on the plane.

"You want to try it?" Mr. Pete Estey asked.

Jack looked at him like he was talking a foreign language. I must have looked at him funny too. Finally it was Mr. Lou Rucker who said something.

"Hey, Pete, there's some limits here, boy. I can show you around and all, but I got no business —"

"Lou," Mr. Pete Estey said, "that's Cappy Haynes, isn't it?" He was looking at the two men again.

"Sure," Mr. Lou Rucker said. "Special assistant to the general manager. He's gonna work out that kid, who's been on the disabled list, I guess. Hijko's his name. He's got a knee. Probably run him around with fungoes a little, see how he moves."

"Cappy Haynes could have been Henry Aaron's twin brother

when I first saw him," Mr. Pete Estey told me. "Except that he came before Aaron, I guess. Cannon for an arm. Wrists like you wouldn't have believed. Magic wrists. And then he got in a car accident and tore up his shoulder and never could throw after that. He could run too. You would have sworn he could hit a ball up the middle and then make it to second base in time to field it and throw himself out at first. Besides all that, he was smart. Not like this clown."

"Jeez, I'd forgotten," Mr. Lou Rucker said. "You signed Cappy too, didn't you? This must be like old home week."

"I don't understand how you could forget it," Mr. Pete Estey said. "It can't have been more than thirty-five years ago."

"You're lucky, though," Mr. Lou Rucker went on. "I bet I haven't seen Cappy on the field six times this year. They usually got him off with one of the minor-league clubs somewhere — two days in the Eastern League, three days in the International League, and then a week in Florida teaching a bunch of eighteen-year-old hotshots to run the bases, only they think they already know all about it, of course. Dog's life."

"Hunting dogs, at that," Mr. Pete Estey said. "That's what we used to say."

"Bird dogs," Mr. Lou Rucker agreed with a nod. "I guess you did have to teach some, at that."

We could hear the fly balls now. The sound was hollow and strange to me, the first time I ever heard anybody hit a baseball inside. Then, between swings, Mr. Pete Estey shouted "Cappy" at the hitter, but it came out only a little croak, and the man couldn't hear it. Mr. Pete Estey coughed and cleared his throat and spat into the plastic grass, where it shimmered in a little puddle, like Jell-O. "What the hell do the boys do who chew?" he said.

Mr. Lou Rucker shrugged. "They got a big machine, like they use for cleaning a hockey rink. Bring it out after every game, like a big vacuum cleaner."

"Cappy!" Mr. Pete Estey yelled again, and this time the other man heard it. He turned toward us and squinted. He *was* a powerful-looking man, and nimble. He hit the fly balls like he didn't have to work at it, flicking them to the fielder's right or left, in and out, watching him move one way or the other. And the funny thing was how he hit 'em with just his one hand on the bat. Just the right hand. Under the edges of his cap his hair was gray, though, and when we got up closer to him, he was breathing hard enough for you to know he was working.

"I'll be go to hell," he said. "Who's this, now? Ol' man of the mountain or somethin'? Naw, they got no mountains down Florida. Must be the ol' man of the swamp. How you doin', Pete?"

"I didn't know you were with the Lions," Mr. Pete Estey said.

"Hah!" Cappy Haynes laughed. "Sometimes I don't think the Lions know about that either. What the hell are you doin' up here, ol' man? And who's the stud?" He'd seen Jack by then, you see.

"Cappy," Mr. Pete Estey said, "meet Jack Brown. Jack, Cappy Haynes."

"Hello, sir," said Jack.

"I'll be damn," Cappy Haynes said. "You a ballplayer, aren't you? This ol' man still scoutin'."

"Sure he is," I said. "I'm Louise Brown. I saw you play."

"Then you looked quick," Cappy Haynes said, "and you saw one of the best. This your boy?"

"Lord, no!" I said. "My husband's brother's grandson."

"Hah!" he snorted. "So this ol' white man here never had nothing to do with him? That's good. No genes for runnin' in ol' Pete Estey."

"How'd you like to hit him some ground balls when you're through, see what he can do on the turf?" Mr. Pete Estey asked.

"Shit, ol' man, what are you on about?" Cappy Haynes said. "What are you up to, ol' Pete? You want a tryout for this Jack Brown?"

"Hell, Cappy," Mr. Pete Estey said, "hit him some ground balls. See what he can do."

Now Cappy Haynes was laughing, but it wasn't at Mr. Pete Estey. Not exactly at him. And he wasn't laughing at us. He'd seen right away that Jack was a ballplayer. He'd said that. "We'll see what he can do, if you want," he said, and then he spat through his teeth. "Trouble is, what can *I* do after he shows us what *he* can do?"

"Just hit him some ground balls," Mr. Pete Estey said.

"I can do that, all right." Cappy Haynes nodded. "No doubt about it. Hit 'em to his right, hit 'em to his left, hit one'll bounce up his nose if he stand still. But then you gonna want me to talk to somebody upstairs, get him signed to a contract somewhere. Maybe Flanagan. Maybe skip Flanagan and go right to the boss. Hell with the minor leagues and bring this Jack Brown right up to the show."

"Cappy," Mr. Pete Estey said, "I don't expect —"

"Up, up, up. I *know* what you expectin'," Cappy Haynes said. "And I know what you *not* expectin', too. You not expectin' to live forever. How old *are* you, ol' Pete? Must be seventy-five, anyway. You already an ol' man when you signed me, and look at me now. *I'm* an ol' man. Ol' one-arm man. So you an ol' man who wants this magical boy to get himself signed up before time runs out on you."

"I was retired," Mr. Pete Estey said.

"Well, you don't look retired to me," Cappy Haynes told him. "You look like a man with something to sell. And you sellin' it under this crazy dome here, so that makes the somethin' a ballplayer, you hope."

"Why don't you just hit him some ground balls?" Mr. Pete Estey asked.

"But maybe you got the wrong man when you found me," Cappy Haynes went on.

"You're here." Mr. Pete Estey smiled. It almost seemed for a minute there that he could see the signs and indications. Cappy

Haynes was where he was supposed to be. But maybe he was just making a joke to himself about Mr. Emmett Flanagan missing the appointment upstairs.

Anyway, I couldn't hold my peace anymore, so I told Cappy Haynes, "You're a special assistant to the general manager, aren't you? Seems to me you're just the right man."

"Mrs. Brown," Cappy Haynes said, "lemme explain to you about special assistants to the general manager. There's a couple different kinds. One kind's old drunks that drink with the general manager, sometimes the manager too. Some guys have it right in their contracts that they get to keep one around. Then there's the sons and cousins and nephews of the owner, who got to have a job. Some of 'em can do somethin' useful and some of 'em can't. Then there's me, and folks like me. I'm a very useful man, because I do what I'm told. Travel all the hell over the place when they say, help punks all down in the farm teams who don't ever stop talkin' to listen. But mostly I'm a useful fellow because my ass is black, Mrs. Brown. So when the club starts hearin' about how baseball doesn't have places for blacks anywhere but on the field, they say, 'Well, ahem, that may be true elsewhere, but not here. Cappy Haynes is an assistant to the general manager. Been here for years. Very substantial position. Roll your eyes, there, Cappy, and show 'em how black you are.' "

"I'm sorry to hear that," Mr. Pete Estey said.

"Don't pity me, ol' Pete," Cappy Haynes told him. "I got the last laugh, don't I? I got it because I'm the best there is at what I do. Any kid listens to me learns somethin'. I can put a fly ball in a bucket out there. And I'm still in baseball, aren't I? Still makin' a livin' in the game. All I'm tellin' you is, nobody's likely to pay any attention just because I tell 'em I saw a kid who could pick ground balls on the slate here."

"Hit him some anyway," Mr. Pete Estey said.

" 'Course I'll hit him some ground balls," Cappy Haynes said.

"Never said I wouldn't. Go on in the clubhouse, Jack. Man in there's name Ray. Tell him I said to fix you up with a uniform and some shoes, and a glove if you didn't come with one. He gives you any trouble, come back out here and find this fool Rucker and tell him you need his gun."

Me, I'd've been scared to death, but Jack Brown just turned around and disappeared down the tunnel in the dugout as if this was fine with him. Cappy Haynes went back to his business of hitting fly balls to the boy in the outfield, and I tugged on Mr. Pete Estey's sleeve to get him over where I could talk to him a little bit.

"Well, now," I said. "So he's a shortstop."

"Today he's a shortstop," Mr. Pete Estey said. "He can show Cappy more picking up ground balls at short than he could doing anything else except hitting, and there's nobody to pitch to him. Besides, how do we know what he'd do with a fly ball in here?" Mr. Pete Estey pointed a bony finger toward the dome over our heads. "That's not so easy," he said, "picking a fly ball out of that plastic sky. And you got a different sound off the bat in here from the one Jack's used to, so that might take a step away from him. It's quicker getting used to ground balls on this turf than flies under the roof. Once Cappy gets a look at Jack's hands and feet in the infield, he can see he's a ballplayer, anyway. That's about all we're going to accomplish today."

"He won't see the best part," I said. "He won't see him hit."

"Not unless you can materialize somebody to throw batting practice," he said. "That one arm Cappy hits with is not the one he used to throw with. If he can't even put his left hand on a bat anymore, he sure as hell can't pitch. And I'm an old man, in case you'd forgotten."

Meanwhile, Cappy Haynes was running that boy in the outfield until his tongue was hanging. He finally waved him in with his bat. That's when I noticed that Jack was already standing at the corner of the dugout, waiting for his turn. He had on a home white uniform with "Lions" in red across the front, and on his head was a red cap with a white W.

As the boy who'd been in the outfield was crossing the first-base line on his way into the clubhouse, Cappy Haynes yelled at him that he wasn't through yet, and the boy stopped and looked at him, gloomier than you'd think a ballplayer ought to look.

"Go on over and play first base a minute," Cappy Haynes shouted. "Let's see can this Jack Brown throw." Then he waved his bat for Jack to go out to shortstop, and I found I'd been holding my breath.

There was nothing to worry about, though. Jack scooped those ground balls up just as fast as Cappy Haynes could slap them out, kept his glove down and watched those balls in like he'd been a shortstop all along, then threw strikes to first base, one after another. After a while Cappy Haynes began hitting them a little further to Jack's left, then up the middle. Didn't matter. He went and got 'em all. It looked like a mechanical wheel, but smooth, like it was running on a current or something. The ball went on the ground hard to Jack, and he picked it up wherever it was, took just the one step for balance if he could and threw hard to first, then that boy at first base sort of half lobbed it in to Cappy Haynes. It was like on the half-lob the ball kind of gained strength to bust off the bat again, hard and true.

Watching it sort of hypnotized me, so it was no surprise that I didn't notice at first when Mr. Lou Rucker had come up behind Mr. Pete Estey and me, and he had on a uniform too. Or at least the shirt. He was still wearing his security guard pants, and the Lions shirt was hanging over them, like an old man had somehow got into a little boy's nightshirt. He was carrying a glove, and beside him was a shopping cart full of baseballs. I only saw he was there when Mr. Pete Estey spoke to him. "What the hell are you up to?" is what he said.

"What the hell kind of tryout is it if Cappy can't see him hit?" Mr. Lou Rucker said.

"How long since you threw a ball in anger?" Mr. Pete Estey asked him.

"Don't worry about that," Mr. Lou Rucker said. "It's like riding a bicycle. You never forget how."

"He won't look so good standing there watching your pitches sail over his head or bounce off the plate," Mr. Pete Estey said.

"Oh, for God's sake, Pete, you come this far. I'll throw him some strikes all right."

"You got a screen?"

"Right up the ramp here, behind the stands," Mr. Lou Rucker said. "You give me a hand with it, we'll have it set up in no time."

So before Cappy Haynes could even wear Jack out at shortstop, here came two old men, pushing and pulling at the wire screen that goes in front of the pitcher when they have batting practice, so he can throw through the cut-out part of it and then duck behind the rest to get away from balls hit back at him. That screen was on wheels, but it kind of collapsed on itself when it rolled. Or at least it did when Mr. Pete Estey and Mr. Lou Rucker rolled it. They made such a commotion pushing and pulling and shouting to each other about which way it should go that Cappy Haynes got distracted from hitting his ground balls. When he saw what they were doing, he just stood and stared, watching the screen lurch forward in fits and starts. Finally he said, "Well, that's fine. Now go back in the clubhouse again and get Mrs. Brown here some catcher's equipment, and we'll be all set."

"Get out of the way," Mr. Lou Rucker shouted, and what do you think? Cappy Haynes did step back from the plate. It wasn't encouragement, not exactly, but he wasn't standing in the way.

When Jack saw what was up, he ran in from shortstop to help, and they got that screen moving faster.

Mr. Pete Estey said maybe he'd watch the rest of the tryout from the bench in the dugout, and when I went in to sit with him, I could hear him wheezing, like something was loose in his chest. His color didn't seem so good either, even if part of that might have been the funny light in that indoor ballpark. I asked him if he wanted some water, and he just shook his head no.

Meanwhile Jack had himself a bat, and Mr. Lou Rucker was explaining how batting practice would work. "Just let the bad ones go, son," he said. "We got this whole cart full of balls, and I'll get some good ones in."

Cappy Haynes came into the dugout beside us. "What a circus," he said. "Your boy deserves better, ol' Pete."

It looked like he was right for the first couple pitches, too. But after he sailed a couple high and outside, Mr. Lou Rucker took a deep breath and stopped trying to wind up. He just kind of rocked back and forth and threw easy, but straight. Jack swung just as easy at first. And then balls started bouncing around the place until that shopping cart was half empty, with us just watchin' 'em fly. Then Cappy Haynes put his hand up and shouted for everybody to stop for a minute.

"I'm enjoyin' this," he said. "I think it's just fine. But let's do a little thinkin' out there now, Jack. Let's see can you do some situation hitting. I call out the situation, you hit where you're supposed to."

Jack nodded and stepped back into the batter's box.

"How much you got left?" Cappy Haynes shouted out at Mr. Lou Rucker.

"I'm not savin' anything, Cappy," Mr. Lou Rucker shouted back. "It's a dead cinch I don't have to pitch tomorrow."

"All right." Cappy Haynes nodded. "Step it up, then. Push him off the plate a little, move the ball around." He turned back to Jack and said, "Man on second, Bud. Nobody out."

Jack Brown whacked the next pitch toward what would have been the hole between second and first, just like you're supposed to when you want to move the runner over. Cappy Haynes jumped up and took two steps toward Mr. Lou Rucker, though, before the ball stopped rolling.

"What are you, holding some stock in this boy?" he shouted. "You in a partnership out there? Don't just hang the ball out so he can hit it where he's supposed to. Push him around. I want to see can he move his hands in there."

Mr. Lou Rucker did look kind of sheepish, like he was caught at something.

"Okay, kid," Cappy Haynes said to Jack. "Now that guy's over at third, one out."

Mr. Pete Estey told me later what was going on. Or more like I let him tell me, because I could see it as plain as he could. Man on third, less than two out, the idea was to get the ball in the air somewhere to get the run home. Sacrifice fly if it had to be. But Mr. Lou Rucker threw a low pitch, hard ball to get under, and threw it a little harder than he had been, like he had to show Cappy Haynes that he'd heard him. Jack went right down and got it, but it *was* too low to really get under, so he hit a line drive about waist high, right back up the middle. That was right at Mr. Lou Rucker, except for the screen he was behind, and if the ball had just hit the screen, it would have been fine. No more than it was there for. Only Mr. Lou Rucker was kind of falling forward from throwing the pitch harder. So when the line drive hit the bar in the middle of the screen and it kind of bucked back, Mr. Lou Rucker was already moving in toward it from the other direction, instead of falling off to one side like he should have been. And when the screen jumped, the top bar of it caught him under the chin and he fell over backward like somebody shot him.

We all went out to the mound as fast as we could, Cappy Haynes and Jack getting there about the same time, Mr. Pete Estey bringing up the rear, still wheezing a little. Mr. Lou Rucker's chin was cut from where the screen hit it, and there was blood all over his Lions shirt, but it looked worse than it was, I could tell.

"Jeez," Jack said. "Is he going to be all right?"

"No dumber than when he started, that's for sure," Cappy Haynes said. He was helping Mr. Lou Rucker up then.

"Hell of a shot, son," Mr. Lou Rucker said.

"Tryout's over," said Cappy Haynes.

I looked at my watch and saw it was just as well. Time to get back to the airport.

Pete

ALWAYS MY WIFE WAS QUICKER THAN I WAS TO KNOW what was wrong. I might be moping around the house or staring at a newspaper, not really reading it, and she would say, "You're worried about how much it's going to cost to fix the furnace, aren't you?" I wouldn't even have been able to say that was it.

With the bigger issues she could do it too. Each time I tried to quit baseball and stay home, working at one thing or another, she always knew before I did that it hadn't worked again. Once, in the middle of an afternoon when it was nearly too hot to breathe, I walked into our bedroom and found her packing my suitcase. I hadn't even known I'd be going anywhere.

My first concern about the jinx came up while we were still together, and though it must have sounded completely crazy to her, she listened in polite silence. Maybe she had some sense that it was coming. When I was through, she said, "It's no more nuts than a lot of things you've told me about baseball."

"Such as?"

She shrugged. "Players who don't change their socks when they're hitting well, as if dirty socks could cast a spell. The third baseman who was so careful to walk the same path from his position back to the dugout after each inning that by July you could see his footprints in the grass, like shadows. The pitcher who always parked his car in the same space on days when he was pitching, and flew into a rage when somebody beat him to it. Actually fought about it, you said."

"All true," I said.

"The fan who came out of the stands in Milwaukee and gave the other team's pitching coach a rock. What did he say? 'Carry this rock with you and you'll win the pennant,' and the pitching coach did it, and they won."

"That too," I said. "Happened to the Red Sox."

"The business about never mentioning a no-hitter while it's going on, or not talking about a hitting streak, or walking the bats. You told me once about a manager who picked up all the bats and took them for a walk in the sun when his team wasn't hitting."

"Lots of managers," I said.

"All right," she said. She was out of examples and illustrations.

"So you think I'm being foolish," I said.

"I didn't say that," she told me. "I just think you're behaving like everybody else in that game behaves. Like there are connections, secret formulas, whatever, that the rest of us can't understand. Lines of power between a man and his socks. Sometimes it makes me tired."

"*I* don't understand it."

"Well, maybe understanding doesn't have much to do with it. Baseball's a world of scared little boys looking for help from lucky charms and rituals. Or that's *one* of the things it is."

"Maybe because what they're trying to do is so hard," I said. "Or at least it's hard to do well, or to do perfectly. Some of them are trying to be perfect. And some players explain losses by saying, 'God didn't intend for us to win today.' "

"All right," she said, "try that, if you think it'll help. Maybe God didn't intend for these boys you've been talking about to have major-league careers."

"That doesn't make any sense," I told her, but I suppose it made as much sense as the jinx.

She would listen to the litany of names over the years, though, periodically. She was a practical, level-headed, no-nonsense woman, and it must have nearly driven her crazy sometimes, but she rarely complained about how I went on. And the irony of it was that I never did quit scouting until long after we separated for the second time, even with the jinx. And when I *did* quit, I couldn't say how much the jinx had to do with my decision, because there were so many other reasons to quit by then. The new machinery, of course, the centralized system. Fewer jobs. The travel was harder and harder on an old man, and I was sure as hell old. Then there was seeing Whit Cullinane bleed to death in that motel room, no different from a thousand other motel rooms where I'd waited for games, or tried to sleep after one, or watched the rain that had killed one slam against the windows far from home.

There is no growing old gracefully. It's a lovely idea, but it doesn't happen. There's no adventure in it, in a motel or anywhere else. You slow down and start to fail just at the time when the people who're likely to tolerate your decline quit themselves. You leave a meeting early with pains in your chest. You find you aren't driving as fast as you used to, because you can't see as well, or you don't trust your reflexes as you once did, so you miss an at-bat or an inning or even a game you would have seen. Maybe you get lost. You have to ask the guy on the other end of the phone to shout, because otherwise you can't hear him over the singing that's come into your ears.

And the guy who called that meeting's not an old friend anymore, not some guy you knew in the Pacific Coast League fifty years ago, who's getting as slow and blind as you are. Instead he's a kid who wants your "input" now to "maximize the potential of his data base." If your chest hurts, he'll be solicitous, but while you're catching your breath, he'll be telling somebody at his side with a notepad that it just doesn't make any sense to have all these individual scouts wandering around with their quirky opinions, their bits of information, and their hunches that can't be replicated or accessed because darn it, the old guys haven't learned how to file it so everybody else can call it up on the screen when they need it. "When you try to teach them, they get chest pains," he says. "Or headaches from trying to read the print on the screen." And finally he says, "Look, how much of a favor are we doing them anyway, keeping these guys out there at their ages?"

On the other end of the phone the guy you can't hear doesn't want to know that the kid you saw pitch throws a little bit of a cut fastball that jumps when he's right, sort of like a guy you remember facing when the Lions had a club in the Appalachian League, only that kid was bigger and so old by the time he *did* come up for a cup of coffee in the bigs that he was throwing mostly knuckleballs . . . and what the hell was his name, anyway?

"Just tell me what his numbers were on the gun," the voice comes back, and then you have to admit that you left the damn gun back at the motel room, or some damn kid stole it out of your car, and you saw him, dammit, but you couldn't catch him.

So at first the jinx was just something on top of everything else. I'd been aware of it, wondering about it, for years. I don't even remember when I first noticed it. But like a stiff neck I'd wake up with every once in a while, it got worse the longer I had it.

When I tried to explain it to Louise one afternoon at the kitchen table, she was skeptical. "Wait just a minute now," she said. "You're trying to tell me that you quit scouting because those boys you signed caught bad luck from you?"

"Something like that," I told her. "You met Cappy Haynes and Lou Rucker."

"So?" she said. "Two fine men doin' their jobs, seems to me. I'm proud to know 'em both."

"Rucker could have been a genuine stopper," I said. "You know what that means? He could have been one of those pitchers who stops losing streaks just because every time he goes out to the mound, his teammates look at each other and say, by God, today we're a tough club to beat! He had all the tools, and they brought him along slowly, and he wasn't stupid."

"Where'd he go wrong?"

"He drank himself down to a .500 pitcher for a couple of years. Then he drank himself out of baseball. I didn't know he'd gotten himself sober enough to hold a job until he showed up in that office that day."

"Well, now, this is crazy talk," Louise said. "How can you go and blame yourself for another man's drinkin' problem? What kind of —"

I shook my head and held up one hand to stop her. "Not blame," I said. "Not in the sense you mean. But things happened to Rucker and the others. Do you remember how Cappy Haynes put it when you said you'd seen him play?"

"Said I musta looked quick and I'd seen one of the best." Louise snorted. " 'Course I remember. You're the one's always talkin' 'bout bein' old, not me. My memory's just fine."

"All right," I said. "That's good. Then maybe you also remember how he hurt his shoulder."

"Humph," Louise said, and I took that to mean that she didn't.

"He was flying a damn kite!" I said. "He and a kid in the park. And he got so involved with it he backed out into the street. The car that hit him picked him right up off his feet. He went over the hood, slid across the windshield, and flipped off the car on his shoulder. That was the end of him in baseball. Before that he threw like Willie Mays."

"That's some throwing," Louise said. "But he's still in baseball."

"And it's a good thing I didn't sign Willie Mays too," I told her. "Because if I had, he'd probably have stepped in a drain when he was still playing in Birmingham, and he'd never have made it to the major leagues. Or Leo Durocher would have given up on him because he couldn't hit when he first came up. Or some redneck who didn't like colored boys would have spiked him in the knee in 1951, and that would have been that."

"You sure give yourself credit for some serious power," Louise said. "Anybody else listenin' to you'd think you were a crazy man, sayin' everything you touch withers and dies. I'd worry about you myself, except that you're the wrong color entirely for the hoodoo."

I didn't laugh, but that only caught her off guard for a minute. "Come on, now," she said. "I'm not fool enough to believe everybody you signed stepped in a hole or got knocked down by a car or drank himself out of a job. I don't know what your game is yet, but —"

"Not everybody," I said. "You haven't been listening. I signed lots of boys who played. But none of the real good ones I signed ever had the opportunity to show people how good they were. Not one. It's only the real good ones I've been talking about, Louise. And I could tell you about a half a dozen more . . . hunting accidents, freak things. One guy, an outfielder from so far out in the sticks in Louisiana that nobody else would have found him in a hundred years, got all through two seasons at double-A and triple-A, broke every record for assists, triples, stolen bases in both leagues. The winter before we were supposed to get him on the big club he decided he'd marry his high school sweetheart, because a major-league contract was going to be enough money to marry on. Three days after the wedding, she stabbed him in their bed. She finally told the police she was afraid that when her man got to the big leagues, he'd have so many beautiful women hanging around him all the time that he'd forget about her and sleep with one of them. She couldn't stand the thought, and she didn't know what else to do about it."

We were talking, as I said, in Louise's kitchen. She had cooked dinner, cleared and cleaned the dishes, wiped the few crumbs from the wooden table. There was coffee before us, and more

on the stove. There were chewy chocolate cookies, homemade.
The kitchen light overhead was bright and rational. The neighborhood outside echoed with the comfortable sounds of late
chores, garbage cans on the move. Far down the block, somebody fiddled with a carburetor that sounded as if it couldn't quite
clear its throat. It was no place or time for ghost stories, and I'm
sure she wasn't entirely kidding when she said she thought I was
nuts.

"How long'd it take you to learn all this?" she asked. "When'd
you start believin' it?"

Hard questions. When do you stop running out leg cramps
and wonder whether they might be symptoms of some deficiency
in your diet, or tendinitis or arthritis, or cracked bones? When
do you feel the first suspicion that you'd be crazy to go skiing
one especially cold morning? And how long after that do you
find yourself staring into the winter space, wondering how you
ever got up the nerve to slide down a mountain? You don't eat
spicy foods anymore, but when did you stop? Did a doctor suggest
it? Order it? Warn against it with a sly laugh? And did you try
it again six months later, just to be sure it wouldn't work?

All you know is what you know now. How much temperance
comes from wisdom, how much from fear? How many good
deeds from charity, how many from guilt? How much love from
desire, how much from deprivation? Questions for younger men.

"I don't know," I said.

"But you're worried Jack Brown might be one of those good
ones," she said. "Is that it? Well, I'll tell you something. He
doesn't care anything about your superstitions and hoodoo. Your
jinx. He's just gonna play baseball, whether you sit there and
hang your head or whether you help him out. But maybe you
should think about another thing too, which is how he can help
you. How he already has. You should see yourself when that
boy plays. You got life in you then, and not just that smart-
alecky sass, either. Real life."

"He's a pure joy to watch," I admitted.

"Maybe too good to be true, huh?" Louise said. "Is that what you're thinkin'? Don't crush it with that baggage you been carryin', old man. Let it fly. It's a dream that wants air to breathe and space to spread its wings." She sipped her coffee, and looked at me for a moment over the rim of her cup. "I'll tell you what I think. I think you up and quit before you knew you did it. And then you had to think up the reasons you did. One's this spooky blaming yourself for what happened to Mr. Lou Rucker and Cappy Haynes and the rest. But you know what? I never heard either of them say a thing about a jinx. Mr. Lou Rucker was so pleased to see you he could hardly keep his arms from huggin' you to him. I could see it. 'Course you standing there lookin' so beat up on by that woman with the eyebrow, he was probably afraid if he hugged you, you'd've broke. But I bet otherwise he would've done it. And then he got out there on the mound and started throwin' those balls in, Jack hittin' 'em out all over the place. You think he was worryin' about some old jinx?"

"Then he got his brains beaten in," I said. I couldn't resist it.

"And he's wearing that cut chin like a badge right now," Louise said. "You can bet on it. Standing in the quiet of that dome before anybody's there to fill it up, some other old security man like himself is askin' him was he in a bar fight or somethin', thinkin' maybe he's drinking again, and Mr. Lou Rucker stands up straight and looks that other fellow in the eye and says he broke it pitching to Jack Brown. 'Remember that name,' he says, ' 'cause you're gonna hear about Jack Brown.' I'm not sure which he tells first, whether it's how he could still throw 'em up there over the plate or how Jack could hit. Maybe he's mixin' 'em together. I bet it gets better and better with the telling, too."

I laughed despite myself. Louise was a wonder.

"And what about Cappy Haynes?" she said. "Didn't he kid me about Jack bein' my son? Wasn't he enjoying himself, though?"

"You really haven't been listening, have you?" I said. "Cappy Haynes could have had a great career. He had all the tools there are — he could run and throw and hit to all fields with power. He was young and strong, and he grinned like Ernie Banks. He was the kind of player who came to the park early for the pure pleasure of putting on his uniform and warming up for the game. Now look at him. Full of bitterness at the organization that keeps him around to prove there's no discrimination there, angry in his middle age, nothing to look back on but —"

"Oh, Lord, Lord, *Lord*, Mr. Pete Estey! How close *you* been listening? You think that man believes all the trash he was talking?"

"What do you mean?" I said.

"How'd you live so long, bein' so stupid? Don't you think that man still has power? He's not a strong man? That Cappy Haynes was settin' you up for a surprise, just as sure as you're a fool. You don't think he liked what he saw when he saw Jack Brown?"

"He said nobody'd listen to him."

"He said! He said! What do you think? You expect him to tell you Jack'd be on the team in no time? Brag that he'd have a contract in the mail before you got home? He's workin' on it right now, certain as we're sitting here talking about it. Don't you worry about that man. You'll see what he can do."

I was sure she was wrong. What was there to work on? Cappy Haynes was a guy who fungoed fly balls to guys on the disabled list. I'd watched him do it. He was a guy who went where he was told, and sometimes got forgotten for weeks and just traveled around to any team in the organization where he thought he might do some good, or maybe just so he'd have an answer when somebody asked him where he'd been. And half the time when he got there, nobody paid any attention to him. I'd heard him say all that.

"Working on it how?" I asked Louise.

"*You're* the baseball man," she snapped. "You figure it out."

*

That night I slept hard in the little room off the kitchen until just before dawn. Then I woke up in one of those sweats that was common enough so that it was no surprise. But what was surprising was that the dream I'd been having — maybe it was what had waked me — was full and finished before me. Ordinarily I don't remember my dreams. This one wasn't much for length, but it was vivid, all the same. In it, Jack and I were playing catch. The strange thing about it was that I was nearly his equal at it, rocking back and throwing to get loose, shoulder and arm and wrist into it, popping the ball. We were in a backyard somewhere, not a ballfield. It didn't seem to be Florida. There were oak and maple trees. We were both in shirtsleeves.

Eventually he tipped his glove at me to indicate that he'd thrown enough, and then he walked toward me. When he reached me, he extended his right arm toward me, palm up, as if I'd asked to examine it. This seemed perfectly natural in the dream, and I took his arm in both my hands. I pressed my thumbs down and the arm was warm in my hands, alive.

"Good, good," I said. "I was thinking that Louise had just made you up."

Then Jack must have curled his wrist, because suddenly the arm went hard, and a vein running up the middle jumped. And then Jack Brown said, "Forearms like fuckin' John Henry."

"Can't make up arms like that," I marveled.

"No, sir," said Jack.

And that was the end of the dream.

The next morning there was no French toast. As usual, Louise was up much earlier than she had to be to get to Fair Haven on time, but she fired around the kitchen as if somebody had a stopwatch on her. I came out of the bedroom to a clatter of dishes and pans worthy of a whole cafeteria, and she banged a bowl of cold cereal down on the kitchen table in front of me. When the coffee came, it was burned. Meanwhile, she wiped down the stove top with a sponge and found a spot on the refrigerator to work on.

"Look," I finally said, "you can't be doing yourself any good working so hard this early in the morning. Give yourself a break here. Sit down and have some coffee with me."

"Coffee's burned," she said.

"Have some tea," I said. "For God's sake, you're making me edgy, storming around in here. What's the matter with you this morning?"

Finally she did quit cleaning and polishing. She looked hard at me, as if I were a bug that had somehow, impossibly, survived the diligence of her housekeeping. And then she sat down in the other kitchen chair with a bang.

"When you were married," she said levelly, "what were the rules?"

"Rules?" I asked.

"You live with somebody, got to have some rules," she went on. "Everybody knows that. You don't need a lot of 'em, but you got to have 'em."

"What kind of rules?"

"No secrets," she said. "That's one. Edward Baker Brown and me had no secrets from each other. I knew what he wanted, and the other way, too. If something hurt him, I knew that, too. He was man enough to talk about being hurt."

"What are you getting at?"

"Another rule," she said. "No goin' to bed mad at each other. One of us'd get mad, we'd stay up half the night until it was talked out and settled between us."

"I'm not mad," I said. "And besides, we're not married."

"I know that, fool," she said. "What kind of crazy person'd marry a man so blind and dumb as you are? Anyone did, they'd have to have a special rule about keepin' your eyes open or you'd miss the world goin' by."

"No sense of signs and indications, I guess."

"Signs and indications!" Louise sputtered. "You don't even see the headlines! What do you think? Every old man who goes to Washington finds two old friends to help him out? It's everybody who walks into that crazy dome and there's two fine men happy to see him there?"

"Quite a coincidence," I said. "But baseball men stay in baseball, you know. That's how it works."

"Don't tell *me* how it works," Louise said. "What if your scouting man, your Mr. Flanagan, had been in? What if Miss Eyebrow there wasn't havin' her time of the month? Think she couldn't've brushed us off? Think you would ever have seen Mr. Lou Rucker, security guard *and* batting-practice pitcher? And what was it Mr. Lou Rucker said about Cappy Haynes? He's out there on the field in Washington, what, six times a year? How he's too smart to hang around much, and usually he's off doin' his business down in the farm leagues? How come we were there on that day he was, and he could look at Jack Brown?"

"I see your point," I said.

"Oh, you see my point." Louise sniffed. "What do you see? And what do you feel? Listen to me. Back when you were a ballplayer, when you went up to bat, did you just think maybe you'd get a hit?"

"You go up with an idea, if you're any good," I said. "You look for a pitch where you know you can hit it. If you're any good, you're patient about it."

"No, no, no," Louise said. "I'm not talkin' about lookin' for something and patient. I'm talkin' about . . ." She looked at me hard and said again, "Did you just think you could get a hit? Or sometimes did you *know* it?"

"All right," I said. "Sometimes I knew it. Or I thought I did. Sometimes you can get in a streak where you see the ball so well, it looks like somebody's hung it out there for you on a string. Then when you don't hit it on the sweet part of the bat, you can't believe it. You're surprised. You look at the bat and you run your hand over it, as if you might find a hole in it."

"But mostly you do," she said with a nod.

"Do what?"

"Hit it right on the sweet part of the bat, fool. Hit it up the middle. Hit it over the wall, up and out and over everything. We're talkin' about batting streaks, right?"

"Right."

"And there never was a hitter so dumb that he didn't know a batting streak when he was on one. Isn't that right?"

"I guess so," I admitted.

"You *guess* so," Louise said. "There's a feeling that goes with it, isn't it? Like you said, the ball's just hangin' there for you? And you know so hard you're gonna hit it, if you don't, you have to rub your eyes, like somebody'd pulled a trick on you."

"Sure," I said. "And when you're on a streak, your appetite's better, too. I remember that. Your food tastes better. And you catch the green lights when you drive anywhere."

"And you don't wash your socks," Louise said.

"Some don't wash their socks," I agreed.

"So somebody'd have to know he was on a streak, so he'd know not to wash his socks," she said triumphantly.

"All right," I said.

"All right." She nodded. "Then how do you suppose you could be so dumb that you don't know you're on a streak right now? I'll tell you somethin'. You're a fortunate man, but a stubborn one. I'm not sayin' you haven't had troubles —"

"Thank you," I said.

"Don't sass me now," Louise hissed. "I got to finish. You've had your troubles with your wife, like half the other folks that go and get married. And you got no children of your own. That's hard and sad. And you're old. That's hard too. So you've had your troubles. But you got a warm, dry place, Mr. Pete Estey. And when you went to Washington, what do you know but you find two men ready to lead you by the hand along just the way you wanted to go? What do you think of that? And what do you do but moan that they weren't the *top* men? Cappy Haynes can't do Jack any good, you say. Mr. Lou Rucker was a fool to go back out on the pitcher's mound. And then there's this jinx you talk about. That makes the whole business a waste of time, you say."

"Louise," I said.

She held up her hand. "I'm almost finished," she said. "You can run up one side of me and down the other when I am. But I'm gonna say what there is to say before you do. You're blessed, Mr. Pete Estey, if you'd see it. There's still a need for you. There's still a use. And people to take you down on the ballfield and look at that boy you brought with you. There's still watchin' what Jack Brown can do, too. Did he look like a jinx was on him, pickin' up those ground balls at shortstop, where he doesn't play, never mind what you said? Or hittin' line drives under that roof? Accept the pleasure in it. Celebrate it. You're on a streak, blessed, and you don't know it, even when any dumb hitter would. Now I'm finished. You go on and have your say."

"Let's have dinner at Fair Haven tonight," I said.

"Dinner," Louise said.

"Early dinner," I said. "The first seating. Then we'll go out to the ballpark and watch Jack's game."

"I got hamburger out of the freezer," she said.

"Put it back in," I told her. "Maybe we'll find somebody at Fair Haven who wants to go see the game too."

"Don't tell me what to do in my own kitchen," she said.

"I apologize."

"All right," she said. "I accept it. But don't tell me what to do in my kitchen."

She grabbed up her pocketbook and headed for the door. Without turning around, she said, "I'll call you when I get in there and let you know what they're servin'."

Then it was quiet in the apartment. Louise hadn't left the radio on, as she sometimes did. There was coffee on the stove, and I warmed it up and set the steaming cup on the kitchen table. I put my head down on my arm, right there at the table, just to rest for a minute until the coffee had cooled enough so I could drink it. When I woke up it was cold.

Fair Haven looked smaller when I went back. That was a surprise. And another surprise was that I had been a topic of conversation since I'd been gone. Moses Labine told me that as we sat at the table, waiting for the other residents to finish filing in so the staff could serve dinner.

"Well, Pete," he said, "you don't look too bad to me. Maybe shacking up suits an old man like you after all."

"I'm not shacking up, Moses," I told him. "Louise took me into her home after the fire. It was an act of pure kindness. Or almost pure."

"The way I hear it, you're shacking up," he said. "Me, I admire your courage. I don't have it in me anymore. More power to you, I say. Even though I bet you wouldn't last six weeks."

Sarah Graham joined us before I could think of what to say next. She looked at me, bright-eyed as usual, and said, "How's your career progressing?"

"My career," I said.

"Your career," she said. "Yes." And then her face clouded over, and she said, "Oh, dear, have I got it wrong? I understood that you wanted to be a baseball player."

"Oh, he's running the bases, all right," Moses said.

"Sarah," I said, "where did you get a notion like that? Look at me. Do I look like a baseball player?"

"Well, goodness," she said, "I hear lots of things, you know. I'm not sure where I heard that."

"I was a ballplayer years ago," I said.

"Of course." She nodded, and she bent to her plate. Moses was eating too.

I'd done the unimaginable, and I hadn't even realized it. The residents at Fair Haven only saw their fellows leave when they'd died, or when they'd been tied to tubes and machinery. I'd walked out, albeit on Louise's arm. Love or a new career could explain it for them, maybe. What else could? Kindness had its limits. Some of them had families — children, nieces, nephews — who were perhaps genuinely kind. But kind enough to spring them from Fair Haven? Kind enough to circumscribe their own lives with the terrible needs of Mom, who was too blind to cook for herself now, or Uncle, who was so deaf he'd drive them crazy with his "What? What?" Or worse, Aunt Grace, who might wander hollow-eyed into the street in her bathrobe at any time to stop traffic. How could even the kindest of them manage lives around such disorder and distraction? It is something plenty of married people ask themselves regarding their partners, and children amplify the question plenty. But the terrible demands of the old, who soil sheets and sip and gobble the medicines that can't revive them, and hurt in ways and places unimaginable to the young . . .

I'd forgotten. I was an outsider now, and though I'd never worked at belonging before I'd left Fair Haven, now I saw that I had belonged. And saw also that belonging somewhere else was a double risk. My bridges were burned; my mooring lines were hanging slack. This was why Louise said she didn't think about her age, I thought. Not because she was any more afraid of death than I was, or anyone might be. Not because she was without pain or imagination. She was simply on her own. Or at least enough on her own not to identify herself with a group of old people, or against a world where everyone was younger. For the residents of Fair Haven, the former was impossible. When neighbors fell down in the bathroom, you found out how old they were and wondered if you'd be next. And in baseball, as I'd explained to Louise, you got older while the players all stayed the same age. Too soon you couldn't talk to them as you'd once been able to do, because even your stories were full of names that might as well have been made up as far as they were concerned. Baseball was cruel, too, because on any new day you might see a swing so similar to the one you'd owned twenty years before, or forty, or sixty. And if you'd gone soft enough in the head, you might even try to recapture it later and hobble yourself for days.

As far as baseball is concerned, you are an outsider as soon as you stop playing, and I'd been an outsider for years. On the field I blinked like a miner in the sun. Now circumstances and Louise had cut me away from Fair Haven too, for better or for worse. Better, of course, as far as Louise was concerned. Different, certainly. But I didn't understand the finality of the separation at first, and I bumbled on, the way a former player relocated to the broadcasting booth might still try to pal around with the boys in the locker room.

"But what about you?" I said to Sarah. "What's the news hereabouts?"

What could she possibly have said? In my ignorance I'd already corrected her once, made her feel as if she'd been a fool. A month earlier I'd have known better. It wasn't likely she'd tell me about visits from her daughters now. But she went on, God bless her for it.

"They are painting everywhere," she said. "You know how it is. They had to paint in the back of the building after the fire, and once they started, they didn't know where to stop. Even the rooms that had looked fine seemed dreary next to the new paint somewhere else."

"So there's fights," Moses said through a mouthful of dinner. He swallowed noisily and jerked his hands with real enthusiasm, kind of like a boxer. "Everybody wants to know the painters' schedule, you see, and why the hell they're not next."

"For goodness' sake, Moses," Sarah said.

" 'Course, some of us *know* why they haven't painted our rooms," he went on. "Some of us aren't so dopey yet that we can't see we're being snookered."

"Well, you're a lucky man then," Sarah said. "When they do paint, the smell is awful. And you have no choice about the color, of course. And they knock your things off the bedside table."

"And I'm pretty sure they're stealing," Moses said softly. "Pretty sure. It's hard to know, of course, because when someone around here says something is missing one morning, it might be something that's been gone for thirty years. You don't get the world's most reliable witnesses here. But I've got a couple of people working on a plan to trap 'em, and by God, we'll blow the lid right off this place, if I'm any judge of it. When they get around to painting some of the rooms where my agents are, look out."

"The other thing is *finding* your room when you've been out," Sarah said. "You know, to the dining room or somewhere. The garden."

"There's no garden here," mumbled Moses.

"Well, the front porch then," Sarah said. "There's a front porch, certainly . . ."

"Right out front," Moses said.

"Well then," she said. But then she frowned. "What was I saying?"

"About finding your room again," I said.

"Well, of course," she said. "If it was blue when you went out and it's green when you come back, how are you supposed to know if you're in the right place or not?"

"We're none of us in the right place," Moses said through another mouthful of dinner, but Sarah wasn't paying any attention to him.

Still, only Sarah took me up on my invitation to go and see Jack play ball that evening. She thought it was a wonderful idea, and told me she'd never seen a baseball game. I had sense enough not to disagree. Meanwhile Moses said no, he couldn't go, because if the word got out that he'd left Fair Haven, even briefly, God knew what sort of mischief they'd try to work on the place.

So after dinner Sarah, Louise, and I headed down the hall for the parking lot, Sarah bubbling with the enthusiasm of a first-time fan and Louise uncharacteristically quiet, I suppose because she was still mad at me. But before we could get out there was a terrible shriek from one of the rooms on the corridor. Soon heads appeared in the other doorways. What was up? they all wanted to know. Now there was whimpering from the room.

Louise, sprier than anyone else, reached the door first, but didn't go in. "Oh, Lordy," she said. When I caught up with her, she hadn't gone a step farther. From the doorway I could see a woman sitting on the floor, with her hands up over her head. Every now and then her fingers fluttered and she whimpered again. I didn't recognize her. She must have come to Fair Haven since I'd gone.

The source of the problem was a bat, knocking around the room from wall to wall, lost and chittering. Louise wanted no part of it.

"All right," I said. "I'll go in. Once I get the window open, you shut off the light from the wall switch here."

"What are you up to?" she asked. "Wait for the maintenance. They got gloves and hats. They know how to get rid of it. That thing bites you, you got rabies and all kinds of trouble. Come on out of there."

"It doesn't want to bite me," I said. "Doesn't even want to get tangled in my hair. Wouldn't want to even if I had hair enough to tangle it. Just get the light."

I stepped around the woman on the floor. Luckily, the window opened without a struggle. "Okay," I told Louise. "Shut off the light and close the door."

"You're crazy," she said. But she hit the switch and pulled the door shut.

The woman on the floor shrieked again when the lights went out, then she was quiet. I could hear the bat chittering and swooping. I stepped away from the window and waited for my eyes to adjust to the darkness. But before they could, I felt the bat go by, purposeful and quick. Then the room was silent.

I shut the window and shouted, "Louise, open the door and turn the lights on. I can't see a thing."

When the lights came on, the woman on the floor looked up. Half a dozen people reached in to help her, and in no time she was in her chair with a cold drink, recounting the ordeal.

In the hall, Sarah Graham wanted to know if we were still going to the ball game.

"Of course," I said.

"What went on in there?" Louise said.

"Just what I said. The bat flew out the window. He needed the dark to find his way."

"How'd you know to do that?" she asked.

"I read about it once," I told her. "It was a long time ago. I always wondered whether I'd have the chance to see if it worked."

"Bats," she said. "Ugh. Give me the shivers."

"Well," I said, "this one just wanted out."

In the car, Sarah did the talking. She hadn't been out of Fair Haven since the other game we'd taken her to, and of course she didn't remember that.

"Baseball," she said. "Now, let me see . . . will there be prizes?"

I couldn't read Louise while she drove. Maybe she was accepting my suggestion to go see Jack play in the spirit I'd intended. Maybe she understood it as a peace offering. But maybe not. She was a careful driver, and all her attention was on the road.

"No prizes," I said. "Just a good game to see, if we're lucky. And Louise's grandnephew, of course. He's a joy to watch."

"No such thing as a *bad* game," Louise said.

When we arrived, Louise hauled out the lawn chairs and we established ourselves again at the corner of the bleachers. Jack's team had taken the field for infield practice, but the pitcher warming up on the opposite sideline wasn't Jack. "Where is he?" I asked Louise.

"Where you put him," she said. "Can't you see out to shortstop from here?"

Sure enough, Jack was taking ground balls at short. The boy who'd played there before had moved to second.

"I'll be damned," I said.

And that wasn't the only surprise I was in for. No sooner had the game started, with Jack's team still in the field, than who should appear from around the other side of the backstop but Cappy Haynes. I don't know whether Louise saw him coming, but I didn't, and it gave me a jolt.

"Don't get up, ol' Pete," he said when he reached my chair, though I hadn't tried to get out of it. "You look too comfortable here between these two lovely ladies. Hello, Mrs. Brown. How you been?"

"Just fine, thank you, Mr. Haynes," Louise said, just as if he'd been a neighbor from across the street. Why should it have surprised her? God's hand was always at work. What was the distance between Washington and Vernon to him? "Nice to see you in Florida," she said.

"Oh, I'm here a good deal," Cappy said. "Me and Florida go back a long way. Maybe thirty years. Somewhere in there."

"How'd you ever find your way here?" I asked him.

"What do you mean by that?" he asked. "Your map was all right, ol' Pete. Don't you trust your own map?"

"Aren't you going to introduce me to your friend?" Sarah Graham asked.

"Sarah, Cappy Haynes. He's a coach with the Lions. Cappy, this is my friend Sarah Graham."

"What do you coach them to do?" Sarah asked.

"Oh, a little of this, little of that," Cappy said. "Hit, run, throw. Whatever it looks like they need."

"What could lions possibly throw?" Sarah asked.

I didn't know which of them was more confused. Or whether maybe it was me. Louise meanwhile watched the game impassively, without surprise.

Jack's team's pitcher retired the side in order, a strikeout and two fly balls to the outfield. Whatever he was throwing, they were under it, and it would be at least another inning before they caught up to him. Jack came out into the on-deck circle and knelt to watch his team's lead-off hitter at work. It was the boy he'd displaced at shortstop, and he ducked into his crouch as the other team's pitcher swung into his motion.

"So," Cappy said, "we'll see tonight whether your boy can just knock line drives off Lou Rucker, former pitcher, or whether he's really a hitter."

"He's a hitter, all right," I said.

"Yeah, that's what you wrote, ol' Pete," Cappy said. "Musta wrote it good, too."

Louise was still looking straight ahead at the game. The former shortstop had worked the count to three-one. While the pitcher wound to deliver again, he shuffled his feet in the batter's box, stuck his bat across the plate as if to bunt, then pulled it back at the last moment and crouched to take the pitch high — ball four.

"Look at that boy devil the pitcher," Louise said. "What do you think? Man on first, Jack Brown at the plate."

"What the hell's going on here, Louise?" I said it right in her ear, so it was just between the two of us. "What's this business about a letter? What the hell is Cappy Haynes doing down here? And when did Jack start playing short on this team?"

"Stop asking so many questions and enjoy the game," she said. She was still looking straight ahead. "Jack's up, man on first. See if you don't see him do something now. Pitcher won't even want to throw to him."

She was right about that much. While Jack stood quietly at the plate, the pitcher threw over to first base twice. The lead-off hitter had his walking lead again each time before the pitcher could turn to face Jack. He was doing what he did best.

"Look at him devil that pitcher," Louise said.

"Throw the ball, boy," Cappy shouted. Then he turned to me and said, "Base runner like that'll screw up some hitters."

When the first pitch finally came, it was up and away, just short of a pitchout. The right pitch for a catcher to handle if he's got somebody going down to second, but it didn't matter. Jack waved at the pitch to distract the catcher, who came up out of his crouch throwing. But the boy on first had had a fair jump, and when the throw came in head high to the second baseman covering, he slid under the tag. The umpire waved him safe, then turned his back on the second baseman's mild argument and spat into the dirt behind the bag.

"There's a boy who has some fun in the game," Cappy said. "What if you coulda run like that, ol' Pete?"

Jack stood in again, one strike the count. The next pitch was well inside, and as he leaned away from it, he threw his hands up instinctively, and the ball hit his bat. Strike two.

"Have to teach him to get his hands outta the way," Cappy said.

"Nothing and two," Louise muttered. "Tough to hit out of a hole like that."

Jack pushed his hands up the bat an inch and dug into the dust with his right foot. Then he was still again in the batter's box, no wasted motion. With two strikes, most pitchers will waste one, trying to get the hitter to go after something he can't reach. But the pitcher Jack was facing this time must have felt luck was running with him, with the gift strike while Jack was protecting the runner and with the foul ball. He threw a pretty good fastball in on Jack's hands — a strike, and a hell of a pitch. Jack got his hands out quick, though, and lined the ball into the hole between first and second. The boy at second should have been off as soon as the ball was hit, of course, since it was behind him and a ball hit there should always move a runner from second to third, even if they keep it in the infield. But he hesitated for some reason. Hell, it wasn't the major leagues. When the ball went through, the third-base coach waved the boy in, despite his slow start.

Coming around first, Jack must have seen there would be a play at the plate, though there never would have been if that boy in front of him had been on his toes. So Jack never hesitated making his turn, heading for second to take advantage of the throw the right fielder would have to make to cut down the runner at the plate. When it came, the throw was on line and all the catcher had to do was hold the ball while the runner slid through it. But to his credit, the kid who'd hesitated gave the catcher a pretty good lick going by, got him kind of half turned around away from the play. He was out at home, but Jack, who'd never hesitated coming around second either, saw that the catcher was off balance and went for third. The throw there was late and high.

"Heads up play," Cappy said.

The part of the crowd that was cheering the other team had been clapping and shouting at the runner cut down at the plate, and the sudden explosion of noise had shaken Sarah Graham out of whatever reverie she'd been in. Now her head bobbed, and she looked around nervously. "Is it over?" she asked.

"No, ma'am," Cappy said, his eyes still on the field. "It's just gettin' started."

Cappy did know Florida. He knew the ballparks, of course, and not just the ones where the big-league clubs trained in the spring. He'd watched high school and college players all over the state. He knew something about the restaurants too, and the day after he showed up to see Jack play he took me out for lunch, insisting that the Lions would take care of everything.

"One of the pleasures of the job," he said. "They can't give everybody else an expense account and not give me one. So I got one. Today we'll put you on it. How long since you had lunch on the Lions?"

"Long time," I told him.

"Try some of the blackened redfish," he said. "It's good here. That and the shrimp creole, and a bottle of dark beer."

I told him that was a little racy for me, and ordered a tuna sandwich and iced tea. Cappy wrinkled his nose once at it, but he let me alone after that. Except after our plates arrived, he said, "Terrible thing when a man can't eat."

After he'd made sure his redfish was satisfactory and taken a long drink of his beer, he said, "Our boy plays again tonight, doesn't he?"

"Same time, same place," I said. He knew it already, of course. Otherwise why would he still have been around?

"How's the tunafish?" he asked.

"Soothing," I said.

"Fine," he said.

We ate in silence for a while. The restaurant was air-conditioned, and pleasant enough. We sat in a booth on the wall opposite a bar that ran almost the length of the room. Two fellows who might have been fishermen sat on stools and sipped beer, and the rest of the place was empty. It struck me that I couldn't remember the last time I'd been out to a restaurant.

"I gotta hand it to you, ol' Pete," Cappy finally said. "You really stirred 'em up in the front office with that letter. I never saw Flanagan so mad."

"He sent you right down here, did he?" I asked.

Cappy nodded. "Called me right into his office. Told me nobody was gonna call him a racist. Asked me, 'Cappy, you think I'm a racist? You think the Lions are racist?' "

"What did you say?"

Cappy laughed. "I didn't have to say anything," he said. "He didn't slow down long enough for me to say a word. Just kept rumbling and roaring about nobody was gonna call him a racist for Chrissakes, and then told me to get the hell down to Florida and look at Jack Brown."

"So here you are," I said.

"Here I am," Cappy agreed. "And I've seen Jack Brown. Gonna see him again tonight."

"And you're seeing a good one," I said.

"I know that," Cappy said. "Knew that before I came down here."

"I didn't write any letter," I said.

"I know that too," he said. He took a pull at his beer and I finished my iced tea. Then he said, "You really got somethin' in that Louise. Jack could do worse than turn out to have a lot of her in him."

"She's only his father's aunt by marriage," I said.

"She's not *only* anything," Cappy said. "You want another iced tea? Live a little. I'm gonna have another beer. Then we'll go back to Mrs. Brown's and you and I'll play cribbage till she gets home, and then I'll be sure and make a profit on this trip."

"I haven't played cribbage in years," I told him.

"That's what I thought," he said. He caught the waitress's eye and pointed to both our glasses. "So I'll teach you again if I have to. Be patient with you while you learn. Good things come to those who wait."

"That sounds like something Louise would say," I told him.

"I'll accept the compliment, ol' Pete." Cappy smiled.

"Tell me something, Cappy. What exactly did that letter say?"

"I never saw it," Cappy said. "Or, I mean, I saw it, saw the piece of paper, but I never read it. Wasn't addressed to me. Flanagan got it and read it. Gave me the map and told me to come down here. Told me he was no racist. That's it."

"What do you suppose she wrote?"

Cappy spread his hands and smiled again. "What do you care?" he said. "Here I am."

Maybe it was the air conditioning in the restaurant. Maybe it was just *being* in a restaurant, out in a crowd of people, I don't know. It could have been the caffeine in the iced tea, I suppose. I wasn't used to two glasses of iced tea. Whatever it was, I was beginning to feel a little dizzy, or that's how I would have described it to a doctor if I'd had to, but that was only part of it. I was feeling kind of absent, too, almost as if in some way I wasn't there in the chair anymore, or even there in my own skin. I sat there spooked for a minute, and then I thought maybe it was something else entirely. "It kind of makes you wonder why she got me involved at all, doesn't it?" I said. "Why she's been carrying me along for the ride."

Cappy shook his head and said no, he didn't think it was like that. "Far as I can tell, she was just guessin' about Jack at the beginning. Real games she'd seen were a long time ago. How's she gonna know how good her boy is when he's playin' with a bunch of other boys nobody ever paid any attention to? Old boys that saw him, you know, at the camps, they let him go. So that had to make her doubt some, even if they did see him at the wrong position. 'Cause she didn't know that. So she needed you to look at him and tell her what she was pretty sure she knew already."

"All right," I said. I was having trouble staying upright in my chair by then. My voice sounded like it was coming from somewhere else. And I thought, *Well, here's the stroke, then. Out here in a public place after all, where I'll fall flat on my face with a crash of dishes and glass, then flop around on the floor for everyone to marvel at, bug-eyed and terrified.* Later someone who had seen it all would say, "You know, I wondered about it when that old man came in. He looked a little shaky, you know? Looked like maybe he should have been resting somewhere with his feet up and an oxygen tank nearby, just in case. Don't know what he was doing out there eating fish."

Apparently Cappy hadn't noticed, though.

"Besides that," he said, "where do you think that letter would have ended up if she'd just gone and signed her own name? It only got where it did because your name was on it, ol' Pete."

My name, my name, I thought. *What is my name?* And I looked down on the wreck of a thing Cappy Haynes was talking to, the stooped old fool with his half-eaten tunafish and his iced tea, his startled eyes . . . looked down from a mysterious, dispassionate distance and said to my sailing self, *My name won't mean a damn much longer, that's certain, but at least it won't be dragging that awful baggage around after it when this stroke is finished. And then my name can rest in peace somewhere, no use to anyone, but no trouble either, as it was before my mother thought of it, "Peter," or before my father, the shortstop with the stumpy legs, long before that married her and made it possible. My name and I are headed back to a darkness complete as that before the dawn. Bye-bye, baby. See you later. Tell it goodbye. This one's outta here.*

"Look, miss," Cappy was saying, "my wallet's right out there in the car. Gimme two minutes. I'll be back with it."

The waitress stood over him with her hands on her hips, eyes wary. The check sat in front of him.

"You gonna leave this old man as a hostage, I guess," she said.

I reached into my pocket, which is how I knew I was back. I took two bills out of my wallet and laid them on the check. The waitress picked up the check and the money without looking at me or Cappy again.

When I got up my foot had gone to sleep, and I sat down again, hard.

"You not finished eatin'?" Cappy asked.

"Just give me a minute," I told him.

"Long as you need," he said. "Even though that waitress just as soon see us gone. She must be new. I never had anything like that happen before. Place used to be all right. 'Course I never brought a white guy in here with me other times."

"Now you'll know," I said.

"I guess," he said.

Out in the parking lot the sun banged down off the cars. It was difficult to see after the cool semidarkness of the restaurant. I squinted hard, but that was all right. I was behind my own eyes again, not looking down from overhead. *Must have been just a trial run,* I thought. *Just practice. And not so bad either, if that's what the real thing is like.* And I had another funny thought then too, which was that I hoped I wouldn't die just yet, because I was looking forward to seeing how this Jack Brown business would turn out. Whatever my part in it had been or might be, I thought, well, I'd just as soon see what happened next.

Once we were in the car, Cappy flipped on the air conditioning, then reached across me to the glove compartment, where his wallet was. He took two bills out and gave them to me, then made a note on a little pad that folded out of the inside of the wallet.

"I appreciate it," I said.

"I'll be gettin' it right back, soon as we go and play some cribbage," he said. "Only I won't tell the Lions that."

"You may be sorry you ate all that lunch," I told him.

"Nothin' wrong with that fish," Cappy said.

"No," I said. "But you're gonna find Louise wants to feed you again before we go to the ball game. And she doesn't believe in just a sandwich and a glass of milk for dinner. She'll have a roast or something in the oven. Chops, maybe, or a chicken. Potatoes. Two vegetables, probably."

"All that," Cappy mused.

"Rolls too," I said. "And a pie if she can get away from work early enough to bake it."

"Well," he said, "we're just gonna have to play some hard cards, work up an appetite again."

"She was married to the same man for forty years," I said.

"And she said he was home all those years, except for a stretch in the service during the war. You'd think he'd have weighed three hundred pounds. But I'm wearing his pants."

"Maybe you're growin' into them," Cappy said.

"What do you think of that, though?" I said. "A man and woman married all that time. I imagine it can be the finest thing there is."

"Could be awful," Cappy said. "Could be two old folks sittin' on the front porch with nothin' to say to each other. Two old husks, all talked out. Could be like that."

"But not Louise, Cappy," I said. "You can't imagine her silent or defeated, can you?"

"Maybe not, at that," Cappy said.

"No," I said. "One day maybe we'll hear her explain how it wasn't really wrong to write whatever it was she wrote and sign my name to it. She'll have our own good in it, and Jack's, of course, and the good of the Lions. She'll have God in it too, if we press her."

"You gonna ask her about it?" Cappy said.

"I don't know," I said.

"It's a mistake if you do," he said. "Be like tinkering with Jack's swing because you maybe like to see him uppercut a little more, hit some more home runs. But his swing's fine the way it is right now."

"No argument there," I said.

"All right," he said. "Same with his aunt, or his great-aunt, whatever she is. She's doin' fine. Don't mess with her. Seems to me she's a natural, like Jack."

Maybe he was right. A natural was just someone smart or lucky enough to find the way toward doing exactly what he was meant to do. You could foul it up, of course. Somebody blessed with a green thumb, loving the soil, could think himself around to believing he needed more money and go into selling cars or insurance or stocks. Then maybe he'd be miserable all his life. Or if you had the right person to love, you could listen to some idiot tell you that variety was more exciting, and foul that up too. Or you could get hurt or lost somehow, so you *couldn't* do what you seemed to be meant to do with beauty and pride, which is what happened to the best of those boys I'd signed, although Cappy seemed to be holding up.

"What would you 'complish, anyway?" he went on. "You want to argue what she did was wrong? She knows otherwise already. Save your breath. I mean, she knows."

"Were you ever married?" I asked him.

"Once, almost," he said. "You don't remember that?"

"No," I said.

"Supposed to be married, and then I got hurt that time, when the car hit me. We put if off 'cause I was in the hospital. And then the two operations, and after the second one the doctor said nothing else he could do, you know, and I still couldn't throw. Didn't seem much point to it then, I guess."

"She left you?"

"We come to an understanding," he said.

"She found someone else?"

"Found a ballplayer who could throw," he said.

We were back at Louise's apartment by then, but we hadn't made it upstairs to play cards. We just sat on the steps in front. It was out of the sun and there was a breeze — enough of one, anyway, to keep the worst of the heat moving.

After we'd sat for a while, Cappy said, "Baseball weather, all right."

"Not for me," I told him. "I hated this kind of weather when I was still playing. You could hit a ball into it and it would just seem to get heavy and die on you, and then fall into the out-fielder's glove like the Sunday paper hitting the porch. Heat like this could take all the carry out of a fly ball."

"You a lazy hitter, all right, ol' Pete." Cappy laughed.

"What could you like about this weather?" I asked him. "It must have been as hot for you as for anybody else."

"Hot days like this," he said, "I'd be warmed up soon as I

stepped on the field. I could go right out to the outfield fence and throw strikes to the plate. My arm'd be up and hummin'. Get loose just puttin' on your shoes. No better day to play the game than a hot day."

"I remember the first time I saw you play," I said. "It was a high school game."

"Tournament game," he said. "You said you came down to see somebody else. Boy from the other team. You just happened to catch sight of me and thought maybe you'd say hello."

"Well, that's what they used to tell us to say," I said. "Pretty stupid, wasn't it? I imagine a kid like you were then knew what was up. You knew you were getting a look, even then. I was still doing it the way they told us, trying to save a dollar. Like the guy who signed me."

"I'll tell you what I knew then," Cappy said. "I knew there wasn't one other boy on any team we played who could throw like I could. Some of 'em could hit, and some could run. Nobody could throw like me."

"You hit pretty well too," I told him. "Couple of line drives, I think."

"Two for four with a walk," Cappy said. "Doubled in the tying run in the sixth or seventh inning, then scored the winning run from second on a single back through the box. Ran right through the sign at third, because I didn't think the outfielder could make a throw good enough to get me. He threw it up the line at third, and I was home safe. Slid, but I prob'ly didn't have to. And nobody would run on me all night. Time the tournament came around, everybody knew it was no use to run on me. But boy, I wanted 'em to that night. Wanted all you boys to see my arm."

I laughed, and he looked at me for a minute like he was going to get angry. Then before I could explain, his face softened and he said, "You laugh, ol' Pete. You think it's funny I remember just what I did that night. But you think back on it, I bet you can tell me what pitches you hit the first night a scout saw you play. I bet you can feel the flannel shirt on your back too, and smell the hot dogs, or whatever the hell they ate at ball games in the Stone Age."

"Two hits," I told him. "I was in the outfield, and my dad played shortstop, just like most nights. The scout talked to my dad, mostly."

"Two hits," Cappy said. He gestured with the tips of his fingers — *come on, come on* — as if he knew there was more to it and I should keep talking.

"A triple off a hanging curveball," I said. "Anybody could have hit that one. But the home run was off a rising fastball, up in my eyes. A good pitch if you couldn't tell where it was going. I bet the pitcher'd say so today if he were alive."

Now Cappy was laughing. "So some ol' scout saw you tomahawk a fastball up, and he signed you anyway. Didn't know enough to write you off. Nobody catches up to that pitch for long in the show."

"He must have liked something he saw," I said.

"Maybe the way you ran," Cappy said.

"Maybe that was it," I said.

"Prob'ly the way you ran when you hit the home run," he said.

We sat for a while and watched the cars go by. Later that night we'd see another game. It hung in the air like a prize at the end of the long afternoon. But I could wait. Didn't want it to come along too soon. There was room and time for baseball talk. What a long, long time had gone by without it.

"You ever pitch?" Cappy asked.

I must have looked at him like I thought he was crazy.

"I mean when you were just a kid," he said. "Little League or somethin' like that."

"Never pitched," I said. "Never played in Little League either, because there was no Little League. There was just the teams that the towns had, you know. And if your dad played and you were a likely-looking boy, you'd start to practice with 'em a little at some point, maybe when you were fifteen, I guess. That's after you'd been playin' ball in the pasture for however many years, ten or so."

"Well, lotta major leaguers pitched sometime," Cappy said. "Lot of 'em were the biggest, strongest kids, you know. So they pitched."

"I didn't pitch," I said. "The first serious baseball I played was for the team my dad was on, the Ducks. Town team with some ringers. Semi-pro. I was an outfielder from the beginning with 'em. They had some good pitchers."

"You were a hitter," Cappy said.

"Right." I nodded. "A hitter, but they had to put me somewhere. They had the same infield for years and years. My dad was the shortstop, it seemed like forever. He was still playing shortstop when I signed and went away to play ball. It was a pretty good team."

"Well, what I'm tryin' to tell you, I *was* a pitcher," Cappy said. "What kind of pitcher you think I was?"

I looked at him in the afternoon sun. Though he'd put on some weight since his playing days all those years ago, he was still a powerful-looking man. His arms were thick and obviously muscled, even in the loose sport shirt he wore. Up in Washington I'd noticed that he still moved pretty well, even as a one-armed hitter. Still bounced a little on the balls of his feet sometimes when he walked.

"You don't have the height to come over the top at anybody," I said, "but with those arms, you probably were a little strong boy thrower. Probably reached back and found all you could, showed your teeth, and tried to throw it by everybody."

"Hah!" Cappy said. "That's what everybody thought when they first saw me. Strong boy gonna just crank that fastball up here, throw it hard as he can till he runs outta gas. They'd dig in on me like they was gonna go to war. Then you know what I'd throw 'em? Knuckleballs. Little nickel curve they call a slider now. Make 'em pop it up and hammer it into the ground."

"I wouldn't have guessed it," I said.

"I liked it," he said. "I liked foolin' em. But it got so I liked the days I played in the outfield more. And then one year there was a coach who made me stop throwin' the way I was. Said my arm wasn't old enough for all that breakin' and twistin' yet. That was all right, 'cause I liked the outfield a *lot* more by then. Other teams' best hitters come up, try and hit it over my head, couldn't do it. Even though I played in so short their eyes lit up and they had to try. Other teams' best runners try comin' in from second on a ball hit to me, try scorin' on a sacrifice fly, couldn't do it. I liked throwin' 'em out from way back there even better than foolin' 'em, twistin' 'em up at the plate with my soft stuff. Liked to watch 'em start from second, you know, think they gonna score, and then throw from way back and watch that ball catch 'em, even though sometimes it look like it never could. Watch that ball come in on a line, and then that runner looks like, whoops, seems like he's runnin' in one of those bad dreams where you just work at it but you're goin' nowhere. Took a lot of fun out of it when they stopped runnin' on me after a while, wherever I was playin'."

"You had a cannon," I said.

"You remember a boy named Applegate? Billy Applegate?" he said.

"Sure," I said. "He was a joke. All he could do was run."

"Well, he was no joke, though, when he *was* runnin'," Cappy said. "No joke then. And the White Sox weren't the only team that thought it was a good idea to get a hold of a sprinter and put him out there on a base when he could do 'em some good."

"That was the year they ran out of catchers in the middle of a game one night and had to use a kid who'd never caught a day in his life beyond high school," I said. "That was one game they would have traded your Billy Applegate for somebody who could handle a catcher's mitt, I'll tell you that. Because that other boy had four or five men steal on him in one inning and then lost the game on a passed ball. The third catcher was probably the guy who was in the minor leagues somewhere because Billy Applegate was sitting in the dugout, waiting for a chance to run. Oakland tried it years later with a kid named Herb Washington. World-class sprinter. Didn't work with him, either, but you could understand it, at least, with Charlie Finley running the club."

"All right, all right," Cappy said. "But what I'm tellin' you, this kid Billy Applegate could really run. They took him off the track and taught him how to cut down his turns and hit the bag with his right foot and all that. Taught him how to slide. And he could run like a bastard. So one night in Chicago, he's on the bench as usual, and the White Sox get a guy on second with nobody out, ninth inning, tie game, so here he comes out to run."

"Probably the catcher they took out," I said. "Manager was probably looking up and down the bench, wondering who the hell he was going to catch if Billy Applegate didn't score."

"I don't remember," Cappy said. "That isn't the story I'm tellin'. But this kid Applegate took his lead, you know, and damn if Minnie Minoso didn't club one out between left and center. Kid was off at the crack of the bat, of course. Third-base coach was windmilling him around, *Go home, go home.* Wasn't anything else he was in there for. But I got a pretty good jump on the ball out there in left, got to it pretty quick, and threw a strike home. Kid was out six feet. He never reached the plate. Just slid into the catcher, *bam!*, and kind of shook his head. Then when he saw what had happened, kid turned around to left field there and started out toward where I was, and he was shouting at me in this squeaky voice, 'How the hell you do that, man? How the hell you *do* it?' He was so mad, see, because he didn't believe he could be caught on a play like that. He'd had his lead and taken his tight turn, just like they told him. Run like hell, you know. But when he got there, why, there's the ball. If it hadda been replays in the clubhouse in those days, he'd been the first one in to have a look. But there wasn't one, so he was lost, you see? It all happened behind his back. Magic. So there he was, screaming out at me, walking through the infield, and damn if anybody knew what was gonna happen next. You know, anyone who's gone to some ball games has seen a hitter charge the pitcher sometime, maybe a runner and an infielder mix it up after a hard tag. But nobody ever saw a guy walking out toward left field screaming out of his mind like that. So I don't know how it would have gone if it hadna been for Minoso. He was on second base. Took second on the throw. And I happened to look over there at him while this kid was heading out toward me, and Minnie was bent over double, both feet on the bag, almost falling on his face he was laughing so hard. You never heard a man laugh like that. And the kid, Applegate, looked over at him too, and that was kind of the end of it."

When I'd stopped laughing with him, I said, "I remember Minnie Minoso. He was one of those guys who looked like he'd never stop playing. Didn't he go down to Mexico to play when he was finished in the majors?"

"Somewhere," Cappy said. "Maybe he's still playin' somewhere."

"I scouted a little bit down there," I said. "Couple of different times I went. Mexico, and Venezuela too. And Cuba. Saw Luis Tiant's father pitch."

"But see, the reason I was talkin' about pitchin'," Cappy said, "I think you see the game a little different if you been a pitcher. Lotta guys who come up to the show, they been the best athlete wherever they been, so they're pitchers for a time. Biggest kids, strongest kids. Maybe the first kids can reach the plate in the air. But anyway, they come to understand how everything starts, you see? How the ball's put in play. Gives 'em a little bit of an advantage, ol' Pete. Like they can see things the other guys can't see."

"You're talking about Jack now?"

"Could be Jack has that," Cappy agreed. "Could be that's one more thing in his favor."

"Besides his quick hands and his glove," I said.

"And his great-aunt," Cappy said.

I told him the story then about the first night I'd seen Jack hit. I mentioned the hitters he'd reminded me of, and his instincts and stillness at the plate. How Louise had had to take the others back to Fair Haven, but that was all right, because I'd been left alone to study Jack without distraction. I even told him about swinging Jack's bat in the room off the kitchen.

"Ol' Pete," he asked, "you get as excited about all the boys you scouted before you retired? You take it all back home with you and start swingin' a baseball bat around the furniture? Because I'm beginnin' to see why your wife decided she'd had enough."

And I realized — had realized, really — that I hadn't been so excited about a prospect in many years. I acknowledged it. Here was the possibility of more heartbreak, wide as Jack's shoulders and sure as his eye. It must have shown.

"What are you scared of?" Cappy finally asked.

"It's almost too much to expect," I said.

"How you figure that?" Cappy asked. "He's a ballplayer. Good one, too. What's wrong with expectin' he'd have himself a chance?"

"You get to a certain age, you don't believe you'll be a part of it again," I said. "Your time has passed. It'd be like winning the lottery and then wondering what an old man like me could do with the money."

Cappy shrugged. "Lottery wheel don't care what numbers come up," he said. "People watchin' Jack ain't watchin' you. Don't mix it up."

"He's a hell of a player, isn't he?" I said.

"Looks like," Cappy said. "Sure does look like it."

We sat for a while, each of us seeing our own pictures of Jack, I suppose.

Eventually Cappy said, "You ever see Brooks Robinson play much?"

"Of course," I said. "A hundred times, I guess, one place or another."

"He was a funny one, wasn't he?" Cappy said. "I mean, you could look at him, he was never as smooth as some of those Latin boys that come up so much now, but Christ, he never seemed to miss. I'd like to have played behind him."

"Wagner's the one I'd like to have played behind," I said. "Him I never did see. My dad said he was the best, though. And all they had then were those little bitty gloves, not the baskets the kids come up with now."

"Billy Cox," Cappy said. "There's some soft hands."

"How about in the outfield?" I said. "Who'd you like to have played alongside of?"

"Clemente," Cappy said. "But I wouldn't have been any good then. Woulda been watchin' him 'stead of playin'. And Mays. I always thought Mays was probably the one *players* liked to watch most."

"I'd like to have played beside DiMaggio," I said. "He played like some kind of lord of the outfield. People who saw him all the time said in his whole career they never saw him miss a cut-off man or throw to the wrong base. Same with base running. Just one time, they say, he tried to stretch a single into a double and got thrown out. But then later the umpire admitted he'd blown the call."

"*Years* later, I bet," Cappy said.

We were silent again for a while, and then I said, "Cappy, do you ever wonder about the player you might have been?"

"I don't have to, ol' Pete," he said. "I *know* it."

"You think it was just bad luck?"

"Whatever," he said. "Was what it was. Maybe I had no business flyin' a damn kite."

"It broke my heart," I said.

Cappy looked at me for a long minute then, as if he were trying to decide what to say. "Shit," he said finally, " 'nother boy'll always come along."

"You know what happened to the best boys I signed," I said. "Yourself included." I rattled off a few names and accompanying disasters and disappointments — just a sampler.

"Oh, for God's sake, ol' Pete, who you think you are? A Jonah? A midget in the dugout? Look what happens to some of those boys you didn't sign. You didn't sign Pete Reiser, did you, and he ran into the outfield wall until he finally beat himself crooked. You never signed Clemente, did you, and he went down in a plane. Or Eddie Waitkus, who got shot in his hotel room. You mighta done the best you could to do it, but nobody collected all the bad luck that shows up for ballplayers. Don't act like *you* got it. I bet you never signed Roy Campanella, did you? But he managed to get himself into a wheelchair anyway. Probably never signed Dizzy Dean either, who got hit in the toe with a line drive and was never the same again."

"My wife used to say it was just the kind of thing a baseball man would think of," I said.

"Naw, it's worse than that," Cappy said. "Nothin' like that at all. Players' superstitions may sound crazy, but they need 'em. Helps 'em concentrate. Hell, you know that. Man's in a groove, he does what he can to stay there. Maybe lines his bats up the same way each day, plays catch with the same guy to warm up, spits three times in the on-deck circle . . . helps him keep that groove just the same and stay in it. Or he *thinks* it does, which is just the same, isn't it?"

"I imagine so," I said.

"You got so old now you have to imagine it?" Cappy laughed. "You musta had somethin' you did when you were goin' good."

And for some reason, I remembered something I probably hadn't thought about in fifty years. "I'll be damned if you're not right," I said. "I did things in fives."

Cappy wrinkled his brow.

"I did things in fives," I said again. "If I tapped my bat on my shoe to get the dirt out of my spikes, I did it five times. If I got a cup of water from the cooler in the dugout, I took it in five sips. Scratched my head five times if it itched."

"Musta been hell on your wife sometimes," Cappy said. "Maybe *that's* why she left."

"I never took it off the ballfield," I told him. "It was just there in the park that it counted."

"All right." Cappy nodded. "Probably helped you out, anyway. Kept your mind on your work. Kept things balanced for you. No different from what other guys do. But how's this Jonah business gonna serve you? What you gonna get from that? Just messes up your mind for when you need it. I say walk away from it."

"That's what Louise thinks," I said.

"Sure," he said. "She's a good thinker, too."

A little later Louise showed up, arms full of groceries, as usual. Cappy went out to the car to help her, and I held the door for them when they got to the steps.

"What's goin' on here?" she said. "You lose your key? How long you been standin' out here?"

"I still have my key," I told her. "We just never got any further than the steps after lunch. It's nice enough."

Louise sniffed. "Nice enough," she said. "You wait just a few more minutes and you're gonna be wet enough."

She was right. While Cappy and I had been talking, dark clouds had piled up overhead. The sky was full of them, except for a streak of blue off to the east, which is where it seemed to me the weather should have been coming from. We hadn't even noticed.

"Maybe it'll blow over," I said to no one in particular. "I'd hate to miss Jack's game."

"You won't miss it, 'cause it won't happen," Louise said. "This is rain comin'. We need it, too. Be another game soon enough."

While she was putting the groceries away, Louise kept two lines of chatter going simultaneously. "What all you want for dinner?" she said. And then before either of us could answer, she was muttering about two old men so dumb they couldn't see it was about to rain, and it was a good thing she'd come home when she did or we might have been standing there astonished, with our mouths hanging open, stupid as chickens caught in a storm.

"What do you think?" I said to Cappy. "Do you suppose Jack spends game days telling baseball stories? Does he feel it coming all day, like I do now? Like you do?"

"He's too young," Cappy said. "How many stories could he know?"

"He's fixin' cars," Louise said. "You the only ones don't have anything to do but tell baseball stories."

"Well, look," I said, "it could have been a lot worse. We could have gone over to the ballpark already, couldn't we? Could have been sitting there in the first row of the bleachers, waiting like shaky drunks in the morning heat for the bartender to come to work."

"Huh," Louise said. "Seems more like a couple fidgety kids with their noses pressed up against the window, waitin' for the candy store to open."

Louise

OLD PEOPLE SURPRISE YOU ALL THE TIME. YOU THINK you learned all there is to know about them, workin' in a place like Fair Haven, and then they fool you. You take Mrs. Sarah Graham. Who'd've thought she'd be flirting with Cappy Haynes at the ballpark that way? Some ol' mixed-up part of a high school girl playin' inside her, sweet as it ever was. "Aren't you going to introduce me to your friend?" she said. Then askin' him baseball questions every time she could think of one to ask. And the truth was she didn't know a baseball from a beanbag.

Before we left the park that night, she told me what she really liked about it was the way the public-address man said everybody's name twice when they came up to the plate, in case you might be going to forget it. "Now batting, Jack Brown," he'd say. "Shortstop, Jack Brown."

"He must be a kind man," she said to me.

Of course she forgot things all the time, like old people do. Next day she didn't know she'd been to a baseball game. Just maybe remembered a dream with lights and colors and a lotta boys runnin' all around. Maybe not even that. Then when you were just sure there was nothin' much that she recalled of what she had seen or heard, she said, "Pete Estey certainly has gotten young again, hasn't he? His eyes are a boy's eyes now. What do you think? Maybe he'd like to meet one of my daughters. Sometimes they're lonely, they say. They could see themselves in his eyes."

I've seen people come and go at Fair Haven, naturally, all the years I've worked there — cooks and nurses, orderlies, maids, schoolchildren volunteering — and a lot of 'em leave real quick, just shakin' their heads. They say, "My, how can you stand it, all of 'em so crazy? I feel like I'll be crazy myself if I'm around 'em too long." But what they never do, they never stay around long enough to listen past the cryin' out and the whinin' for a pillow or something for the pain, or how mean you are when you have to roll them over to keep them from the bedsores. The ones who leave so fast just hear the shoutin' and the moanin'. They see the plates pushed off the table, still full of food, or someone crying in the bathroom at night because she can't find her way out. But I've been there long enough to hear the singing, you see.

One time I heard a little squeaky voice in the middle of the day, sounded like it was singing a high school football song. Fact is, I heard it through the wall of Mrs. Sarah Graham's room, and we both sat silent, listening together. After a while it was only humming, and maybe tapping feet, just one person, and light, light tapping, if that's what it was. We listened until there was no sound anymore, and then Mrs. Sarah Graham looked straight at me and said, "She was a cheerleader. What do you think? And she loved the boys on the football team. All of them. After games, sometimes, or after practices. Before it had gotten dark. The grass was cool and soft, and better out beyond the field, where it was trampled down from the running, you see? She was so eager. Her father had to take her out of school finally and send her away to avoid the scandal. But she still sings sometimes. She remembers all of the words."

"How long have you known that lady?" I asked her.

"Who?" she said.

I get caught like that all the time, after all the years I've been at Fair Haven. And sometimes I even think, *Lord, I hope I don't just go on and on, lose my wits and just keep wanderin' through the days, maybe not even knowing which is which.* But those are times I recover from fast, and I remember that my worryin' about it doesn't amount to scraps. The Lord took care of me through all the years of childhood danger, helped me to a marriage full of love, saw me through the raising of my children. He gave me eyes to see the world and the sense to appreciate it. I got up every morning with plenty to do and strength enough to do it, that was the main thing.

Besides, who says stories like the one about the woman who was a cheerleader aren't true? Could be, easy as some others I've heard. Some of the baseball stories Mr. Pete Estey and Cappy Haynes told each other! There was one about a boy in the minor leagues somewhere — little stringy boy, Cappy said, when Mr. Pete Estey finally described him enough so Cappy could place him. Anyway, this boy was an infielder. They played him at every position and he dug in and gave 'em their money's worth at each one, small as he was. To hear those old men remember it, nobody ever worked so hard to be a ballplayer, even though Cappy couldn't remember him until Mr. Pete Estey about painted a picture of him on the kitchen table. And one day this boy was at second base and his pitcher just lost it. Just couldn't throw a strike. Couldn't even come close. But this is the minor leagues, and either the manager was gonna teach this pitcher a lesson about finding his control, or he was maybe just out of pitchers entirely. Anyway, this boy stayed in the game, giving up walk after walk, and all those base runners just parading past that stringy boy at second base, some of 'em laughin', probably. And this boy's working to convince the coaches and manager that he's gonna be a major leaguer, you see? Been working just at that ever since the first time someone told him he'd never be big enough for it. But it's gettin' harder and harder for him to manage, with these other boys, one after another, just dancing around the bases, four pitches and move up again. It must have felt like an insult to his dream. And finally he couldn't stand it anymore, and the way Mr. Pete Estey told it, he just burst into tears and threw his glove down at his feet and shouted, "Throw strikes, you bastard! Goddamn you, throw strikes!"

Cappy and Mr. Pete Estey laughed then, but you could hear that they felt for what that stringy boy was trying to do, too. It was just that he had nothing to say at all about the pitching part of it. And he couldn't just scratch in the dirt with the toe of his baseball shoe or look over at the pretty girl in the second row behind the dugout, like most second basemen might do if it happened to them. He had nothing clever to say to the base runners as they went by. I imagine he was not a clever boy.

I was talkin' about how old people are bound to surprise you, but there's some things you can predict about 'em. They lose what it was that drove that boy to throw his glove down and weep, those who ever had it. It kind of gets worn away over the years, when life shows 'em more and more things that are gonna happen, whatever way they might feel about it, whatever they might do. Mr. Pete Estey sat there in Fair Haven, protesting that there was nothin' he could do for anyone anymore, and anyone could see all he needed was a little nudge in the right direction. But most old people with any sense come to see how people will go on makin' their mistakes — can't throw strikes, whatever — and they don't take it on themselves so, don't suffer with it.

There was some of that learning in Cappy Haynes already, even though he wasn't what anybody'd really call old yet. Maybe he'd earned it, losing his career the way he did. Anyway, the rain on the second night he was supposed to see Jack play didn't bother him any. He just said, "What the hell? We'll play some cards." Which he knew I wouldn't be doing, so what he was up to, of course, was tryin' to win Mr. Pete Estey's money. Except that he knew as well as I did that there wasn't anything much to win. But it was something to do while it rained and rained.

Except that Mr. Pete Estey wasn't any more able to sit at the table and play cards than he could fly to the moon. Almost right up until game time, he paced over to the kitchen window every couple of minutes to see if maybe it would clear off after all and they'd get the game in. Long after he must've felt like a fool saying it, he'd be tellin' us about some little patch of clear sky he thought he could still make out up between the clouds. If we'd just look out the window, we'd see it, he told us. And then he stopped saying anything about it and just paced back to the window every few minutes to see how his piece of blue sky was making out.

"Come on and play cards," Cappy'd say. And Mr. Pete Estey would sit a minute, maybe even pick up his hand to look at it. Then he'd be up to see about the sky again.

Cappy stayed over that night, though he already had a motel room somewhere. It was fine to have him, too. I'd liked him right from that afternoon in Washington. But a funny thing happened with him there all that time — through dinner and then all the while it rained, and then breakfast the next morning before he got back in his car to go to the airport. Somewhere in there I got to thinking it would be nice when Mr. Pete Estey and I had the place to ourselves again. I didn't realize until then how comfortable it had begun to feel. It took Cappy Haynes being there to make me see it. And it caught me by surprise a little.

But then I came to think about it, and what did I expect? Mr. Pete Estey was good company, and someone to cook for, so I ate better. Someone to chat with too, when there was something to tell about the day at Fair Haven. He acted at first like he didn't enjoy that. Too much like gossip for him. But he warmed up to it, same as anyone would. It was just stories about people he knew, and some who'd come along since he'd moved in with me. We'd talk along into the night. And it wasn't just the Fair Haven stories, because there was baseball to talk about too, like I'd said there would be when I first said he should come home with me. Old players. Old ballparks. Just like you'd think, Mr. Pete Estey had plenty of stories stored up, and they came along in their time. Cappy being there reminded him of more stories, naturally, so once Cappy'd gone on back to Washington, there were some later nights. Nights after we saw Jack play, and some when we didn't, Mr. Pete Estey would sit with me and call up players he could remember. Sometimes those stories about the players and the stories about the old men and old women at Fair Haven, they were more like each other than you'd think.

And that wasn't all. Mr. Pete Estey, mostly late on the latest nights we were up, would tell stories about himself. He told me his wife was the most beautiful woman he ever saw, and how when he saw her the first time, he couldn't think about anything else for days. "She was the cautious one from the beginning," he said. "After I'd called her up or seen her every day for a couple of weeks, she told me, 'Look, maybe we should go a little more slowly, and consider what we've got here. Why don't you wait a week or so to call me again?' So I went home and fretted about it for the rest of the day, and then I called her that night and said it was no good, and I wanted to have dinner with her. And she said she hadn't gone out because she thought maybe I'd call."

They were like two children then. He could tell me this from where he was, an old man. He could look back and see it. But only *like* two children, he said, because they weren't children at all.

"She wanted a family," he said. "And I did too. Maybe if we'd met earlier, we'd have had one. Anyway, we didn't have any luck with it."

I asked him did she blame him for that, because sometimes some women will. A woman can work herself around to believin' it's the man that's somehow not tryin', holdin' somethin' back. Seems as if there's gotta be some special give in him to make a baby, ready as she feels for it. Some women say that. But he said no, there was no blame. There was just a kind of sadness that came into things for them.

"Some sadness brings folks together," I told him. But he said that wasn't so with them. Or it wasn't enough.

"Finally," he said, "I think it was that she felt I'd gone ahead and had a family without her. I'd come home full of news about this boy or that one I'd seen — boys who really were just kids, you know. And she'd try to be enthusiastic about them. She liked them all right. Some more than others, of course. But they were mine, she knew. My work. Maybe I'd never have been so involved with them if we had made a family of our own. I don't know."

"So I guess you just worked more and more," I said. "Most anyone would. Get away from the sadness."

He smiled and said maybe that was it, like it would be with anyone else. But he told me about scouting trips where she went with him, too. He said there were days so bright he could still see them, and so full of music he could still call it back. He could hear it at night sometimes, before he went off to sleep.

"Dumb music," he said. "Mariachi bands and steel drums, the corniest music for tourists. The same songs, over and over. We'd lie in bed and talk about how if we heard 'em one more time, we'd go out into the street and strangle the singer. Except who wanted to risk a Latin American jail? That's how they knew they had you."

But the trips got to be routine, like other routines, he told me. And sometimes the front office complained about how he was taking her along with him, only he didn't want to blame the Lions. He didn't make a case of it because after a while she was less interested in the travel anyway. Less interested in him too, he thought.

"Or maybe not less interested, exactly," he said. "But frightened, in a way, so she pulled back. She came to see, I guess, how the rest of her life would be. It was a pattern of doing for me when I was home, then waiting for me when I was gone, or tagging along somewhere. And it scared her, I think, to see so clearly how it would go."

"Didn't scare you?" I asked him.

"Well, that was a way we were different," he said. "I was always so caught up in one kid or another, running around trying to see this fella pitch or that fella run. Trying to figure out this coach or that one, who was maybe telling one scout one thing and me something else. Talking with the parents of those boys, of course, who all thought they had the next Babe Ruth or Dizzy Dean at the kitchen table, and how could I miss it? It was all full days for me. I didn't know anything."

"And she saw the days goin' by." I nodded.

"Goin' by, and gone," he said.

"No fun in the games for her," I said.

"Oh, fun, sure," he told me. "It was fun to be out there in your shirtsleeves, just watching the boys play. She couldn't have missed that. She was smart, and she knew how to watch a ball game. She recognized an outfielder who got a jump on the ball, or a hitter who could foul off a good pitch to stay alive. But it was *my* game first. It couldn't be any different for her. And she wasn't going to be one of those women who followed half a step behind a man and chattered with the other wives and kept the icebox full of beer for poker nights. Which I never played, come to think of it. . . . I'm not explaining it very well, am I?"

Better than most, I thought. And he was charitable, too. Or that's what I guessed, because that was all there was for me to do. I just know that Fair Haven was full of stories of folks picking at their marriages. Women who'd outlived their husbands would scold the old men, long gone, for dying. If they had loved them, why'd they gone and died? And the men would creep up on

things their wives had said or done, you know, look at them
from everyplace they could find, pick at them like they had a
stick, look under them. And the wives left behind remembered
looks they'd caught their men at, hot looks across the table at
the church social or the dinner party, or when they were just
waiting for a bus — "How could he look at her that way, and
him just engaged to me two weeks? And didn't he stutter when
he tried to explain?"

I listened to it. Some of them at Fair Haven would ask me to
listen, or to sit with them, anyway. And after a while they would
be more like talkin' to themselves. If I'd stepped out, some of
'em wouldn't have noticed. But I didn't. I stayed and listened.
I heard about marriages that started with rape and turned quiet,
gentle. And I heard about the children, of course, some of 'em
wonderful and some not so good.

I did what I could to help. I listened, even if I could not walk
in their shoes. Because my Brown, I don't think he ever loved
anyone else but me. I know it. Neither of us did. And the life
we shared, we *shared*. Some of it was the children. Like Mr.
Pete Estey said, they might have made a difference for him. But
the children came and went. Might sound like a bad thing to
say, but that's how it was. And we were there all along. So I
would listen to the stories in the afternoons at Fair Haven, or to
Mr. Pete Estey at night, and I would find myself thinking, *Lord,
Louise, you're blessed*. But I didn't talk about that.

"She wasn't a baseball fan before we got together," Mr. Pete
Estey said. "Maybe that's why it was always my game as far as
she was concerned."

"Well, some come to it early, and some late," I said. "Some
not ever."

"Anyway, we ran out of gas. And what I missed most when
she was gone was not having her to talk to when I came back
from looking at some boy throw or hit. I liked telling her about
it."

"But she came back," I said. I told you I was a listener. "She must have missed something too. Maybe hearing about those boys."

Mr. Pete Estey smiled and said yes, he was getting ahead of himself. "She did come back. But it wasn't to hear more baseball stories. I think it was just to make sure. She was lonely, she said. And I was lonely as hell. And she came back to find out whether that was better or worse than what she'd left. She must have decided she was better off lonely than with me."

"Maybe she was a fool," I said. I wouldn't have said that to anyone at Fair Haven. I don't know why I said it to Mr. Pete Estey.

"Hah!" he snorted. "No, I don't think so. I'm not doing it justice, Louise. Not doing her justice. We loved each other both times we were married, and she was no more a fool than I was. And we did work at it. It just didn't turn out."

Then we sat for a while, looking across the table at each other. I don't know how much he was sleepin' during the day, when I was at work, but it seemed like he didn't need to sleep much at night. He'd sit up and talk as long as I'd listen. And I'd talk too, more than I had in a long time. And outside in the world, whatever wheels were grindin' kept on grindin'. The world kept turnin'.

After one of those times when we had nothing else to say, both thinking back over what to tell or what wasn't for telling that night, Mr. Pete Estey said, "Well, Louise, what do you suppose they'll do about Jack?"

And I said, "What do you think? It's been three weeks" — or six weeks, or whatever it had been — "since Cappy Haynes saw that boy play. When do you think we'll hear something?"

Because we didn't know. Or that is, we knew something, but only a little of it. We saw just what Cappy Haynes saw, of course, the night he was in town to watch Jack play. When his heart was where it should be, Mr. Pete Estey *knew* that was enough.

"I signed boys when I'd only seen 'em play an inning sometimes," he'd say, "let alone a whole game. I could decide with some of 'em with one at-bat. One damn swing while they were waiting to hit, some of 'em. He saw enough."

But other nights, like this one, he'd fret about it, curse the rain that had washed out the second time Cappy'd have seen Jack play, mumble about politics and tokenism. "What he might have done that second night could have put him over the top," he said. "Might have stolen a couple of bases, hit a couple of long balls. Might have been facing a better pitcher. Cappy'd have seen that."

"He said he saw enough," I told him. "The rain didn't seem to bother him."

"What's it matter?" Mr. Pete Estey said. "Where's the guarantee they'll pay any attention to Cappy anyway, whatever he says he saw? What kind of weight could he carry? Hell, the day we saw him in Washington, he was out on the field hitting fungoes."

"Good thing for us he was," I said.

"Maybe," Mr. Pete Estey said. "And then maybe it doesn't make any difference at all."

"Look," I told him, "you were the one told me Jack Brown would be a pitcher down here in Florida for as long as he liked. Somebody'd always be after him to pitch for 'em. He'd have the game, all that goes with it, for years to come. Have himself a fine time, too. So what if all this we've tried to do doesn't make a difference and he plays here, if that's all that's given to us? All right. We will go watch him as long as we can, come back home afterward and have some tea, like we are now, and talk about how he did. We can do that. We can have that."

He sat still for a while, stopped fidgeting at least. Then he said, "Louise, think now, for a minute. Look at what we've done. Jack's had a look. He thinks he can play ball in the big leagues. Cappy Haynes thinks so too. That's our doing. How do you think he'll forget it?"

"Well, why should he?" I asked him. "It oughta make him proud."

"When he's fifty, maybe even forty, it'll make him proud," Mr. Pete Estey said.

I must have looked like I didn't understand him, because after looking at me for another minute across the kitchen table, he went on. "Have you ever heard of a ballplayer named Buck Weaver?" he asked me.

"Weaver," I said. "Where did he play?"

"You've heard of Joe Jackson," Mr. Pete Estey said.

"Shoeless Joe Jackson," I said. "Everybody's heard of him."

"All right," Mr. Pete Estey said. "Well, Buck Weaver was one of his teammates in Chicago. He played third base. Some people say he was a great third baseman. I never saw him play, but some people say that. And everybody who ever knew him knows there was never anybody who loved playing the game any more than Buck Weaver did. I never knew him until after he'd stopped playing, been stopped from playing, but he couldn't let it go."

"So he was one of the Black Sox," I said. "He took money to lose the World Series."

"He was banned from baseball," Mr. Pete Estey said, "just like Chick Gandil and Eddie Cicotte and Joe Jackson himself. But they say he never got any money at all. And he never could go along with the idea of losing that series. He played like he always did. Maybe even better. Even his teammates laughed about it afterward. They said Buck Weaver was too dumb to play to lose, even when that was the plan." Mr. Pete Estey was smiling when he said that, but it was a sad kind of smile. "Judge Landis didn't take brains into account, though. Or statistics either. I suppose if he had, he'd have allowed both Buck Weaver and Joe Jackson to play again. Jackson hit way over .300 in that series."

"And Weaver didn't even get the money," I said. I never knew much about the Black Sox, only that a little boy was supposed to have stopped Shoeless Joe outside the courtroom and begged him to say it wasn't so. But of course it was. That's what I'd always thought.

"Well," Mr. Pete Estey said, "the money part of it was a mess from the beginning. The gamblers who were supposed to pay the players were slow to come up with the cash. From game to game, some of the ballplayers didn't know what was supposed to happen. And Buck Weaver had stopped going to the meetings the others were having to decide what to do. What he'd found, I guess, was that once the game started, he couldn't play any differently from the way he always had, no matter what. So he sort of dropped out and didn't tell anybody about it. A year later, when they investigated the series, that's all anyone really could say against him. He knew about the fix, and he didn't say so. And a lot of people felt he should have been pardoned or whatever, given the chance to play again. There were petitions for it, with thousands of names. John McGraw said he wanted him to come over and play third base for the Giants. Buck Weaver was still a young guy, you see. Younger than Joe Jackson. Younger than Cicotte."

"What it must have been like," I said. "What it must have been. He knew those other boys were looking for a way to lose, and him out there playing as hard as he knew how. And nobody to tell about it, either."

"Not until a season later," Mr. Pete Estey said. "And then Landis apparently led him to believe he might reinstate him. But he never did. Weaver stayed away from Joe Jackson and Gandil and the rest. They put together a kind of All-Star team, traveled and played for money where they could. Buck wouldn't play, but the game still drew him, you see, and when they saw him in the crowd one day, they asked him to come on down on the field and play with them. Then. That minute. Here's an extra glove, Buck. But he didn't. He said he'd be back in the majors the next season. So he sat and watched. The best third baseman there was, some say."

I didn't know right then if Mr. Pete Estey even remembered why he'd decided to tell me that story, or what it had to do with Jack Brown at all. But I saw it, anyway. What if Jack didn't get his chance, now that it was real? Now that it was right there in front of him? Would it make him bitter and sour the game for him?

"What happened to him?" I said.

"He got old," Mr. Pete Estey said. He spread his hands out and looked at them on the table, big, beat-up hands that must have surprised him sometimes with their spots and their jumpy veins. *Where are that ballplayer's hands?* he must have thought sometimes, even if anybody could see that's what they still were. "He got old petitioning the commissioner and writing letters, calling his friends for help, long after he ever could have played again. It was a crusade to clear his name by then. Playing baseball didn't have anything to do with it after a while."

"What you said, though, about how Buck Weaver couldn't help but play hard as he could, even though he knew what he knew . . ."

Mr. Pete Estey looked at me across the table then and smiled. "You think that redeemed him?" he asked.

I must have showed the hurt, because Mr. Pete Estey's face changed. He hadn't said it with meanness, hadn't meant to mock me, I don't think. But he said it hard, like the word pulled something out with it.

"Louise," Mr. Pete Estey said, "I'm sorry."

"Don't matter," I said. "I never knew him."

"He would have had that, yes," he said. "He would have known he'd given all he could, played as well as he could ever play. And he had someone as shrewd as John McGraw to see it too."

"But he only could watch the game. That's what you're sayin'.

He only could sit and watch those other boys, none of 'em as good as he was. And he got older and older, watchin'."

Mr. Pete Estey looked at me sadly, like maybe he was sorry he'd said anything at all. "Well, maybe you're right, though," he offered. "Maybe it was enough for him to have played the way he did. All I have to go on is what other folks have guessed about him. I didn't know him well. Maybe there was that satisfaction. Maybe even redemption."

And what about you, Mr. Pete Estey? I wanted to ask him that, but I swallowed it. "You think Jack Brown would have that?" I asked him.

At first I thought he wasn't going to answer at all. He just sat, looking at me, like it was a question that didn't need an answer. Or maybe I surprised him with it.

Finally he said, "You saw him cut around first base on the single when the boy in front of him was headed home on the night Cappy was here, didn't you? And you heard Cappy say, 'Heads up play.' So you know how his feet were involved, and his head. And you've seen his hands enough times to know how good they are. Soft hands."

"All right," I said.

"All right," Mr. Pete Estey said. "These are the parts that are easy to talk about. The parts scouts talk about."

He was turning it over in his mind, you see? How much more would he say?

A couple of days later, sitting at the same table, he told me a story. For once it was about a boy he didn't sign. This one was a pitcher, and Mr. Pete Estey mostly signed hitters. This one was strong and tall and fast, like a lot of 'em, and cocky, Mr. Pete Estey said. Cockier than most.

"That was what caused some of the boys who looked at him to hesitate," he told me. "It made you wonder if it was all flash. So some of 'em who saw him weren't sure. But there was a

Cleveland scout who thought that boy'd be all right, and he got the Indians to offer him a bonus so he could sign him. Kid used the bonus to buy himself a car, then took one of his girlfriends out in it the same day he bought it, wrecked it, crushed his leg. Years later I ran into him. He was coaching ball at the high school where he'd made such a big name for himself when he was a kid. Now he was up around three hundred pounds, and drunk. He wouldn't have that job long. I don't know what made me think about that boy after all these years. Much as he drank, much as he weighed, dumb as he drove, he's probably dead by now. But maybe it was that conversation the other night that stirred it up. Louise," he said, "I don't think that Jack would throw it away. I can't imagine that. He plays with too much love. You can see it every time he moves."

I started to say yes, that was so, but Mr. Pete Estey went on.

"Maybe that's redemption enough," he said. "I don't know. But in a situation like Buck Weaver's . . . how would he handle that?"

"He never would get messed up with it in the first place," I told him.

"Well, that's sure to have been what Buck Weaver thought too," Mr. Pete Estey said. "But that's not what I mean. I'm just thinking about Buck Weaver watching that game he knew he could play in, maybe watching a lot of them. You see, we've given Jack some indication, some sense of how good he is. Good enough for me to take him seriously, he knows. Good enough for Cappy to come all the way down here to look at him. Now, what if nothing happens? What if the Lions feel like they've done all they have to do? They're paying into the scouting bureau, you know. And paying lots of their own scouts. Or some, anyway. To offer Jack anything at all would be as much as to suggest that their system's incomplete. They aren't going to want to say that. Maybe you don't realize how unlikely this all is."

"You're the one not realizin'," I told him. "This is simpler than you think. Jack's a ballplayer. What could be simpler? And he ought to have his chance. I'm not gonna have to convince you all over again, am I? You sound like you're still back in Fair Haven, trying to decide can you get up for breakfast or not. Maybe it won't be any good when you get there, stale toast or somethin'. Somebody might spill coffee on your shoes. Better stay in bed and think about it."

"I just wouldn't want to see him bitter," Mr. Pete Estey said. "Not the way he can play."

And then he stood up about halfway — stood up like the conversation was over, far as he was concerned, and he had somewhere else he had to be. But halfway was as far as he got, and then he started leaning forward, like he saw a quarter on the floor. I got there in time and caught him full against my chest, and the oddest feeling came to me then, standing there with Mr. Pete Estey in my arms. I didn't know what I was gonna do with him. Could have kissed him, you see. Or I could have crushed him. Could have just squeezed the life out of him right there. And God forgive me, I thought about it, for his cowardice when he needed to have faith. I could have done it. But I only held him, hugged him to me, and listened to him when he sighed. What we want from people is their courage and strength and their believing, and sometimes we forget that these come with their doubts and fears and their secrets, and we have to hug all that to us too when we hold 'em. But sometimes it comes to us to help 'em, too.

"My feet are asleep," he said. "Let me down, Louise."

I held him just a minute longer than I guess I had to, and then I put him back in his chair. Conversation wasn't over after all. So I took a deep breath and I pulled my chair right around to his and sat down hard and asked him, "What do you think, you're God? You gonna not want for someone somethin' he can have because it might not work out? You gonna not do what you can? Besides that, you've already done it! You think Jack Brown's a fool? You think he's bound to mope his life away if he's never in the big leagues? Did you mope your *own* life away, fool? Is that it? What? You think if that old cracker with the bad teeth hadn't come and taken you away, promised you a career, you'd still be standin' out in left field in the corn patch behind your daddy the shortstop? You think time mighta stopped for you? What you do is what you *can*. Or I'll tell you what, maybe you think, *Damn, that Jack Brown's gonna make it to the big leagues, and I never did*. Maybe there's somethin' in you wants him to stay right here in the twilight leagues with you. Maybe just so you can keep watchin' him, the way we have. Maybe 'cause the father don't like to see the son jump over him, and you got some father in you after all. Corn patch was good enough for you, why not for Jack? Who's he think he is?"

"That's foolishness, Louise," Mr. Pete Estey said.

"Huh!" I told him. "That's not foolishness. Foolishness is you ever thinkin' Jack'd be better off without his chance. We don't *know* anything, can't you see? Future's not given us to know on earth. What we do is what we *can* do, like I say."

"All right," Mr. Pete Estey said, but his heart wasn't in it. I wished Cappy Haynes was there with us then, so it would've been two against one. He'd've been with me. And where was the bitter in *him*? I wished later I'd thought to say that to Mr. Pete Estey, too.

"All right nothin'," I said, because I didn't know what else to say. I'd talked myself out. Then it came to me, before he could try to get up again. I took his old hands in mine and I said, "Pray with me."

He looked doubtful, but he didn't pull his hands away. Maybe he was afraid his feet were still asleep.

"Help us to know, Lord, our limitations," I said. "But teach us our duty, too. Give us the will to persevere, and wisdom enough to rest when we can. Show us the angel in us, weak as we are. Lord," I said, "give these hands I'm holdin' power, and make these eyes see. What we can know, let us understand with serenity. What we can't know, let us trust in you to deliver."

That was just another moment when I was afraid. Mr. Pete Estey might have mocked me again. He might have laughed, or anything. But his hands stayed right there in mine. Maybe he was too tired to pull them away. I thought about that later. Or maybe he heard me.

"That was nice, when you held me," he said.

I stood up. I still had his hands. "You want to get up now?" I asked him.

"I'm all right here," he said. "I'm fine. But as long as you're up, maybe you could heat up some coffee."

"I'll make it fresh," I told him.

"Even better," he said.

A few days later, Cappy Haynes called. I was the one who picked up the phone.

"How you doin', Mrs. Brown?" he said.

"I'll be doin' better when you start calling me Louise, like I told you to," I said.

"All right," he said. "Louise, your boarder there?"

"He's right here, sittin' at the kitchen table," I said. "Same place you left him."

"Tell him to get on the other extension," Cappy said. I told him we just had the one phone here in the kitchen, and he said, well, we better put our heads together on it, because he didn't want to say his news twice.

We got settled with the phone between us — "like a pair of old gossips," Mr. Pete Estey said — and Cappy said, "Jack don't know it yet, because they still got paperwork to do here, but the Lions want him to go up near Albany and play for their double-A club."

I don't know what I said then, but Mr. Pete Estey beside me

was all business. "That doesn't make any damn sense, Cappy," he complained.

"Yeah, well, maybe some," Cappy Haynes said. "They aren't gonna win anything up there this year anyway. Just seein' what's gonna percolate on up. Kid who usually plays short is hurt and they're pitcher-rich, so they don't have room for a utility in-fielder, really. Our A-ball shortstop's a spooky Latin kid who can't tie his shoes without the Spanish-speaking coach we got for him there in Daytona, so he isn't goin' anywhere right now. They got another kid plays some short in the other A-ball league, but he can't hit where he is now, so they don't want to send him up. Anyway, that's what they say. Maybe they're afraid somebody'll see whoever they send and steal him in the next draft. But they don't worry about Jack, because they never heard of him and ain't nobody else did either. So maybe he'll just fill the need."

I started to say it sounded real good to me, but Mr. Pete Estey said, "You tell them he'd work cheap?"

"He isn't screwing around with any agent, is he?" Cappy asked. "Because I told 'em he wasn't. He'll do all right. Better than he is pounding out fenders. And he'll play ball every night. Or be on a team that does, anyway. I told 'em up here, I said Jack's playin' in a better than A-ball league right now. And I said he don't care what he makes."

"I think he can play double-A ball," Mr. Pete Estey said. Sounded almost like he was talkin' to himself.

"Should do fine," Cappy said. "He'll get some coachin' up there, but it prob'ly won't hurt him. You pin a note on his shirt, say nobody should screw up his swing. And then lousy as the Lions are goin' this season, anything's liable to happen. Last two years they already looked at everybody they thought was worth a shit at triple-A — 'scuse my language, Mrs. Brown. Jack hits good, steals some bases in Albany, he's gonna maybe get himself called up here for a couple weeks in September."

"Doesn't cost 'em anything to look," Mr. Pete Estey said.

"Not a dime," Cappy Haynes said.

"Especially when you told 'em he didn't care what he made," Mr. Pete Estey said.

"Jack's goin' to the big leagues!" I shouted, and Mr. Pete Estey jumped. I was up away from the phone and the table now, sashaying around the kitchen floor.

"What's goin' on down there?" Cappy Haynes said.

"Louise is dancing," Mr. Pete Estey said. "I wish you could see what you've done."

"I'd like to see it," Cappy said. "Mrs. Brown, you save me a dance."

"You gotta call me Louise!" I shouted. I wasn't on the phone anymore.

"One day she'll call me Pete," Mr. Pete Estey told Cappy Haynes, and I sang, "Pete! Pete! Pete the scout found Jack Brown after all, or did Jack Brown find you, Pete? Old Pete? What do you think?"

Mr. Pete Estey was flapping his hand and shushing me now, so he could hear somethin' else Cappy Haynes had to say. I was winded anyhow, so I sat back down at the table and made him put the phone up between us again.

"So," Cappy was saying, "you're the one's gonna sign him. Papers comin' down to you."

Mr. Pete Estey didn't say anything. Just looked like he was worrying the idea around.

I nudged him and said, " 'Course you'll sign him."

"The kiss of death," Mr. Pete Estey said. I couldn't see if he was smilin' or not.

"Bullshit," Cappy said. " 'Scuse me, Mrs. Brown."

So it was still there for him, all that doubt, whatever else you want to call it — whatever had him thinking back in Fair Haven that there was nothin' for him but to wait and die. Getting him out, seeing Jack on the ballfield, feeling the bat in his own hands again that night . . . it just shook up the coins in the bank, I guess. But when the shaking stopped, it was still just the same coins in there. All my shouting at him, too.

But doubt or no, Mr. Pete Estey was in it now, deeper than ever. In it like a bug in a flood, maybe, but in it just the same, with Cappy Haynes tellin' him, "Sign Jack Brown." He could grunt and grumble about it, and 'course he would, but he couldn't ever act like it made no difference to him, like he had back in Fair Haven. Couldn't say that and anyone believe him. Jack Brown caught him up good. Some of the coins in that bank were baseball coins still, and they were shined up with the shaking now, and sitting near the top. Doubt like he might, Mr. Pete Estey couldn't deny it. All the ghosts he told about, hard luck, busted promises — he was alive in it, anyway. Alive in baseball. Maybe that was all there'd be — that he wasn't quit of it. Maybe it would be more, and he'd come to see the glory of every day of his life. I didn't know. I prayed, though.

But all I was thinking that afternoon was *Jack's gonna play ball for the Lions. Jack Brown up in the big leagues.* I knew Mr. Pete Estey would snort at that too when he got off the phone. "Long way from double-A to the majors," he'd say. "Hell, I played as high as double-A, and I never got so much as a sniff of the big leagues on the best day I ever had." Somethin' like that. But the news bubbled in me. Cappy Haynes was still on the phone, but I couldn't just sit still and listen. I walked around the kitchen touching things for a few minutes, watching Mr. Pete Estey just listen, or sometimes he'd nod. Maybe Cappy wasn't even talking about Jack anymore. Lots of baseball news he mighta been telling Mr. Pete Estey.

Then it came to me that 'course we better celebrate this day. Wasn't every day a man got a contract to play baseball. Or a boy. So I started looking through the cabinets to see what was there, and then pushing things outta my way on the refrigerator shelves. Seemed like a day like this we should have a roast chicken at least, or a big turkey maybe, with stuffin' and potatoes, gravy, cake for dessert, with candles. But maybe a roast beef would be better, or a big steak. I couldn't decide. Then Mr. Pete Estey got off the phone, so I just asked him, "What do you want?" I said, "Turkey'd be good for a celebration, but maybe you baseball men'd rather have a steak. What about some champagne? And what kind of cake do you like?"

"Maybe we ought to just have French toast," he said. He said it with a straight face, too. Could've been one of those sphinxes.

"I'll take care of it myself," I told him. "I don't need your nonsense. You call Jack while I'm shopping. Tell him to get over here quick as he can, and bring his appetite."

I got halfway out the door, then I stopped myself and turned around to him again. "It's too bad Cappy Haynes can't come down here tonight," I said. "He should be celebrating with us."

"Well, he's got important fungoes to hit," Mr. Pete Estey said. "But I asked him to see if he could arrange to have that woman from the front office up there join us, since I thought you'd want to celebrate. You remember that lady who works for Emmett Flanagan? She's been looking forward to seeing you again for some time."

"It's fine the excitement hasn't messed up your sense of humor any," I told him. And I hope it hurt his ears when I slammed the door.

Jack was already there when I came back. When I came in the front door, he jumped up from his chair in the kitchen and took the bag of groceries I was carrying. "More in the car?" he asked me, heading for the stairs. I blocked his way, though, and I wouldn't let him dodge around me when he tried it.

"Come here and let me hold you, Mr. Baseball Player," I said. "Mr. Professional Baseball Player. Come and tell me you're gonna remember us when you're a famous star."

Jack just laughed and shook his head, picked me right up off
the floor, spun me half around, and put me down again so he
could get past.

"I'll get the rest of the bags," he said on his way out. "I'm
starved."

They stayed right there in the kitchen, the two of 'em, while
I was cooking, so I heard what Mr. Pete Estey was telling him.
A time or two I thought I was gonna bite right through my lip
trying to stop myself from saying somethin', but I just got busier
with the cooking when the temptation almost got too much.
Later, after Jack was gone, Mr. Pete Estey told me he knew
when I didn't like somethin' he was telling Jack because it
sounded like I was warring with the pots and pans, somethin'
like that. But I didn't say a thing. It was Mr. Pete Estey's time
to talk. I don't remember all that he said, but it wasn't telling
Jack what to do or not to do, anything like that. It was just
stories.

"I remember one fella when I started playing A-ball," he said.
"It wasn't exactly your situation because I'd already been in the
system a couple of years and I was cocky enough to think nothing
could surprise me. And then one day I came out to the park on
a day we weren't playing to see if I could find somebody to throw
me a little extra batting practice, and here was our shortstop,
boy about your age or so, stripped to the waist and out there in
the infield with the groundskeeper — who wasn't a real groundskeeper at all, of course, but just an old fella who worked four
or five different jobs to make the nut, and one of them was
taking care of this little minor-league ballpark infield as well as
he could after the kids got in there and tore it up. But this fella
who played shortstop for us was out there with the old guy in
the heat of the day with a rake and a hose and one of those old-
fashioned rollers you had to fill with water until it was so heavy
you got a running start to move it, and then you were lucky to
stop it before it rolled right off the field and into a light pole or

something, which it would have knocked down on that field. And this boy was explaining the field, you see, showing that old man, who probably hadn't ever thought about how the infield played as long as he got his ten or twelve dollars every Friday — showing him how to take care of it.

" 'You don't want to chop it all up,' he was saying, just gently scratching around second base with a rake. 'Chop it up too much and it'll get soft. We're a line-drive, ground-ball hitting team, see? Keep the infield hard, and some of those ground balls go through. That's hits for us. Plus I'm a shortstop with good range, so a hard infield's okay with me. So you just wet it down and roll it, wet it down and roll it. Then we'll have a nice, hard, true infield here, and no surprises.' "

Mr. Pete Estey smiled at the memory of it. "You see how much that boy loved the game?" he said. "And then that old man looked at him like he didn't know what the hell the boy was talking about. As far as he was concerned, his job was just to chop the weeds out of the dirt around the bases every couple of days. So the shortstop started all over again, showing how to just sort of agitate the dirt a little to clean it up, no chopping, and then water it and roll it, water it and roll it. 'Give us what you can,' that boy told him. 'A nice true infield. Make it mean something when we're playing at home.' How many other boys on that team ever felt like that? And when was the last time before that day that anyone had tried to teach that old man something?"

"Sometimes we have to shovel dirt into the puddles here before we can play," Jack said. "When the park department's a little slow gettin' to it. People come out from the seats and help."

"Well, you come to the park, you want to see a game," Mr. Pete Estey said. Then he sat still for a minute so he could think of something else to tell Jack while I was getting dinner ready. Somethin' must've smelled good to him, because he said, "I've seen boys eat their way right out of baseball, Jack. Some guys drink their way out, and now it's drugs too, of course. That's a fast way to go."

I *did* stick my nose into it then. I said, "Jack, you don't have anything to do with those kind of people in Albany, any more than you do around home."

But Mr. Pete Estey said, "Well, they're around, though. Bound to be some, even on your team. I know *managers* who killed themselves drinking, and a boy Jack's age, he's going to know some people using drugs unless he stays locked up in his room all day. But we've seen you play, Jack. You know what you're doing out there, don't you? You know it's something more than a game and something more than just making a living too, don't you? You know how the real good ones . . ." Mr. Pete Estey made a shape with his hands on the table in front of him, like he had a ball in them he was rubbing. "You know how they make something out there that's special. Magic, almost. Hell," he said, "I know a lot of old bastards whose whole lives were shit except what they did in a ballpark. But what they did there they did with beauty, with grace, like God meant for it to happen, for us to see it."

I turned around from the stove because I never had heard him talk like that — not just the *hell* and the *shit*, but being so mad because he wasn't sure he could make it clear, get it right. But he never saw me looking at him.

"The way a real good one can stay down on a hard ground ball — keep his hands down, and his head, and his ass. Or a hitter who can wait and wait and then hit a good pitch nine miles with his wrists. One time a newspaper writer I used to know said Willie Mays made a new harmony of geometry when he went after a fly ball in the old Polo Grounds. You never saw a center field like that in your life, Jack. It went on just as far as Willie Mays could run."

He opened his hands, and there was no baseball there. "All you have to do is remember how beautiful it is," he said. "Then you won't let anything foul it up."

That was another time biting my tongue wouldn't do it, and I said, "All this about Willie Mays, what are you trying to do? You don't want to send this boy to Albany thinking he's gotta be Willie Mays."

Mr. Pete Estey laughed when I said that, and then he turned to Jack and said, "You already know that too, don't you?"

"I never saw Willie Mays," Jack said.

"No," Mr. Pete Estey said. "You make your own geometry."

We ate then, and it was quieter than you might think. Between the stories there was time for considering that Jack would be gone.

Pete

IF YOU TELL ME THAT LAST NIGHT AT A BALL GAME you saw somebody double to left center field, I can see it. I can see the batter start out of the box with his eyes coming up to follow the ball he's hit, see the two outfielders dig after the ball and then decide as they go who's got the better shot at it, even as it carries past one of them and the other cuts it off, back-handed, and turns to throw to second. I can see the hitter making the decision to take the extra base when he's a stride or two past first, and speeding up on the curve of the infield, and hooking away to the inside part of the bag so the second baseman taking the throw will have to reach back to get him and maybe only catch a shoulder with the late, high tag, or maybe nothing at all.

The imagination, the mind's eye, will do that for you, run the whole play back, dress it up even, because it will give you the dirt off the hitter's spikes as he cuts the first-base bag at the same time you see the center fielder stretch for the ball and lose his balance for just a split second, then plant his right foot to throw — two things you really couldn't see at once. You'd have to decide what you'd watch as the play was developing. Easy enough if you were there to scout one player or the other, but otherwise something you learn only after you've seen a lot of games: how to pick your pleasure.

Louise, of course, could do it. She knew more about baseball than she told anybody but me, and she didn't tell me all she knew. Instead she let me tell *her*, pretending she was learning something about pick-off moves or how an outfielder could decoy a runner by acting like he was about to catch a ball that was going to hit the wall over his head, or what a catcher could do to frame a low pitch so it looked like a strike. She was too sharp to ask a dumb question, but she'd let me explain framing a ball, and then she'd say, "Ol' Roy Campanella sure could do that, and it looked like he didn't even have to think about what he was doing. He'd be talking to the batter and the umpire and encouraging his pitcher — maybe Joe Black or somebody — with a little nod or somethin', same time he was doing it."

"What did you let me go on about framing pitches for if you've seen all that?" I'd ask her.

"Just wanted to see if you knew what you were talkin' about," she'd say.

Jack called a couple of times a week at first, then less often when he'd settled in. There were box scores of the Albany games in the *Sporting News*, and we went over them every week, first one of us, then the other, doing the best we could with the small print and our old eyes. We would imagine what was happening from those box scores, and I was harder on Louise than I should have been sometimes.

"Look," she'd say, "a walk again when they played Thursday. His eye's getting sharper. He's laying off the bad pitch."

"Might mean he just faced some boy who couldn't find the plate," I'd say. "How many other guys walked?"

But it never touched her, or never seemed to. "No matter," she'd say. "When you see a lotta bad pitches, just learn to lay off 'em faster. He's learning all the time."

The truth was that Jack didn't have to learn that, because a bad pitch was a bad pitch in New York as well as Florida, and he had always been a disciplined hitter. Louise knew that as well

as I did, or better, since she'd watched him for years before I'd
ever seen him. But it was something to say on a night when he
didn't hit.

Worse were the nights when he didn't play. We'd hear about
them from Jack sometimes, when he called, or we'd open up
the *Sporting News* to the back pages and there would be Albany's
games and Jack's name not in the box scores at all. I tried to
explain to him how it worked in the minors, how sometimes
even the manager couldn't play the guy he might want to play
because the major-league front office wanted to see what somebody else could do, or they might send a big-league shortstop
down for rehabilitation or to get his confidence back up. Some
owners even do it for punishment, shuttling their marginal players back and forth between the big club and the farms, looking
for a good combination of players instead of letting one develop.

Some nights we'd go over and watch Jack's old team play.
They all knew where he'd gone, of course, and they followed
his progress the way we did, or they asked when they saw us.
Two things they wanted to know each time Louise and I showed
up with our lawn chairs and our iced tea along the first-base
line: how long until Jack would make the big leagues? and who
was I looking at next for the Lions to sign?

"I'm retired," I told them. Then Louise would laugh, and
those boys would laugh with her. And they would go out on
that sandlot ballfield and play for the hours it lasted, all pointed
in the same direction. Some nights one player or another would
get hot, hit three or four balls right on the button, or get a jump
on a ball he had no business reaching and then catch it, sprawl-
ing full-length and skinny on the outfield grass when he had it,
then get up businesslike and nonchalant, like he did it every
day.

I knew how those boys felt in their moments. Anyone could
tell it, looking in their eyes, though they tried to be even more
casual, more cool than usual when they were having those days.

But I knew it because I'd felt it myself on ballfields no better than the ones they were playing on, sometimes in front of crowds no bigger. I'd had moments too, had those stretches when I'd hit so well . . . You hear players when they're interviewed about a hitting streak and they say they saw the ball well or it looked big as a melon to them, but that's not it. What happens is that you come to know you're going to hit. You go up to the plate knowing. I suppose it's the same for a fielder sometimes, that he knows nobody can hit anything to center field that he won't catch. But with me it was hitting. I was so sure sometimes that I had to swallow the urge to laugh at how hard everybody said it was. During those streaks, hitting would just happen, over and over again, easy as breathing or your own young, thoughtless heartbeat. And you could fool yourself, or I could, about what that meant. Not that you would hit like that forever — nobody who's learned the game anywhere could believe that. But that you could hold on to a piece of it, enough of it to carry you past the limitations elsewhere in your talent or your luck, that you could ride it all the way to the big leagues. It was a feeling I'd forgotten about until it came to me watching Jack and those other boys some of those nights.

On nights when one of those boys Jack had played with found it, caught fire, he might look over at me to see if I saw what was up — just sneak a look over. I might have thought it was a sad thing, but Louise wouldn't have tolerated that. For her (and she could see as well as I could) there was none of the complication. If I'd said anything, I'd have said, "Ride it, son, until it's gone. Because it sure as hell will be gone one day." But Louise just clapped her big palms and shouted under those lights, shouted that boy's name. And sometimes I did too, and the pure pleasure of the moment would be enough. Sometimes I forgot myself, as I had that night when I'd held on to Jack's bat. If we'd brought anyone with us from Fair Haven, Moses Labine or Sarah Graham or one of the others, one of them would maybe shout too. And then in a minute they'd look at each other and feel a little sheepish. Except for Louise. She never thought it was silly. How else would you watch a ball game? How else would you live your life?

On the morning she died, I overslept. I suppose what finally woke me was the sun, streaming through the window where the curtains didn't quite meet.

At first I didn't know where I was. I stared at the white corner where the ceiling and the two walls met as if I'd never seen it before and thought, *God, I have to piss, and I don't know where there's a bathroom.* In a minute or so I realized that for months I'd been waking up to the sound of Louise in the kitchen. Over the rattle of pots and pans or the hiss of bacon frying she would sing high in her throat, the same tunes she'd sung or hummed at Fair Haven, hymns of praise or thanks, with the words worn smooth as ocean stones so she really didn't have to sing them at all, just kind of suggest them over the tune she carried around the kitchen. If I'd told her she was singing, she would have been surprised.

On this morning there was no sound from the kitchen at all. Outside the traffic ran by, louder than I remembered it. We weren't far from the expressway. There were birds, too, and it sounded as if they were fighting over something. I hauled myself out of bed finally, thinking I'd give Louise a hard time for sleeping so long. At Fair Haven she was always after someone to get up, get fed, get the day started, and here it was — I squinted at my watch now, and saw it was nearly nine-thirty, probably later than I'd slept in ten years. She was late for work. I'd give her hell, all right.

At the foot of the stairs that led up to her bedroom I shouted, "Louise, Fair Haven called. There's an old people's lie-down strike. Nobody made it to breakfast without you. It sounded like they were desperate."

There was no sound but the traffic and the birds, which seemed to have eased up a little. Then there was a kind of rustling, sheets maybe, and after a minute a crash. I started up the stairs too fast, and lost my balance halfway up. Or maybe it was worrying about what I'd see when I got there that slowed me down. I caught myself on the wooden railing before I banged my knee on the step, and kept climbing.

I'd never been in Louise's room before, never been upstairs at all. Now the first thing I noticed was the heat. She was up under the slant of the roof in that room, with only one small window for ventilation. No wonder she was always up early, I thought. On a pine dresser there were pictures — Louise's husband and her children, I supposed, and one of Jack, laughing on a bench at the ballfield. Her white shoes sat side by side under a straight-backed chair next to the dresser. On the opposite wall was a closed door, a small closet probably. Beside the bed a night table lay on its side — the crash I'd heard. In the bed, under a white blanket, lay Louise.

She was on her back, and under the blanket her arms and legs were still. Her face was wet with sweat, because she'd been working hard. What it was — I realized it in the first moment in the doorway — she had moved the bed by rocking herself side to side until she could topple the night table. Beyond the rocking, she could not move at all.

I pulled the chair up to her bed and sat beside her. "I'll call the hospital," I said. "Do you have a doctor I should call too? Someone who'll meet you there?"

Why didn't I go downstairs to make that call as soon as I saw she'd had a stroke? I can say now that what she was asking for then, with her eyes and with the effort she'd made to knock the table over, was not so much help as company. That's how I understand it now. Beyond that, I don't know. I'm not sure what I knew then. Maybe that she was dying, no matter where or who knew.

"Hold my hand," she said. Her voice was a whisper from her chest.

I reached under the blanket and found her right hand, and held it in my own, like clay, out where she could see it.

"That's fine," she said.

"Are you in pain?" I asked her.

"I was afraid," she whispered. "When my eyes opened and I couldn' move, I was afraid. Didn' know if you ever would wake up. How'd you sleep so long?"

"Do you want something?" I asked her. "Water?"

"Stay," she said.

Her breathing was regular, and her eyes were bright. From just the few minutes in her room, I was soaked with sweat. Under the blanket she must have been burning up.

"I'm going to call the hospital," I said.

But she whispered "Stay" again before I could get up out of the chair. Then she said, "You think of anything I left undone?"

"I don't understand," I said.

"Oh, you understand," she whispered. "You understand pretty good, I think. Sometimes you just forget."

When my father died, I was away playing baseball. When my mother died, I was watching a game. Someday Alice would die, probably not before me. We'd promised twice to love and comfort each other until death parted us, and twice we'd reneged. We'd separated friends, or we respected each other anyway, or each other's wishes. I wouldn't send for her when I was dying, though, nor she for me, I suppose. We'd worn each other out trying.

Louise knew all this. She knew more about me than anyone else knew, living or dead.

"Were you afraid to die alone too?" I asked her.

"Days I'm afraid are my greatest days," she whispered. "Sometimes that's what I think. It brings me close to the Lord, the days when I'm afraid, filled up with fear. Reminds me to call on him."

She was quiet again for a minute, then she said, "You remember your friend who died on the road?" I didn't know what she was talking about, until she said, "In the motel there, with you beside him, same as you're beside me now." Then I understood she meant Whit Cullinane. It seemed like a long time ago that I'd told her the story.

"Yes," I said.

"You were afraid of it," she whispered, and I nodded that yes, it was true. "You see how dyin's dyin' now?"

"Are you teaching me to die?" I said.

"Seems like maybe there's nothin' to it," she said.

God, it was hot. How could she stand it under that blanket? Then I remembered how Whit Cullinane's teeth had chattered, and how the windows there wouldn't open.

"I think you can call that ambulance now," Louise whispered.

I stood up and said, "I'll make the call and be back up here. You think if there's anything I can bring you."

"You do what you can do," she said.

When I got back upstairs she was dead.

In the heat of that room, I picked up the table she'd knocked over. Then I sat on the bed beside her and took her hand again. Later I'd call Jack, call Fair Haven, call her children who'd moved away. I'd call Cappy, too.

What a strange thing, I thought, to be drawn into the weary business of death now.

But the mind plays tricks, makes adjustments. Here I was on Louise's bed, already anticipating the looks I'd get from her children, or the coroner, or the boy who'd be driving the ambulance. When they asked me about my relationship to the deceased, or "What was it you were doing living with my mother?" "friend" wouldn't be much of an answer, would it? And "business partner in the matter of Jack Brown" wouldn't answer much. Maybe I'd say we were lovers.

I heard the sound of the siren outside, and started down the stairs to the door.

*

"Pete," Jack said, "if she'd lived just a little longer, she'd have seen the real thing."

I looked at him across the car seat. We were sitting in front of the house. He seemed as reluctant as I was to go in. The funeral had been strange for him, I think. Mourners, some of them bused over from Fair Haven, others from the neighborhood or members of the church, had filed by Louise's daughters, extending their sympathies and blessings. Those who knew Jack from the ballpark spoke to him too, but we stood off to one side, apart from the others. One by one the old folks she'd comforted, strangers to her children, explained to them how their mother had eased their pain with kind words or encouraged them to eat, to get stronger, to pray. Earlier the minister had praised her devotion to all those who had nobody left to care for them — "her gift for helping God's children home to Him," was the way he put it.

Now in the car Jack said, "I wanted to tell that man — tell them all — that she didn't just prop up people's pillows. Didn't just help folks down the hall, you know? I wanted 'em to see how she helped me too, and I'm not gonna die."

"You would have surprised them if you'd jumped up and said it," I said.

"I could have yelled it out," he said. "I could have shouted right there in the church, I was so full with it."

"You'd have knocked 'em over like tenpins," I said. "It would have been some funeral."

"If she'd lived just a little longer, she'd have seen me in the big leagues. Then everybody'd have heard about her."

"You don't know her children, do you?" I asked him.

"They called sometimes when I was livin' with her," he said. "One or two times one of them'd visit. They wanted to know why she was takin' care of me. They'd as soon forget my father, and my mother never had anything to do with 'em. Never had much to do with anybody."

"But you don't think you had anything you had to prove to Louise, do you, Jack?" I stared hard at him as he tapped his long fingers lightly on the steering wheel. "You know she couldn't have been prouder of you, couldn't have loved you more if she'd seen you make rookie of the year or some damn thing?"

"It would have been something to give her," he said.

"You didn't have to give her anything," I said.

"For me," he said.

"All right," I said, "just so long as you give yourself credit for what you *did* do, though. Your Aunt Louise was a lover. You understand that, don't you? And she loved you. Watching you, seeing you run and hit — hell, seeing you eat, that filled her with love." He'd stopped tapping the wheel and he was looking straight at me, composed. "You filled her heart," I said. "When Cappy called with the news about your contract, she danced in the kitchen like a girl, and she sang your name. But she was happy just to see you, too. When we came to the ball games here, creeping across the parking lot, you know, because Mrs. Graham or one of the others was with us, or hell, because she had to slow down for me, she always had her head up, looking past us to get the first glimpse of you. 'I hope we're gonna be early enough to see him practice,' she'd say. 'See Jack take some ground balls.' "

He was quiet then, and still quiet when we went inside, so I tried again. "Not everybody's lucky enough to love that way, or be loved," I told him. "Mothers don't even always feel that way for their children. Fathers don't either. You know the story about Ty Cobb?"

"I know about Ty Cobb," Jack said.

"But about his father?"

"No," he said.

"Ty Cobb's father was a schoolteacher," I said. "He didn't like the idea that his son wanted to play ball for a living. He was a strict man, a disciplinarian. He told Tyrus that he didn't want anything to do with him if he was going to waste his life playing a game. But eventually Cobb wore him down. Maybe his father saw that the boy was going to be a ballplayer no matter what he said, I don't know. But according to Cobb, when he left home to join the Tigers' minor-league club, his father's last words to him were 'Don't come home a failure.' "

"So he prob'ly thought it worked," Jack said.

"But he never knew," I said. "Because one night not long after Cobb had gone, his father told his wife, Cobb's mother, that he had some late business he had to take care of, and off he went in his buggy. The story was he thought his wife had taken a lover, and he was planning to sneak back into the house and catch her in the act, if he could. But when Mrs. Cobb heard him at the window, trying to get in, she let go with both barrels of a shotgun, and that was that. There was a hearing, I think. No trial. She said she thought it was a burglar."

"Jesus," Jack said.

"All this happened while Cobb was still a kid," I said. "Still a minor leaguer. He felt like he hadn't proved a thing. And he said afterward — long afterward, when he'd retired — that he spent his whole career trying to show his father he was no failure."

"At the end he was crazy, wasn't he?" Jack asked.

"Maybe before the end too," I said. "I never knew him, but I knew lots of fellas who did. Some who played with him. They said he worked harder at baseball than anyone they ever saw."

"I saw a picture of him once, sliding into third base," Jack said. "Looked like he was maybe gonna bite the third baseman if he tagged him. Chew his ankle right off."

"It's a famous picture," I said.

"And they say he sharpened his spikes," Jack said.

"That's what they say."

Jack was quiet for a while again, then he stood up and planted his feet, the left one first, as if he were about to face a pitcher. He rocked gently, easily, from one foot to the other, swung his left arm forward a little from the shoulder, then back, and he cocked both fists behind his right ear, ready to hit. There was a moment of absolute stillness, and then he pulled his imaginary bat back from a fastball, high and tight.

"You know about my father?" he asked me.

"A little," I said.

He rocked on the balls of his feet, getting set in the box. "That's all I knew him too," he said. He stepped back with his left foot and looked over his left shoulder at the third-base coach, then settled into his stance again, hands cocked. "Louise ever tell you about my mother?"

"Only that she moved north with you after your father died," I said. "And then that she talked to Louise after you came back to Florida. Asked her to keep an eye on you."

"Some days she was so frightened she wouldn't answer the door or pick up the phone," he said. "Once she tried to kill herself. She drank bleach."

Suddenly he crouched and squared toward the pitcher, dropping the bat parallel to the ground. Then he jerked his head back, following the ball he'd fouled off the screen.

"Get all the way square around," I said. "Assuming you're sacrificing."

"Man on first, nobody out, one and one," he said. He rocked back into his stance and cocked his fists again behind his ear. The next pitch must have tied him up inside, because his swing started out looking cramped before he could inside-out the ball toward right. It curved foul into the seats while he watched it.

"Quick hands," I said. "Keep the hands quick."

"One and two," he said, looking out at the mound with new respect. He rocked and settled into his stance again. "So she was crazy sometimes too," he said.

"Sounds like it," I said.

"But you played ball with your dad, didn't you? Didn't Louise say that? You must have known him pretty good."

"Sure," I said, "and I watched him for years before I played on his team. And then he watched me a bunch of times after I signed."

"How'd he die?" Jack asked.

"Old age," I said. "His heart quit. But he played ball on that semi-pro team until he was about fifty."

"You think he thought you were a failure because you didn't make it to the big leagues?" Jack said.

"No," I said. I didn't even have to think about it. And then I said, "It hurt him, though, when my wife and I were divorced. He was still alive the first time. He liked her." I looked at him for a minute, standing there, and then I said, "What are they doing, changing pitchers?"

"Conference on the mound," he said. "But they're gonna leave him in." He stood back in. "Big mistake."

"One and two," I said. "He'll probably waste one."

"Louise was the one watched me play," Jack said. "Louise and you." He stepped into his natural stride, rode his hips forward, and cracked a waist-high, outside fastball up the middle, out over second into center field, vast and perfect.

And I thought, *So you find your father where you can, too, and your mother.*

"That was quicker," I said. "Could you feel the difference in your hands that time?"

"Shortened up with the two strikes and went with the pitch," he said.

I got up then to make coffee, and after I'd fumbled around with Louise's old coffeepot for a few minutes, Jack came over to help. The two of us managed to fit it together, but for all the times I'd watched Louise in the kitchen, Jack had to find the coffee for me. We guessed on measuring it, then guessed again on the level of the water. It took longer than it ever had when Louise had done it, and she'd be making a whole meal at the same time. When we finally had the coffee in front of us in two mugs, we agreed it was probably the worst ever made in that kitchen, and we poured it down the sink.

We spent another day together before Jack went back to Albany. The rest of Louise's family had left shortly after the funeral. They'd found a lawyer to put in charge of the details that had to be settled, and he spent two mornings going through her papers, which he told me were thoroughly organized and complete. She'd left what she had to her children and to Jack, the lawyer said. She'd also paid her rent a month in advance, and nobody had any objection to my staying where I was through the fall if I wanted to, though according to the lawyer there'd been some talk of selling the property to developers at the end of the year, so there might not be another lease.

It was strange being alone, especially at first, but people were kind. Cappy called me several times. Jack kept me posted. At first slowly, and then in an avalanche that Louise's refrigerator couldn't accommodate, food came in. Neighbors I'd known a little brought casseroles and plates of chicken or beef. The families of the boys Jack had played ball with sent littler boys over with homemade bread and applesauce, fruit drinks, salads, and pies. I got dinner invitations too, and notes in the mail reminding me of when the ball games were, or asking me to church.

They figured I'd stay on. Louise would have known they would, but I didn't see it right away. She probably could have predicted the dishes people would send over, and which child would return later, big-eyed, knocking softly at the door, for the return of a plate or a bowl. Jack wasn't surprised either.

"You had the right woman on your side," he said when I told him about it. "You were all right with Louise, so you're all right with them. And there's the baseball, too. Some of 'em saw you at a lot of ball games. May be they got kids they think can play, you know?"

He didn't feel it was anything she'd said to anyone about me, or that his own departure to play what his former teammates called "away ball" really had anything to do with it. But nothing I said surprised him. "Maybe they just like you," he said. "Give yourself a break."

One night at a ball game neighbors had driven me to, two boys about eight or nine came up to me with a baseball, a foul ball they'd retrieved from the parking lot. They'd stayed out there with it, I guess, until the umpire'd given up on them and tossed another ball out to the pitcher. Then they crept back around to the side of the bleachers where I was sitting, and the taller, braver of the two handed the ball to me. *Jesus*, I thought in astonishment, *somebody told them I'm famous. They want me to sign it.*

But that wasn't it. The boy said, "You throw a fastball 'cross the seams or with 'em? We got a bet."

So I showed them how to hold a fastball.

On September first, the Lions did call Jack up. Cappy'd had it right. He and Jack phoned me the same night to tell me about it.

"He's been solid these past few weeks," Cappy said. "Done everything they asked him to do. Albany club made up eight games on the league leaders from three weeks ago. He tell you that?"

"He told me he thought they'd finished pretty well," I said.

"He carried 'em for a couple weeks," Cappy said. "Spec Murphy, managin' up there, got right behind him and said he oughta be here in September so we could see for ourselves we oughta invite him to camp with the big club in the spring."

"They're not desperate enough to bring him north with the Lions after six weeks in double-A, are they?"

" 'Course not," Cappy scoffed. "He's got triple-A ahead of him, and that Latin shortstop I told you about, who's almost as good as he ever was. And you can subtract the couple weeks he's gonna be up here now from another year, because they wouldn' give him any more time toward arbitration rights than they have to. So what all that means is you better come up here and see him now."

"You think I won't live another couple of years? Or maybe I'll get senile and I won't know what I'm watching."

"What I think is this," Cappy said. "We'll be in Boston when Jack and the other kids come up. That's where they'll join us. That'll be your last chance this time around to see him in a real ballpark. After Boston we got the Twins in the dome and then that goddamn new mall in Chicago. After that we're home for the rest of the month, and I know how you feel about our building. So you better come to Boston. I'll get the club to pay your way and put you up, or make 'em embarrassed if they don't."

There are a lot of funny stories about Fenway Park. It is in the middle of the city, and the only parking lot looks about right for a medium-sized grocery store. There's no exit for it off the Massachusetts Turnpike, even though the pike runs right by, and there are no signs on the neighborhood streets to tell you you're almost there. It's as if you're supposed to *know* where it is, and if you can't find it, maybe you don't belong there after all.

It's an old ballpark, of course, and though it's been renovated half a dozen times, it still feels old. Smokey Joe Wood pitched in it, and Ted Williams hit there. Those are good reasons for a team to stay in a ballpark. High in the right-field bleachers there's one seat they put a new coat of red paint on each spring. All the other bleacher seats are green. The red one's the one Williams hit with one of his longest home runs.

When Cappy met me at the airport, I'd already been seeing that park again in my mind's eye for some time. I'd never played in it, and I hadn't watched all that many games there, but if you've seen it, you remember it. It's shaped as if the builders had miscalculated, tried to squeeze the ballpark into a grid of city streets that just wouldn't quite let it in. It looks like they had to cut part of left field off with a big cleaver and then put the wall up to keep the game from spilling out of the place.

"I'll tell you about hitting here," Cappy said when we'd settled into our seats up behind the third-base dugout. "If you're a right-handed guy, you see that wall for the first time and you think, 'Jeez, pop-ups I've hit woulda made it over that.' You let it, and that fuckin' wall'll screw up your swing for a month."

I wondered if I'd have had that problem if I'd ever played in Fenway Park. Now I didn't need to worry about it. I couldn't have *walked* that far without help. Louise's friends had put me on the plane in Tampa. Cappy'd met me in Boston. That's the way I traveled now.

We were there early. The visiting team's reserves took batting practice first, and that would probably be the only time I'd see Jack hit. The sky was still blue — pale, but blue — though they'd already turned on the lights so the players could get used to them. The effect was a field unnaturally bright, dazzling. Or maybe it was just my old eyes. But I thought to myself, *God, to hit in a place like this . . .* The background was a perfect green everywhere, and the very shape of the old park seemed to focus your attention on the plate. They used to say Ted Williams could see the stitches on the ball when it came toward him, though he denied it. But when he hit early, before the people filled up the bleachers and spoiled that perfect background in this perfect hitting place, it looked like maybe he could *count* the stitches.

"He wanted to come out to the airport with me," Cappy said. "But I told him you could never tell about the traffic. Didn't want him late getting over here."

Before us, groundskeepers wheeled the batting cage out. The bat boy lugged a big canvas bucket of baseballs to the mound.

The public-address loudspeaker crackled and a disinterested voice said, "Testing. Ladies and gentlemen. Boys and girls."

And suddenly there was Jack. He'd come up out of the dugout, and he was already walking away from me before I could speak. He wore number 51 on his back. There was nobody on the mound to throw to him yet, so he and a few of the other younger players leaned against the cage, trying, I suppose, to look as though playing ball in Fenway Park was nothing special. Eventually a fella with a little gray in his hair where it came out from under his Lions cap appeared out of the dugout and headed for the mound. The first batter was already in the box when the batting-practice pitcher reached into the bucket for a baseball.

When it was Jack's turn to hit, I was happy to see him swing level, hitting the ball where it was pitched. Some players horse around during batting practice, trying to hit the ball out of the park or win bets with the other boys. But the good ones think about situations — hit to the right side to move the runner up, whatever — and they don't try to pull pitches away from them.

"Thinkin' all the time," Cappy said. "You don't see too many kids just up who know how to use batting practice. He did it right in Albany, too. . . . One of the things Murphy said about him when he told us we got to bring him up here for a look, said he takes batting practice like a damn Wade Boggs."

"Hah!" I said to him. "Louise would have been all over you for that."

"I'd have liked it," he said. "We'd have had some fun."

"Comparin' him to Wade Boggs!" I said, trying to work Louise's outrage and huffing into it. "He's just Jack Brown, and not even one at-bat in the big leagues yet, either. What do you want to heap Wade Boggs on him for? Let him be Jack Brown."

Cappy looked at me and shook his head. "You got her voice a little there. You got a little of her."

Jack had seen us, and he came to the dugout and leaned up over the low concrete wall to say hello.

"You look good," I told him.

He looked down at his new gray uniform with "Washington" across his chest and touched the letters for a second.

"I meant your swing," I said, and he laughed.

"I'm glad you made it," he said.

Once the game started it began to get cold fast. There was wind too, and in the wind the beginning of the feeling of fall; not the fall of sweet apples and crisp football afternoons, either, but the early cold that can make a bad joke of a night baseball game in October. The kind of cold that breaks off your connections with summer hard and fast, and when that happens you can't imagine another season of warm days.

My feet had gone to sleep, and my legs started to cramp. Even the good seats we had were hard up against the seatbacks in front of them, and I'd banged my knees a couple of times, trying to shift the legs one way or another.

Cappy finally said, "Hey, Pete, let's get on down into the dugout. You can stretch out a little, and they got cushions on the bench. I shoulda thought to bring us some."

That's how it happened that I saw Jack play his first major-league innings from the bench. Somebody found me a pitcher's jacket, which was nylon, but quilted and half heavy. I could stretch my legs, even walk a few steps along the dugout if I stayed out of the way.

It was the bottom of the eighth when Jack got in. The game was tied, and they sent him out to play short — as good a time as any for them to start seeing what he could do. The first Boston hitter struck out, and the next one popped the first pitch up to right field. It looked as if he was trying to get back into the warm clubhouse as fast as he could. Then with two outs the Red Sox catcher hit a little flare into short center that looked like it was going to drop, but Jack got a good jump on it, and so did the Lions' center fielder, who was a rookie too, named Benjamin.

This Benjamin never called the ball one way or the other, and he and Jack were both closing on it, and on each other, fast. I sat up straight to watch it. I wanted to cry out, but my throat was tight. And what would it have mattered? Who would have heard me? Jack and this other boy were both racing so hard toward the ball as it dropped that they wouldn't have heard the crack of doom. And then it fell and Jack dove and out of the corner of his eye that kid Benjamin must have just caught sight of him, because he jumped like a hurdler, awkward, but it looked like it would be sufficient. Only his trailing foot caught Jack's hip as the ball dropped into Jack's glove, and the two of them rolled over each other out beyond the infield dirt, like puppies. And then in the sharp light of nobody on and two outs or three, Jack jumped to his feet with his glove hand high, showing the umpire the ball.

His spot in the batting order didn't come around in the top of the ninth, but in the bottom of the inning he ran out again to his position, whole and strong, immortal as ever.

"So you're back," Sarah Graham said. "Well, that explains it, anyway."

"Explains what?"

We were having lunch at Fair Haven. I'd sat down at her table because she was the only one I'd recognized when I'd first come in, though during the meal a few others had arrived, squinting our way, nudging their companions, in some cases nodding hello.

"Well, if you're back, it means you were gone," Sarah said. "Perhaps for some time. So that's why you were missed."

"You missed me?" I said.

"Don't be silly," Sarah said. "I didn't even know you were gone until you just now told me. I won't know it again by the time the coffee's ready. How could I miss you? It's Louise I'm talking about."

For a minute I didn't know what to do. This coming back would be a good deal harder if I had to explain again and again that Louise was dead. Already with every blank stare I saw in the hallway, every whimper and moan I heard out there, I worried about whether I'd die as well as she had.

"You better see her as soon as you can," Sarah was saying. "Right after lunch would be good, though she may be napping."

And after lunch I let her take my arm and lead me along the corridors, counting the doors as she went. We passed old men sitting in the dark, women in cranky conversations with themselves, neighbors all. Eventually we came to the room I was to visit, and Sarah peaked in. She bobbed her head out again like a bird and said, "She's awake, but she may have been trying to sleep. I told her you'd tell her a story. That's what she's been asking for, perhaps for as long as you've been gone. How should I know? Anyway, I said you were wonderful at it. Come on."

The woman in the bed looked up, puzzled.

"Don't worry, Louise," Sarah said. "He won't bite you. This is just Pete Estey, the man I was telling you about. The one who tells such good stories."

We sat and looked at each other then, equally baffled, I suppose, and Sarah said, "I'm sorry I can't stay. I've a visitor coming. A daughter. Goodbye, Pete. Goodbye, Louise."

When Sarah had gone, I said to the woman in the bed, "I hope I'm not disturbing you."

"No," she said quietly. Then after a pause she said, "Is it true that you're a storyteller? I love a story."

"I'll do the best I can," I said, but I didn't have any idea where to begin. Sarah was mixed up again. Where had she gotten the idea that this old woman wanted me? Or that I had a story to tell?

"It was Louise she kept calling me, wasn't it?" the woman in the bed said. "Why do you suppose that was? Who's Louise?"

The silence after her question was broken by a fit of desperate coughing down the hall, and then an aide's soft footsteps. I looked at the old woman, who'd heard the coughing too, and I said, "Well, that's one I can tell you." I pulled a chair up to the side of her bed and sat close to her in the small room. "But I'll have to feel my way a little here to know how to tell it. Maybe you can help me out, and then I'll know where to start. Do you know baseball at all? Do you know what it means when a scout looks at a young ballplayer and he says to himself, 'That's a prospect'?"